STEPHANIE'S
REVENGE

STEPHANIE'S REVENGE

Susanna Hughes

First published in Great Britain in 1993 by
Nexus
332 Ladbroke Grove
London W10 5AH

ISBN 0 352 32844 4

A catalogue record for this title is available from the
British Library

Typeset by Phoenix Photosetting, Chatham, Kent.
Printed and bound in Great Britain by
Cox & Wyman Ltd, Reading, Berks.

ONE

Stephanie let the warm water from the shower cascade over her body. The shower was powerful, pumping needle-jets of water at considerable pressure. It was one of the many things about life at the castle that she loved. A real luxury. She turned her back and let the water wash through her long black hair and down the length of her spine, until it hit the slope of her arse and funnelled into the deep gully between the plump cushions of her buttocks. Turning again, she dipped her face briefly into the hard stream of water to wash the sleep from her eyes. She shampooed her hair and soaped her body. The water ran down her neck, down her hollow collar bone, over her firm breasts – seemingly defying gravity with a distinct upward tilt, their nipples puckered and hardened by the water – over her iron-flat stomach and waspy pinched waist, to the fullness of her hips and into her thick, black, curly pubic hair. Here it was momentarily trapped. It accumulated, like rain on the leaf of a tree, then fell away in large drops or ran on further down the long sculptured curves of Stephanie's thighs, over her tight shapely calves to her delicately pinched ankles.

Shutting off the water, Stephanie stepped out of the shower. She ran a thick comb through her long hair to untangle it, and examined her body in the mirror that

1

ran the length of one wall of the white Carrara marble bathroom. The three whip marks on her thighs had almost entirely disappeared. But the one on her inner thigh, the one from the cut of Gianni's whip that had so narrowly missed the soft folds of her sex itself, still displayed a slight bruising on her otherwise flawless tan. The welt across her breasts, from the same source, was also distinctly visible – an angry red scar across the top of her breasts in the middle of their soft, opulent curves.

It made her fume every morning, made her curse his name. It made her think of that night, three weeks ago, when Gianni had used her and inflicted these marks.

Pulling on a white towelling robe without bothering to dry herself, Stephanie walked through her spacious bedroom to the large terrace outside, paved in terra cotta. The morning sun would dry her hair.

She walked to the parapet and looked down at Lake Trasimeno. The sun had just cleared the horizon to the east and hung, a huge fireball, in the clear blue sky. Two or three small fishing boats were rowing for shore, their pre-dawn work done. They left long wakes in the silvery calm water of the lake. Somewhere, a distant solitary church bell tolled an irregular note. Down beneath the terrace she could hear the water of the lake lapping at the jetty. No doubt it had done so since the fourteenth-century castle, in which she now lived, was built. It was a pleasant, hypnotic noise. A slight breeze ruffled the over-hanging jasmine intertwined with bougainvillaea. The air was full of the heady scent of flowers. The breeze took up the calm waters of the lake too, and corrugated them into a pattern that glistened and reflected the sun. It was, Stephanie thought, paradise. And it was hers. For as long as she wanted it.

Every morning she awoke with a sense of incredulity

at her situation. No doubt when she got used to it the disbelief would fade. At the moment, she had to remind herself how it had all happened. The sexual odyssey she had embarked on had been a voyage of self-discovery – a sudden and unexplained need to explore her own sexuality, the desires, lusts and longings she felt so fiercely but did not understand. It had led her through the faltering and painful first steps with Martin, to Devlin and to the castle.

Devlin had brought her to this island castle, on Lake Trasimeno in the middle of Italy, for a weekend. The castle was more than a beautiful and luxurious house with every possible amenity. Its ancient dungeons had been converted into cellars adapted to cater for every conceivable sexual taste and 'staffed' by men and women who had been caught with their hand in one of Devlin's many company tills. Their choice had been simple: come and serve at the castle or face the police.

Whether Devlin expected her reaction she did not know, but Stephanie had found herself responding to the castle in a way she would not have predicted. She had not been shocked or repelled. She had discovered that an ability to control and dominate, to play the ring master in a sexual circus – the power Devlin was only too willing to give to her – had given her feelings she had never even imagined. After three days of sexual excess, of every sort of sexual experience – including Gianni's abuse – she had found herself on a sexual high that was simply beyond her experience.

She had not asked herself where her odyssey might end. She had no idea it would end here, with her relishing the role Devlin had cast her in or, more accurately, the role she had created for herself. She had treated Devlin to a display of total dominance. She had

3

made the master into a slave, her slave. And he had told her it was the most exciting experience of his life. He wanted it repeated. And repeated. Which is why he wanted her at the castle, and why he'd offered her the chance to make the castle hers. Stephanie's Castle.

The sun was already hot. Stephanie slipped off the robe to let it dry her body. She lay on one of the loungers, waiting for her breakfast to arrive. Looking down at her body, she caught sight of the marks on her breasts again and a wave of anger returned, spoiling the peace of the moment.

Her instinct had been right. She had intended to go to Rome to take her revenge on Gianni immediately, the day after he had abused her so wantonly. But when Devlin, on her instructions, had called to make sure Gianni would be at home, he had been told that Gianni was away. And so far he had not returned. If she had been able to get it out of her system, repay him for what he had done to her, Stephanie would have been able to concentrate and enjoy all the considerable delights of the castle and her new position. But while it still lingered, while the marks on her body remained, however faded, the idyll was flawed. The only advantage to the delay was that she had thought long and hard about exactly what she was going to do to Gianni. She had developed an elaborate punishment to fit his heinous and elaborate crime against her. As soon as Devlin discovered Gianni was back home in Rome she would take her revenge.

4

TWO

Two weeks earlier Devlin's private jet had landed at Heathrow. Stephanie was the only passenger. The black Mercedes coupé was waiting to meet her, its driver ready to take her luggage. But there was none. This was a day trip to clear up her affairs in London, put her flat on the market, and give in her resignation at work. She had told the pilot of the plane to be ready to return to Italy by five o'clock that afternoon. It was, she thought, definitely the only way to travel.

The driver brought the Mercedes round to the front of the terminal and got out to open the passenger door. But Stephanie had other plans.

'I'll take the car,' she said. 'Be here at five to pick it up, will you.' It was not a question.

Walking round to the driver's door, Stephanie slipped into the deep leather seat, adjusted its position with the electrics provided, and pulled into the traffic, leaving the hapless driver standing on the kerb.

She hadn't wanted to be chauffeured today. Firstly, she wanted the feeling of driving a big, powerful car. Secondly, she wanted to be alone. She intended to enjoy herself. She soon felt at home in the cocooned double-glazed interior of the big car. Its engine accelerated effortlessly as she cruised past other cars on the motorway into central London. She turned the radio on and let it search the airwaves automatically until it found Radio Three and a concert of English baroque music. The sharp, crisp, brassy sound suited her mood. She adjusted the air conditioning so it blew colder. It was a typical English late summer day, hot and stuffy, and the cool air from the vents was welcome.

She wore a short sleeveless yellow dress that clung to her figure, curving into her slim waist and emphasising the richness of her full hips and the taut firmness of her bust. Apart from a pair of pure silk tanga cut panties and her matching yellow high heels, she wore nothing else, unless a pair of gold-framed Cartier sunglasses count as clothing. Her black hair was pinned up to the back of her head, revealing her long graceful neck.

When Devlin had asked her – begged her, would be a more accurate description – to stay at the castle, she had phoned her boss to say that she was ill. After a couple of days she'd got a friend to tell him she'd be back in a week. Today the week was up. Apparently, her boss had been most concerned about her welfare, sending good wishes for her speedy recovery.

It was fortunate that Stephanie intended to give her notice, because there was no way her boss would ever have believed she had been ill. With the almost continuous sun at the castle, with slaves to massage her with sun screen, she had an almost perfect tan. She looked and felt better than she had ever looked and felt in her entire life. She was relaxed and, most of all, she was in control. That was the feeling Devlin had given her, encouraged in her, created in her. She was her own woman now.

She parked the Mercedes in the curved driveway in front of her company's office building, next to the managing director's rather smaller model. The commissionaire scuttled out of the building immediately, his arms waving in agitation.

'You can't park there, Miss,' he said, coming round to the driver's door. He hadn't recognised her.

Stephanie opened the door of the car and swung her long, tanned legs out, her knees together. The shirt of the dress had ridden up on the leather seat. She could have sworn she heard him gulp.

'I'm sure I can for a little while,' she said, slipping a fifty pound note into his hand.

'Miss Curtis?' he said, looking at her as though she were wearing a mask.

'Look after it for me, Cyril. I won't be long.'

Not waiting for his reply, she left the keys in the ignition and walked into the building.

On the sixth floor she acknowledged the 'How-are-yous?', 'Are-you-betters?' and 'Good mornings' of her colleagues. After her experiences at the castle, after flying into London on a private jet, the office seemed particularly dim and unreal. The person who had worked at her desk in this large open-plan office was very different from the person she was now. Her life had changed irrevocably. She did not want her old life back.

At her desk, she sat down and went through the drawers, looking for anything personal she might want to keep. There was very little. She looked around her. The other people in the office were staring at her as if she were a ghostly apparition, as though trying to reassure themselves that it really was her. She smiled at them angelically.

The phone on her desk rang.

'Stephanie?' She recognised the voice of her boss.

'Norman,' she said.

'You are in, then?'

'It appears so,' she said sarcastically.

'Can you come and see me now?'

'I was just about to.'

'Are you feeling better?' He sounded concerned.

'Much better. I'm coming up now.'

Stephanie made no attempt to hurry. She finished clearing out her desk and found one or two things she did want to keep. Stuffing these into a plastic carrier bag, she walked back to the lifts, ignoring the questions in the faces all around her. As the lift arrived, she turned to the assembled company and flexed her fingers in a tiny wave.

Two floors up on the executive level, the offices were divided into executive suites, unlike the open-plan offices for the menial classes below. Each suite had an outer office for the executive's secretary and, its size depending on the importance of the executive, a large inner office. Some had adjoining conference rooms, some, for the most important in the company hierarchy, had their own toilets. Stephanie's boss was among the latter.

'Mr Hughes is waiting for you,' the petite, mousy-haired, bespectacled secretary said, as Stephanie walked in, as though keeping Mr Hughes waiting were a capital offence.

'I know,' Stephanie said, opening the door beyond the secretary's desk and walking straight in.

'Stephanie . . .' Hughes was obviously about to say something. Instead, he eyed the exquisite vision in yellow that had just walked into his office. 'Stephanie?' he repeated, unable to keep the astonishment out of his voice.

'Norman,' she said, sitting in the chair in front of his desk without waiting to be asked and crossing her legs.

She had always liked Norman Hughes. The resentments and disappointments she had felt in her job were not of his making: she ascribed those to a system dominated by men. Norman had always treated her well and given her credit for her work.

'My God . . .' he said, seemingly hypnotised by her appearance. His eyes were riveted to her legs. Her skirt was so short. 'You've been ill?'

'No. I've been offered a new job. I've come in to give you my notice.'

'You told me you were ill.'

'I lied,' she said, blatantly smiling.

He managed to take his eyes off her thighs for a moment, and looked into her face. He didn't appear angry. 'It doesn't surprise me. You're very good. Is it one of our rivals?'

'No.'

'But in advertising?'

'No. It's a job where I can use all my talents.' It came out more provocatively, more teasingly, than she had intended. She realised she had not taken off her sunglasses. He could not see what was going on in her eyes.

'What talents are those?' he said.

'If I told you, I don't imagine you'd believe me.'

'Really? Sounds very interesting.'

Hughes got up from his desk. He was a tall man, and his face was not unattractive in a rugged, weather-beaten sort of way. His short curly hair was flecked with grey, and his piercing eyes seemed grey too. But his prominent feature, literally, was his belly – a huge hillock of fat rising from just under his chest and only descending again at the top of his thighs, where the belt of his trousers was pushed down by its weight. His shirt struggled to contain the rubbery flesh, the buttons stretched to their limit. White, hairy blubber poked through the gaps created by its own bulk.

He came round the desk and leant on its front edge no more than a foot away from her. His eyes went back to her crossed legs, the finely drawn lines of her thighs.

'Is there something about my legs that interests you, Norman?'

'Everything about you interests me. Surely we can persuade you to stay? I'm sure I could get a sanction to offer you more money . . .'

'It's not a question of money . . .'

'Perhaps even a company car – '

'No,' she said, simply and firmly.

'There's a lot of companies going bust out there. I'd hate for you to walk from a nice, secure job into something that wasn't going to last.'

'It's nice of you to be so concerned.'

'I am. I'd really like you to stay.'

'My mind's made up, Norman. I'm flattered . . .'

'Well, at least I can't be accused of sexual harassment, can I?'

'Sorry?' She did not understand. The tone of his voice had changed.

He leant forward and put his hand on her knee. 'Well, if you're determined to go.' He slid his hand higher, until it was almost half way up her thigh. 'If I tell you I think you're absolutely gorgeous, it isn't sexual harassment since you've given in your notice. And I do – think you're gorgeous, I mean.'

Stephanie measured her reaction. Before her experiences at the castle she would have felt anger, then panic. She wouldn't have known what to do, what to say, or how to react. But now she felt in control. She didn't feel threatened or cowed or put upon. She felt no anger. Instead, she felt a delicious sense of power. She had a power over this man; power she could use, wanted to use, to see how far it could be used. It was like a muscle wanting to be exercised.

She took off her gold-framed Cartier sunglasses and put them down on the desk, leaning forward slightly and looking straight into his grey eyes.

'Your hand is very hot,' she said steadily.

'Is it?'

'Very. I like that.'

'Do you?'

'It makes me hot.'

'You feel very cool.' He was rubbing his hand on her smooth thigh, up and down. In his trousers, under his gut, she could see movement.

'I feel very hot.'

She got up from her chair and walked slowly around the office. She picked up and examined his executive toys, looked at his prints, went over to the window and looked down, seeing her Mercedes parked below. She could feel his eyes following her, burning into her back, the neat curves of her arse, the slimness of her legs, the pinch of her ankles. She felt too her barely covered sex, felt it beginning to want attention. He had woken it up.

'What do you want exactly, Norman?' she said. She knew what she wanted.

'Perhaps we could have dinner.'

'And after dinner?' she smiled, turning so he could see her smile.

'Well . . .'

'Why don't you say it, Norman?'

'Say what?'

'Say that you want to fuck me. You do, don't you?'

'Yes.'

'So what are you waiting for?'

'What?'

'Haven't you ever wondered what it would be like? Haven't you ever fantasised what it would be like to fuck someone over your desk? Perhaps even me. Perhaps you had a little fantasy about calling me in here and getting me to bend over your desk. Did you?'

'No.'

'Oh. How disappointing.'

She reached for the zip in the small of her back and pulled it down. She pulled the dress off her shoulders. 'The door's unlocked,' he said.

'Does it matter?'

She stepped out of the dress and stood in front of him. The tanga panties clung to her hips, forming a deep V-shape pointing down to the junction of her thighs. Norman's mouth was open. His eyes did not know where to look first.

Stephanie leant over the desk, tilting her pert arse into the air and resting her elbows on the blotter. The tiny crotch of the panties did little to conceal her thick forest of pubic hair. She reached behind her back and pulled the thin crotchpiece aside.

'Well, Norman?' she said, tauntingly.

'I didn't . . .'

'Fuck me, Norman.'

'The door . . .'

'Leave it.'

'I could put a chair – '

'Leave it.'

He appeared to be in a frenzy of indecision. He wanted to fuck her but he couldn't lock the office door.

'Fuck me,' she said again, letting her considerable irritation into her voice.

Indecision resolved. For a big man he moved with surprising speed. In seconds, his trousers were around his knees and she felt the hot sword of flesh pushing through the cleft of her arse. Up until now, Stephanie had been experimenting with herself. Seeing what would happen. It had been a game. But suddenly, the game had turned to an urgent need, her urgent need. She wanted him. She had never given him a thought before, never even noticed that he was a man. Now she wanted him. Now.

His cock pried down into the folds of her sex. When it found the entrance to her cunt, it plunged forward. She couldn't stop herself from moaning. There was no resistance. Her cunt was wet. He sunk in to the hilt. In this position, that meant deep, so deep she felt him nudging at the bulb of her womb.

He was out of control. Perhaps this was his fantasy. He was fucking her like an animal, pounding into her with all his strength and energy, with a power that belied his bulk. She could feel his huge belly bouncing into her arse as he thrust forward. She could feel his cock, hard and hot, reaming into her wet sex.

She rested her head on the desk, unable to concentrate enough to keep it raised. Her orgasm was beginning, slow and heavy. She felt herself tensing, her nerves pulsing as Hughes pumped into her, trying even harder, ramming her faster, invading her deeper. She started to moan, rhythmically and loud, as each wave of her climax welled up in her body, each moan louder until she felt her body explode over his cock, broken on it, every locked nerve in her body, released, sprung open, at once, and the moan changed to a long continuous cry.

She pushed him away quickly before he could spunk. She wanted something else.

'Please.' he said.

'Norman,'

He looked at her, his eyes dulled by his passion.

'No, Norman. I want you to do as I say.'

'I want to fuck you.'

'No, Norman. Bend over the desk. Like I was.'

'I want to fuck you.'

'Do it,' she said, with the command she had learnt at the castle.

Reluctantly, he obeyed. His cock rested on his blotter, glistening with her juices. He rested his weight on his elbows. He had no idea why he was doing this. Why wouldn't she let him just fuck her? He'd thought that was what she wanted.

She picked up the wooden ruler on his desk and, before he realised what she was doing, slashed it down on his huge white buttocks. It landed with a sharp smack. She repeated it again, and again. To his own amazement, he made no objection. He couldn't object. It was his fantasy. This was his fantasy.

'Oh my God . . .' he murmured.

'You want it, don't you Norman?' She didn't know how she knew.

'Yes, oh yes.'

Four strokes, five strokes. Harder, fiercer. She could see red marks appearing on the white flesh. Seven strokes.

She raised the ruler for the eighth, but he knew he could not hold out any longer. His cock began to pulse, his spunk ready to jet out. As he felt the wind of the ruler come down, as he braced himself for the shock of delicious pain, the office door opened and the mousy-haired secretary stood in astonishment, the handle of the door still in her hand.

'Mr Hughes . . .'

He came, flooding his blotter with his spunk, more than he could ever remember producing, as the ruler bit into his arse one more time and he saw the look in his

14

secretary's eyes. It went on for ever. He came and came and came.

'Mr Hughes!' the secretary said again, recovering enough to slam the office door behind her.

Norman slumped into the chair in front of his desk. He was sweating profusely and panting for breath.

'Well, Norman . . .' Stephanie said. 'Quite a performance.'

'How did you know?'

'One of my talents, it appears.'

'I've never known . . .'

'Sh . . .'

She stepped out of her knickers. They were too wet to wear now. She dangled them in front of his face then dropped them into his naked lap.

'Souvenir,' she said.

He had still not recovered his breath by the time she had zipped up her dress, adjusted her hair, replaced her sunglasses and picked up her handbag and the plastic bag with the things from her desk.

'Well, time to go.'

'Stephanie . . . Listen . . .' He had so much he wanted to say to her.

'Got to go.'

'But – I want – I mean, can I see you again?'

'No,' she said simply.

'But . . .'

'Think of it as something to remember me by.'

'I really want to see you again.'

For a moment, Stephanie toyed with the idea of inviting him to the castle. She could certainly be sure he'd lose weight after a spell in the cellars. But Norman Hughes, despite his new found ardour, was part of her old life.

'No, Norman.' She patted his cheek as if he were a

15

schoolboy, before walking briskly out of the office.

The mousy-haired secretary blushed scarlet as soon as Stephanie appeared. 'I'm giving in my notice,' she said.

'But now you know what he really likes,' Stephanie said.

'Disgusting,' the secretary said under her breath.

As she waited for the lift, it occurred to Stephanie to go and see Martin. Four months ago it had all started with Martin, her odyssey. In a sense he had created what she was now – he had made her.

He had shown her what was on offer and what she was capable of. Hesitant at first she had soon become his willing accomplice, and she had never looked back. Which is why she took the lift to the ground floor without stopping off. Never look back. She was grateful to Martin. Very grateful. She would never forget him. But Martin was now in the past.

The commissionaire ran to open the door of her car. Perhaps as she slipped into the driving seat and he ogled her legs, he could see she was now totally naked under the dress. She could not tell and did not care.

The rest of the day passed quickly. She had arranged to meet an estate agent at her flat to put it on the market. She went to see her solicitor and gave him power of attorney to sell the flat and store her furniture. She took a huge box of clothes and trinkets to the local charity shop and discovered there was almost nothing of her own she wanted to take to the castle. It was, after all, a new life.

By five o'clock she was back at Heathrow. The chauffeur was waiting at the kerb, seemingly in the exact position she had left him.

Thirty minutes later the Learjet took off on course for

Lake Trasimeno. Devlin had constructed a private airstrip five minutes' drive from the lake.

On board the jet, Stephanie asked Susie, the flight attendant, to fix her a very dry martini with a twist of lemon, while she showered in the plane's lavish bathroom. Towelling herself dry, she slipped on a white satin robe that hung on the bathroom door, and went back into the main cabin. Susie served her drink, pouring it from a silver cocktail shaker into a triangular martini glass. Stephanie sat back in one of the large leather armchairs and sipped at the ice-cold liquid sticking viscously to the sides of the glass.

She smiled to herself. With Devlin and the castle there were so many firsts in her life: the first time she had been in a private plane, the first time in a Cadillac, the first time she'd driven a big Mercedes and now the first time she had sat naked in a robe sipping a martini at thirty thousand feet.

It was certainly a new life.

THREE

The slave arrived with her breakfast, knocking tentatively on the frame of the open terrace doors. Stephanie got up from the lounger, still naked, and indicated for him to come forward and put the tray on the white cast-iron table. Normally, breakfast would have been served by one of the white-linen-coated servants who were paid to work in the castle kitchens. Stephanie, however, had decided she wanted her breakfast brought up by one of the slaves – a different slave every day, in rotation. In this way, she could get to know each individually, get to know who was likely to make trouble and who she could rely on.

Of course, the change had another advantage. It meant there was someone on hand should Stephanie feel the need for some sexual service first thing in the morning.

The change had not pleased Bruno, Devlin's chatelain, the keeper of cellar keys. The mute servant had, prior to Stephanie's arrival, been given the sole charge of the cellars and their occupants. But Devlin had made it clear to him that Stephanie was now in charge, that he must do as she ordered and that, if he didn't like it, he would have to go. Since Bruno was born on the island and had never been across to the mainland, even for a day, he accepted the decision – though with all the bad grace his body language and dark hooded eyes could command.

This morning, the slave was male. He put the large tray down on the table. It was piled with a basket of croissants and brioche, a bowl of fruit, slices of melon grown on the island, orange juice the colour of blood, and a silver pot of coffee, all displayed on a white linen cloth with a matching linen napkin on top of which was a small yellow rose. The man turned to leave.

'I didn't tell you to go. Pour the coffee,' Stephanie said imperiously. The man was about thirty, with strong well-defined muscles and not an inch of fat on his body. As with all the male slaves, his genitals were covered with a black leather pouch stretched over a hard metal frame and chained like a G-string around his waist.

The man immediately picked up the coffee pot and poured the hot black liquid into the delicate white porcelain cup. Stephanie came to stand beside him. She picked up the blood-red orange-juice from the tray and sipped it. She could see the slave was trying not to look at her, trying not to feel her naked body next to his. The hard shell of the leather pouch allowed no room for expansion; getting an erection was an uncomfortable experience.

Stephanie sat at the table and crossed her legs. The man waited for instructions. All the slaves wore small metal chains around their necks; each bore a metal disc engraved with a name. This disc, hanging on the man's hairless chest, was engraved 'FRANK'. When Stephanie had come to the castle the names had all been false. Her orders had ensured that they would now be real, their real Christian names.

'Frank?'

'Yes, madam?'

'I haven't seen you before, have I?'

'Yes, madam.'

'Have I?'

'In the cellars, madam.'

'But you haven't been up here in my bedroom before, have you?'

'No, madam.'

'So you haven't been here long.'

'Two weeks, madam.'

'Look at me, Frank,' she said.

'Yes, madam.'

His eyes reluctantly looked at Stephanie's face: her bright, dark brown eyes; her hair, nearly dry now, falling on to her finely boned shoulders; her perfectly symmetrical mouth and pursed, ripe lips; her high cheek bones and delicate, quite sharp nose. Deliberately and very slowly, she licked her lips with the tip of her very pink tongue.

'Look at my body,' she ordered.

'Please, madam . . .'

But he obeyed. It was too late, anyway. His erection was already pushing against the metal of the pouch. He looked down at her firm breasts, the nipples not at all hard, down into her lap where her crossed legs showed only a neat triangle of tight black curls. He moaned with the pain as his cock tried to swell further and couldn't. It was agony.

Stephanie tired of the game.

'You may go,' she said, standing up and pulling her white towelling robe back around her body.

The slave shuffled out of the room, his discomfort obvious in the difficulty he had walking.

Stephanie sipped at the coffee and buttered a brioche which she ate hungrily. As she began to think of what she would wear, the phone rang. She walked into the bedroom to answer it, and recognised Devlin's voice immediately.

'Good news,' he said. Devlin was in London on business, but his voice sounded as though he were downstairs.

'What?' she asked.

'Gianni's back in Rome. I just heard today.'

'Really?' Stephanie felt a surge of excitement.

'He got back yesterday. I've just spoken to him on some pretext. He'll be there for at least a week.'

'Perfect.'

'I'll send the plane back so you can go this afternoon. You're booked into a suite at the Excelsior. I won't be back for at least three days, so go and enjoy yourself. You've got all the credit cards now. If you go into the safe in my office there's Swiss Francs if you want to take some cash. Do some shopping . . .'

'I do need some clothes. None of my stuff from London is really – '

'Get whatever you want,' Devlin said. 'Oh, and apparently, if you want to catch Gianni alone, tomorrow is the best night. His wife always plays bridge on Tuesday night. Never misses.'

'How did you find that out?'

'I've had her followed.'

'You think of everything.'

'I try. The plane will be ready about two. I'll get the car to pick you up at the airport.'

Stephanie was already making her plans. She could get to the hotel this afternoon, spend Tuesday shopping and then, on Tuesday night, pay her long-awaited visit to Giancarlo Gianni. At last!

The tone of Devlin's voice changed. 'Have you missed me?' he asked.

'What are you doing now?' Stephanie ignored his question deliberately.

'Getting dressed.'

'What are you wearing?'

'Socks, pants, my shirt . . .'

She could hear another change of tone, a slight breathlessness.

'Take your shirt off again, Devlin,' she ordered, her voice hard and imperious. She could picture him in his hotel suite; his squat, awkwardly-shaped body, his bulbous nose and pock-marked face making him appear brutish and ugly. She could imagine his huge, outsized fingers – each the size of a banana – struggling with the buttons of the shirt. 'Hurry up,' she said.

She heard a rustle of material.

'I've done it,' he announced.

Stephanie slipped out of the towelling robe and lay on the bed, the silk sheets cold against her sun-warmed body.

'Stephanie, are you still there?'

'Yes. I'm here. I'm naked now, Devlin. Lying on my bed naked.'

'Are you?'

'You should be here, shouldn't you?'

'Yes . . .' His voice was husky.

'Do you know, Devlin,' she said, stretching out on the bed, feeling the first flush of sexual excitement heating her blood, 'I can imagine that you're here now. What should I have you do to me?'

'I'd do anything, anything you want.'

'Of course you would.' She ran her hand down into her thick, wiry pubic hair. The image of Devlin's enormous gnarled and veined cock, so big her cunt could not contain it, was vivid. How many times it had driven her to distraction, how many times her orgasm had

23

broken over it like waves crashing on a huge rock. The first time seemed a long time ago now, in the days before she had realised her sexual potential: before Martin, before she had discovered another world of sex, a world of fantasy and reality, a world she had come to inhabit, enjoy and ultimately, here in the castle, a world she had come to control.

'So what would I have you do, Devlin? Should I have you lick me, Devlin? Or wank me? Should I have you spunk over my tits?' Her fingers found her cunt lips and she pushed two as deep into her cunt as they would go. There was no resistance. She was not surprised that her body had responded to the images her mind was dwelling on. The first time Devlin had put that cock inside her, that was a feeling she would never forget. She could conjure it up like the genie in the lamp. An exact picture of where, when and how. She, bent over in his bedroom, facing an oil painting, a huge canvas dominated by a woman with a crimson vulva. In those days Devlin could only get an erection if he looked at the painting. Things were very different now.

She started to move her fingers inside her cunt, as deep inside as they would go, scissoring them apart, pushing against the elastic, satiny, wet walls.

'You didn't answer me, Devlin,' she said sharply, the authority in her voice giving her a thrill of pleasure.

'I don't know.'

'Are you erect?'

'Yes.'

'Fully erect?'

'Yes. You've made me hard.'

'Are you touching yourself?'

'Yes.'

'I didn't give you permission to do that, did I, Devlin?'

'No.'

'No what?'

'No, mistress.'

'But since you've started you'd better wank for me right now, hadn't you? If you were here I'd make you wank for me. Make you come all over my tits. Are you wanking?'

'Yes, mistress.'

'I've got my fingers in my cunt, Devlin. It's so wet. My clitoris is all swollen. It feels so good.'

'Yes, mistress.'

'You are not to come until I tell you to.'

'No, mistress.'

Stephanie moved her fingers out of her cunt and on to her clitoris. She pressed it hard down against her pubic bone and gasped at the sensation. She could hear Devlin's excitement, hear little exhalations of breath, little 'ahs' and 'ums'. She could imagine Devlin's huge hand circling his cock. When she wanked him her hand barely covered a third of its length. But in his hand, with his banana-sized fingers making a fist like an American baseball mitt, the cock all but disappeared.

'Do you remember when I had Venetia beat you, Devlin? Beat you while you fucked me?'

'Yes, mistress.' He would never forget it.

'I've been thinking of what I'm going to do to you next, Devlin. When you get back.'

'Oh . . .' Devlin's moan of pleasure was involuntary.

'Have you come?' Stephanie barked.

'No mistress, but I want to. Please let me.'

'Not yet. You have to wait.'

'Please let me,' he whispered.

'I'd love to have that cock inside me now. I'd squeeze every drop of juice out of it . . .'

'Please . . .'

25

'I'm wanking, Devlin. I'm stretched out naked on the bed. I've got my legs wide apart, so wide, so open. You should be here to lick me, service me. I have to do it myself . . .' She was rubbing her clitoris in little circles, knowing she was going to make herself come. She would have loved to pinch her nipples with her other hand, but she had to hold the phone to her ear.

'Please . . .'

She felt her orgasm explode. It surprised her. She thought she could keep it at bay for longer, hold it back, torment herself with anticipation. But her body had other ideas; it had tricked her, found a way through her defences, taken its own pleasure, her nerves racked with sensation.

Devlin heard her long, low gasp for pleasure.

'Please . . .' But it was too late to ask permission. His spunk jetted from his cock, hot wet spunk flowing over his fingers like lava from a volcano.

For a moment, the phone line transmitted nothing but little mewls and whimpers of contentment from both parties.

Devlin was the first to speak. 'Stephanie. Darling. You are so wonderful. You do such things to me. Such wonderful things.'

'I'll call you when I get back from Rome,' she said.

'Be careful.'

'Don't worry. I've got it all planned.'

Stephanie put the receiver down and lay back on the bed, still tingling with the aftermath of her orgasm. She squirmed her naked body on the bed to nudge the nerves to produce another little frisson of pleasure, another tremor in her body like the aftershock of an earthquake. She toyed with the idea of getting Frank back, unlocking his pouch, and getting him to fuck her. But as the orgasm faded, her mind was turning to other things. To the plans she had to make, to her revenge . . .

The Learjet landed smoothly at Leonardo da Vinci Aeroporto in Rome. It had been no more than a twenty minute flight, and most of that had been circling Rome waiting for a runway.

Rome was hot. As Devlin used Rome frequently for business, he kept a car and chauffeur in the city. They were waiting to meet Stephanie off the plane. As she intended to do a great deal of shopping she had brought a number of suitcases with her, though all, bar one, were empty. A smaller case contained everything she would need for her short stay, and the one or two special items she needed to deal with Gianni.

The chauffeur loaded the cases into the Rolls Royce Silver Wraith while Stephanie waited in its air-conditioned interior. The short journey to the five star Excelsior Hotel on the Via Veneto would be accomplished in the utmost comfort.

Stephanie had been to Rome before. She had never dreamt she would return in such style – a private jet, a chauffeur-driven Rolls, a suite at the Excelsior. It was amazing how dramatically her life had changed. But the most important change was not in her circumstances – not in the fact she was now dressed in a cotton Armani shirt-waister, Versace shoes, Cartier sunglasses and La Perla knickers and driving in a Rolls Royce – but in her attitude. She felt free. She felt able to use what she had, able to express herself, able to be herself. She was not cowed by taboos, inhibitions, sexual prohibitions. All the social conventions that she had carried around for so long had turned out to be like the luggage in the boot of the Rolls – empty.

They drove through the Piazza Della Repubblica, where Stephanie remembered sitting to eat a pizza on the steps of a church designed by Michaelangelo, then on up the Via Barberini to the Via Veneto. Rome, like most great cities, presented a beautiful vista at every corner, a particular mixture of the heavenly and the prosaic, of the divine and the sordid. The great statues of the Trevi Fountain mixed inextricably with the thirteen year old girls in red satin mini-skirts and black Lycra halter tops displaying their nascent breasts to passing men as a means of touting for business.

The staff at the Excelsior were appropriately ingratiating, bowing and scraping in a way that suggested Devlin was a valued and important customer. Stephanie was escorted to a suite by a tail-coated manager before whom minions scattered in confusion. He assured her that her every wish would be their command. He assured her the hotel was honoured and privileged beyond mere words by her singular presence.

He showed her around the huge suite on the top floor, its bedroom and sitting room both opening on to a small terrace that overlooked the Via Veneto. He absolutely refused to take the tip she offered him explaining, in the florid language he seemed to favour, that it had been entirely his pleasure.

Stephanie unpacked the few clothes she had brought and wandered downstairs again. She dismissed her driver and wandered aimlessly across the street to Harry's Bar where she ordered a glass of dry spumante – the Italian version of champagne – and a large café nero, and sat quietly on the wide pavement to watch the people go by.

She attracted admiring glances from passing Italian

men, but did not notice them. Her mind was full of her plans for Gianni. She had no doubt her plan would succeed. Gianni was the sort of man who believed he was absolutely irresistible to women. It would not be difficult to convince him that, despite the way he had treated her in the cellars at the castle, she had conceived a great passion for him, a passion she had to satisfy. And then . . .

An Italian man sat down opposite her at the small circular table.

'You are English?' he said.

'Go away.' Stephanie remembered the way Roman men had harried her when she was a student here. She had disliked it intensely then and *that* had not changed.

'Hear what I have to say.'

'Fuck off.'

'Language. For a respectable English woman, I think you have much fire.'

Stephanie looked around for a waiter. They were all inside the bar.

'I give you what you want.'

'I told you to get lost.'

'Anything you want. I can get you anything.'

The waiter came out of the bar with two cups of cappuccino on his tray. Stephanie waved her hand. She was determined not to have to get up and leave. Why should she?

'I know,' the man was saying. 'I know about you. You want a party. I get you a woman. Two men. Anything you want. I can get anything.'

The waiter delivered his order and saw Stephanie's hand. He walked over towards the table and the man immediately got up. He smiled a leering, ogling smile.

'Pity,' he said. 'You are a very sexy lady. 'I know. Very sexy. Molto caldo . . .'

Before the waiter had covered the ground between the five or six tables the man was gone, disappearing as rapidly as he had appeared. Stephanie heard his rather whiny, high voice, 'Molto caldo . . .' Well, he had been right about that. She could not suppress a flicker of a smile.

FOUR

Stephanie had ordered breakfast for nine and it arrived precisely on time. She had it taken out to the balcony and, climbing into a pink silk dressing gown, she drunk her coffee and blood-red orange juice as she watched Rome coming to life in the streets below. The street cleaning trucks spewed out water to clean the gutters, the delivery vans restocked the restaurants and bars with crates of aqua minerale, wine, beer and, inevitably it appeared, with crates of Coca Cola.

After spending an hour on the terrace, enjoying the sun and the sights, she dressed in a light, plain cotton dress which buttoned down the front – and was therefore easy to get in to and out of in the innumerable changing rooms she planned to visit – and selected a pair of low-heeled shoes that would be comfortable to walk in. Armed with the credit cards, store account cards, and thousand Swiss Franc notes she had found in Devlin's safe, she walked out of the hotel and into the sun. It was no longer the height of summer but, though the nights were colder, the days could still be uncomfortably hot.

She walked to the Spanish steps and stood surveying the terracotta-coloured city, before descending to the Piazza and the Via Condotti, at the heart of commercial Rome. As yet there were few people about. In the

Piazza the flower sellers were busy setting up their stalls. The narrow streets were effectively shaded from the early morning sun and felt slightly chill in the dark shadows.

After two hours she had been to Valentino's, St Laurent, Trussadi, Armani and Ferre. She had tried on dresses for all occasions and not bothered to look at the prices. She had bought silk, satin, and leather. And then, with the colours of the clothes she had bought still fresh in her mind, she had gone to Rossetti and Bally and Gucci for shoes and handbags and gloves. All her purchases were to be sent to her hotel.

The hotel had recommended a restaurant for lunch and she found that shopping had made her ravenously hungry. Not wanting to go back to the hotel and order the Rolls she decided to take a taxi, and regretted it immediately. The driver was clearly under the impression that she was a representative of Ferrari looking for a driver for their Formula One team. He drove with such speed she could have sworn the car was cornering on two wheels. As she did not know the Italian for 'slow down', there was nothing that she could do but cling on. They reached the restaurant in three minutes.

The concierge at the hotel had booked a table. Clearly, from the warmth of her welcome, he had also added that she was considered to be a very important client. She was ushered to a large window table overlooking the Piazza Navona. The dining room was beautiful, a black marble floor contrasting with the crisp white linen on the tables. A huge display of fresh flowers on a circular table dominated the room.

Sipping a glass of spumante to calm her nerves after the ordeal in the taxi, Stephanie ordered Tagliatelle al Prosciutto followed by mixed grilled seafood. It was all delicious. She had a salad of what looked like grass –

thin flat leaves of green – but which tasted sweet, dressed with a virgin olive oil and Balsamic vinegar. She declined the dessert trolley and ordered instead a Vino Santo with almond biscotto and a large cappuccino. Following the tradition she had learnt on her first visit, she dunked the biscuits into the golden-coloured wine.

The one area she had not investigated that morning was lingerie and that, she decided, would be her main objective this afternoon, before she returned to the hotel for her siesta.

She didn't ask for the bill. She dropped on the table a thousand Swiss Franc note which seemed to meet with the hearty approval of the restaurant staff, and got into the Rolls. Not wanting to risk a taxi again she had got the restaurant manager to call up the chauffeur. At a dignified pace, she returned to the main shopping drag.

She wandered more aimlessly than she had in the morning. There were two shops devoted entirely to lingerie, but after browsing in both of them she had bought nothing. It was after an hour of haphazard searching, and at the point at which she was almost giving up, that she noticed a very old-fashioned shop tucked away in one of the narrowest streets. A window on each side of a wood-framed, opaque glass door displayed one item of lingerie only. On the left side was a white waspie basque complete with suspenders, mounted on the sort of cloth dummy dress makers use. In the other window was a camiknicker in black silk on an identical dummy. The frame of the windows was dark brown, the paint chipped with age. The door was painted in the same ageing colour, through its brass handle was brightly polished – the only thing on the outside of the shop that looked as though it had been cleaned for years.

Stephanie was intrigued. Both items of lingerie were beautifully designed and made. She had not seen anything in the other shops to rival them. She turned the door knob and the door shuddered as she pushed it open. A bell rang somewhere deep inside the shop, triggered by the frame of the door.

The shop was cool, not from air-conditioning but from the lack of direct sunlight in the narrow street. A long, wooden counter ran the whole length of the room behind which, from floor to ceiling, were glass-fronted wooden drawers, each with a brass finger pull and a neat label written in florid Italian script. In front of the counter there was nothing; no point-of-sale bins, no special offers, no advertising display cards, not so much as a poster of any manufacturer of lingerie. There was a chevalier mirror and an old upright chair with a wooden seat.

A woman, summoned by the bell, appeared from behind a heavy damask curtain hanging at the end of the counter. She was dressed entirely in black; her wrinkled skin was sallow, her hands thin and bony, the fingers crooked with arthritis, her black lisle stockings hanging loose on her thin legs.

The woman said some words in Italian, obviously a question.

'Non parlo italiano,' Stephanie said, determining that learning Italian should be on her list of priorities.

'Fine. I speak a little English. How may I help you?' Her English was spoken with little trace of an accent.

The woman was definitely over seventy, Stephanie thought, but she moved with a grace and energy that belied her obvious age.

'I'm looking for lingerie. Whatever you could show me . . .'

'Of course. You are a very beautiful woman. For you,

34

I think, only the best is good enough.' Her English was precise, her voice strong. 'You have the figure to wear such things. It will be a pleasure to serve you.'

'Thank you,' Stephanie said.

The woman took a bra out of one of the drawers, then some matching knickers and a suspender belt and slip, all in black. She laid them out on the counter. 'Everything we have is made here by our own girls. All our own designs.'

'They're lovely.' Stephanie fingered the garments.

'Try these first for size, and then I will show you all our designs and colours.'

Stephanie picked up the bra. It was exquisitely made, hand-stitched and underwired.

'This way please.' The woman in black came out from behind the counter to guide Stephanie through a small mirrored door into a short corridor where there were two small cubicles made from frosted glass mounted in ornate wooden frames, each with a lace curtain for an entrance.

'Please,' the old woman said, indicating one of the cubicles.

Stephanie stepped inside, stripped off her clothes and slipped into the black lingerie. The size was perfect. The underwear could have been made for her. The bra held her breasts firmly, pushing them together slightly into an alluring cleavage. The knickers fitted perfectly, following the soft curves of her buttocks. Obviously the old woman's experienced eye had judged her size to the millimetre. The material of the garments was soft and silky, but it was more elastic, more supportive and stronger than silk. This shop, Stephanie thought, was a definite find.

She put her dress back on and came out of the cubicle. The old woman stood waiting for her.

'Va bene?' she asked.

'Wonderful,' Stephanie said. 'Exactly the right size.'

'So I show you the styles and the colours. This way please.'

She lead the way through another door and up a narrow flight of stairs. The stairs were dimly lit with no carpeting. Their shoes echoed on the wood. At the top of the stairs was a comparatively large room with two picture windows overlooking the narrow street and the building opposite, which appeared to be no more than feet away. The windows were bare, no curtains or lace. At one end of the room was a small dais, and a large green velvet drape hung behind it. The only items on the polished wooden floor, pitted and marked with age, were five or six gold-painted spoon-backed chairs. The woman indicated that Stephanie should sit. Then she lifted a corner of the drapery and disappeared for a moment behind it.

Stephanie felt a strange sense of excitement. She could still feel the silky material of the lingerie as it had wrapped itself around her body. She looked down at herself and was not surprised to find that her nipples were hard and erect, poking through the thin cotton of the dress.

The old woman reappeared. She hooked the corner of the drapery to a tie-back so it formed a curtained arch. Then she came to stand behind Stephanie and the line of golden chairs. She clapped her hands.

From behind the curtain, a very tall black woman emerged. She was wearing a cream camiknicker in satin and lace, the lace panels positioned over the breasts and at the side on the hips. In white high heels, she pirouetted on the dais, took three or four steps forward towards Stephanie, and then wheeled again, heading back through the curtain. As soon as she disappeared another girl, white this time and blonde, strode out on to the dais wearing the waspie basque Stephanie had seen in the window downstairs, except in a stunning flame red. She wore red stockings too, attached to the long suspenders, and a pair of matching panties that barely covered the pouting triangle of her sex.

There were three girls in all. Each time they appeared in different outfits the old woman gave a running commentary in her precise English: style, material, colour. All the girls were attractive, all with figures that matched the underwear, all aware that their bodies and what they were displaying were special, but it was the black girl, among the array of pulchritude, that most fascinated Stephanie. There was something about her. Something quite exceptional. She was a dark chocolate brown, her skin soft and young, her curly black hair cut to within an inch of her scalp, her long legs and slim waist complementing whatever she was given to wear. She had small breasts with large, prominent nipples and, Stephanie noticed, modelled only the lingerie where the architecture of the bust was not important. The under-wired bras and basques and corsets were all modelled by the other two girls, whose breasts were full and heavy.

'Can I see that more closely?' Stephanie asked innocently, actually wanting to see the girl rather than the lingerie. She was modelling a short, grey, silky slip, no more than a beautifully cut shift supported on two thin spaghetti straps. The old woman beckoned the girl closer. She took two more steps forward, but was still four feet away. Stephanie could see that under the slip she was naked. Dressing and undressing in quick succession obviously left no time to find a pair of knickers to wear under the slip, and a bra would have spoilt the effect of the floating, diaphanous garment.

'I'd like to feel the material,' Stephanie said, wanting her closer still. The old woman nodded, and the black woman advanced again until Stephanie could reach out and rub the hem of the slip between finger and thumb. Picking it up from the front in this way exposed the woman's triangle of pubic hair. To Stephanie's surprise, it was not thick and wiry like the tight curls on her head, but very sparse – only a few black wisps struggling to cover the delta of her sex. Stephanie could see the beginnings of her sex, the delicate folds of her labia. She could see her nipples too. Though her breasts were no more than a gentle swelling on her chest, her nipples were like a stack of pennies, hard and corrugated and distinctly pink in contrast to the surrounding dark brown of her breast.

The woman saw where she was looking. She waited until Stephanie's eyes looked up into her face and then stared back at her, trying to see what Stephanie wanted, what she was doing.

Stephanie felt a surge of passion. As the woman turned and walked away, the light material lifted to reveal her arse, a pert, tight, neat arse, a crescent moon at the top of each thigh where the creases of flesh delineated the bottom of the buttock. Stephanie's palms were sweating and she realised she was breathing in shallow pants. In her mind's eye she could see the woman in her bed, could feel her fingers pinching those huge nipples, could hear her moan as she tongued her clitoris, could see those long brown legs spread open.

'You would like to see more?'

'More?' Stephanie tried to concentrate on reality.

'That is our lingerie collection.' The old woman had been watching, she had felt the tension in the air. 'We have more specialised items. I think for you that they may be of interest. You are a strong woman. That is what men like in you. Is that true?'

Stephanie looked round at the old woman, who stood behind her as upright and straight as if she had been eighteen. Her eyes were sparkling with life. 'Apparently,' she answered truthfully.

'I know these things. Before I started my shop, I too was like you. Men like the young, soft, innocent women. They like the satin and silk and lace. They like the virgin white. Some men, a lot of men, like something else . . . I show you more, yes?'

'Please.' Stephanie was fascinated.

The old woman clapped her hands again. This time through the curtain one of the white models emerged. Instead of the soft, delicate lingerie she was wearing high-heeled, knee-length, lace-up black boots, a black leather basque and a studded leather collar. The basque clung to her body, its bust cut to support the breasts from underneath, pushing them up and leaving them completely exposed. Leather suspenders held black stockings. Elbow-length gloves clad her hands and arms and she held a short riding-crop.

The old woman was giggling. 'This is our more specialised range. You like?'

'Show me more . . .'

It was another half hour before the display of bizarre costumes was finished. There were leather cat-suits, leather bras, knickers and suspender belts. There were dresses laced down both sides from shoulder to mid-thigh. There were mini-skirts and halter tops. The leather was either the softest glove quality or bright, shiny patent leather; tight, elastic and clinging. To Stephanie's disappointment, none of these outfits was worn by the black woman. All required a substantial bust to look their best.

Stephanie went through a catalogue of items and ordered quantities of lingerie and leather. The old woman told her everything was custom made, but she would have delivery within a week. As they did not accept credit cards, Stephanie was grateful she had raided the safe for the Swiss Francs.

After the business was concluded, the woman got up to escort Stephanie downstairs. But Stephanie remained seated.

'Could I just ask . . .' Stephanie said, hoping that after all the money she had spent she could ask for anything.

The old woman was looking at Stephanie with what could only be described as a knowing smile.

'The grey slip. Could I just see that again?' She hoped the woman would understand that the grey slip meant the negress to model it.

The old woman was way ahead of her. 'She is beautiful, isn't she? Most beautiful. So long. So fine. Before I started my shop . . . It is a long time ago now. I was like you, I think. I had another business. A good business. I made a lot of money. I saw what men liked. And women.'

The old woman went to the door and turned a large key in an old-fashioned box mortice lock. She put the key on the chair next to Stephanie, unhooked the drapery in the corner from its tie-back and let it fall.

'It will only take a moment,' she said, and disappeared behind the curtain.

Stephanie waited, feeling her pulse increasing. No more than four months ago she had never even dreamt of having sex with a woman. But now that had changed, like everything else in her life. At the castle, she had experienced such delight in the arms of a woman, it was not something she intended to forgo ever again. Now she could feel, just as she had today with the negress, a surge of desire when she saw an attractive woman, and now she was in a position where she had no need to suppress it. Her sexuality was almost masculine; she could join the hunt like a man, searching for her quarry – male or female. It was a wonderful feeling, to be free to do as she pleased.

The drapery rustled and was pulled aside, and the black woman appeared wearing the grey slip with the spaghetti straps. She paraded on the dais, looking self-conscious now they were alone.

'Do you speak English?' Stephanie asked.

'Yes,' she said.

'Come and sit here please.'

She walked over to the line of gold chairs without looking directly at Stephanie. She sat on one of the chairs, leaving an empty chair between herself and Stephanie. The large key to the door lay on the seat of the chair between them. The young woman looked at it before she looked up at Stephanie, her eyes full of questions.

'You are very beautiful,' Stephanie said.

'Thank you.' Her dark brown eyes searched for an answer, wanting to know what she was doing here. 'You are very beautiful, toi aussi.' Her accent was not Italian, but French.

'What's your name?'

'Jasmina.' She continued to stare into Stephanie's eyes.

'Give me your hand, Jasmina,' Stephanie said firmly.

Jasmina obeyed, holding out her left hand. The fingers were slim and incredibly long, the fingernails cultivated, manicured and painted with brilliant red varnish. Stephanie had a pulse of pleasure at the

41

thought of what such long fingers could do to her. She clasped the hand in both of hers. She had never seduced a woman before (until now she had always been seduced). She hadn't the slightest idea of what to do next, now she was the hunter. She wanted desperately to kiss Jasmina's thick, pouting lips; wanted to feel that slim athletic body pressed against hers.

'If I were to kiss you, what would you feel?' She could think of nothing else but being direct.

Jasmina laughed, a deep throaty laugh, breaking the tension. Her eyes sparkled with energy and life. Stephanie had her answer.

'Je ne sais pas. I don't know. I have never tried this.'

'Would you like – '

But before Stephanie had finished, Jasmina leant over the chair that separated them, her hand reaching round Stephanie's neck, and pulling her over into a kiss. She kissed hard, urgently, her tongue probing between Stephanie's lips. The unexpectedness of her action gave Stephanie an enormous thrill. Jasmina had thrown aside the cloak of apparent shyness.

'There . . .' Jasmina said, breaking the kiss. 'Very good,' she said to herself, as if testing her own reaction. 'It was good?' she asked Stephanie, as though genuinely thinking she might not feel the same.

'Yes.'

'I think so too. Your mouth is very soft. Not like a man.'

She bent forward again, wanting to renew the experiment. This time, she let Stephanie's tongue into her mouth and, when it was firmly between her lips, sucked on it as though it were a penis. At the same time, she let her hand fall on to Stephanie's breasts, squeezing them both in turn.

She broke the kiss again and looked into Stephanie's eyes – a long, searching look.

'I have never done this before, jamais,' she said. 'It excites me.'

'Does it?'

'Mais oui.'

Jasmina stood up and faced the seated Stephanie. 'I saw you looking at my little pussy. I have little to cover my secret parts. You like what you saw.' She parted her legs so that Stephanie's knees were between her thighs and pressed forward until Stephanie's face was up against the silk of the slip. Then she pulled down both spaghetti straps from her shoulders, and the slip fell away until it caught on Stephanie's lap.

'I like this, I think . . .' Jasmina said, laughing with sheer pleasure.

Stephanie sucked the bulbous nipple into her mouth and heard Jasmina moan as she pinched it with her teeth. She ran her hands around to Jasmina's back, feeling its sinewy length, and then down to her tight, muscled buttocks, pulling her forward until their bodies were crushed against each other. The young woman sat on Stephanie's thighs and ran her fingers into her long black hair as she bent to kiss her full on the mouth again.

As their tongues explored, vying for position, each wanting to be first to find new territory, Stephanie ran her hand down under Jasmina's thighs, under the cleft of her arse, to touch the lips of her sex. She felt a shock wave run through Jasmina's body at the first contact of her fingertips, and her whole body tensed. But she did not allow that to stop her. She caressed the outer lips softly, then slowly pushed inward. Jasmina responded by kissing harder, sucking on Stephanie's lips, pushing against her tongue. Stephanie's fingers delved deeper, moving upward to find Jasmina's clitoris. She could feel her heat and her wetness. Her clitoris was swollen.

43

She worked it with the tip of her finger, lightly at first and then firmly, moving the engorged flesh from side to side. Jasmina moaned, a moan muffled by Stephanie's mouth. She felt her whole body relax, its tension gone, suddenly giving in to the pleasure, melting over Stephanie, her hands wrapping round Stephanie's back and clinging to her.

Jasmina broke the kiss. Instead, she began to move her lips against Stephanie's neck in little sucking wet kisses. But it was hard to concentrate. Her whole body was reverberating to the tiny movement of the tip of Stephanie's finger, circling and nudging, stroking and tapping at the tiny pebble of her clitoris.

'Je t'adore . . . My little button is so hard. So hard,' Jasmina whispered in Stephanie's ear.

'You want me to stop?' Stephanie said teasingly.

'Non, je t'en prie . . . Please don't leave it.'

Stephanie plunged her fingers deep into Jasmina's cunt, deep between the wet flesh, and heard her moan. She heard her moan and gasp. Her cunt was hot, burning hot and very tight.

'Is that what you wanted?'

'Oui, oui . . .'

Then Jasmina could not form words. Her body was trembling and her sex contracting around Stephanie's fingers, and she knew she was coming. Stephanie could feel it too, feel it in her cunt and all over her body. She reamed her fingers deeper, wanting to make her come. With her other hand, she found one of the thick, erect nipples and pinched it viciously, digging her nails into the puckered flesh. In this position, thighs resting on thighs, bodies pressed together, Jasmina's head on her shoulder, she could feel every reaction, all the trembling and breathless excitement of the woman's body. She heard her mewl like an animal, little

44

meaningless noises, and then felt her orgasm spreading through her body, up and out from her cunt, spreading to all the nerves in her body, giving them the signal to explode with sensation, locking out everything but total passion. She clung to Stephanie desperately, like a drowning man clinging to a piece of flotsam, her whole body rocking with her pleasure.

In the midst of all this, a movement caught Stephanie's eye. The large windows of the modelling room had no curtains and, because of the narrowness of the Roman street outside, the window was no more than a few feet away from the first floor windows of the building opposite. The movement that had attracted Stephanie's attention was a blind, on the window opposite, being raised. Standing in the window, Stephanie could see a man. He was beckoning for another man to join him, beckoning urgently as if delay were a matter of life and death. This was a show he would not want to miss. The other man arrived, and they both stood staring intently at the tableau across the street – the naked black woman sitting on the knees of the fully-clothed white woman.

Stephanie stroked Jasmina's short curly hair and felt her body relaxing as the waves of passion gently subsided. She looked across at the two men. Jasmina had not seen them. They stood completely still, hoping they would not be noticed, hoping the show was not over. The slow movement of Stephanie's hand on Jasmina's hair was, for several minutes, the only activity.

Then Jasmina moved, raising her head from Stephanie's shoulder, looking into her eyes.

'You knew,' she said, very softly.

'Knew what?'

'That I would like this. Sapphisme.'

'Do you?'

By way of reply, Jasmina began unbuttoning the front of Stephanie's dress. She pushed her hand under the cotton and cupped it over the white silk that held Stephanie's breast, pressing her hand hard into the soft flesh. It was a world of new sensation. She had never touched a woman before. She felt Stephanie's erect nipple against the palm of her hand.

'Très dur. Very hard. Moi aussi. Like mine.'

'Yes . . . But you don't have to . . .'

Jasmina stopped her by pressing her finger against Stephanie's lips.

'I want very much I want . . .'

She slipped off Stephanie's thighs and knelt in front of her on the floor, the discarded grey slip falling to her ankles as she did so. There were still two buttons on the dress to be undone. Unfastening these, she spread the dress apart, exposing Stephanie's white bra and panties.

'Jamais déjà. Never before . . .' Jasmina whispered, almost to herself, as she used her hands to part Stephanie's legs, rather like drawing aside a curtain, pushing them wide apart so she could sink her head down between Stephanie's thighs. She kissed both in turn from the knee up to the very top. She felt Stephanie's pubic hair on her cheek where wisps escaped from her panties.

Stephanie eased forward on the seat of the chair, anxious to feel the negress's lips between her legs. She looked down at the head between her thighs, the hair so rough it almost scratched her skin. But then her eyes were drawn to the two men who watched from the window opposite. Both were in short-sleeved shirts and ties. Both stood stock-still.

Jasmina's mouth settled on the junction of her thighs, probing it gently with her tongue. Then she opened her mouth and sucked on the whole of Stephanie's sex, sucked in silk and cunt lips and clitoris, sucked in hard. It was a wonderful sensation. But Jasmina wanted more; she wanted to feel the lips without the veil of silk. Quickly, she snaked her hands up to the sides of Stephanie's hips and pulled the panties down. Stephanie co-operated, raising her bum off the seat, watching Jasmina's long, red-painted fingers draw the white silk off her thighs.

With no hesitation, Jasmina plunged her mouth on to Stephanie's now naked cunt. Stephanie gasped as she felt her hot tongue teasing out her clitoris from the thick pubic hair, then sucking it eagerly into her mouth. It was not going to take much to make her come. The situation was too exciting. Jasmina's black skin, in such sharp contrast to her own white flesh, was a provocation in itself. But there was so much more. So much provocation. So much stimulation. There was the fact that she knew Jasmina had never done this before, never had a woman, never climaxed on a woman's fingers as she had done with Stephanie, never pressed her mouth to a woman's cunt or played with a woman's clitoris with her tongue as she was doing now. And there were the men's eyes, riveted to her, watching every move, every undulation of her body as it responded to Jasmina's mouth.

Stephanie came suddenly, her orgasm sharp and powerful like a crack of thunder. It came not in waves, slowly getting more intense, but as an electric shock, a jolt of pleasure so great she could not suppress what sounded like a sob of delight.

But Jasmina did not stop. Her hand reached up blindly, searching for Stephanie's breast. When it found the silk covered mound, it closed on the nipple, pinching it just as Stephanie had done to her.

Stephanie moaned. Jasmina moved her hand to the other nipple and pinched this too. At the same time, she sucked Stephanie's nether lips into her mouth, and worked her clitoris with the tip of her tongue. The pleasure from both her nipples flooded to meet this new pleasure from her cunt, and Stephanie felt herself coming again. This orgasm was in waves, big tidal waves rising and falling in her body, each rise higher and harder. As the last waves engulfed her, as Jasmina's tongue relentlessly licked her clit, she fought to keep her eyes open, to look across at the two men watching her, watching her come in the mouth of a woman. The look in their faces, astonishment and lust, took her higher, as she knew it would. Then she could control herself no more, her eyes closed and she abandoned herself to sensation, pure, unadulterated sensation.

Jasmina sat on the chair beside her. She slipped her arm around her and rested her head against Stephanie's shoulder. Another tableau for the two men across the street. A worthy subject for a painter in oils.

It was minutes, perhaps longer, before either woman wanted to move.

'Did I do right?' Jasmina asked finally.

'Wonderful,' Stephanie said, and meant it.

'But I want more. I want to learn. Will you teach me. Please, I want to learn everything.'

'If that's what you want – '

'Of course! It is so good. Ammm . . .' Jasmina was laughing, her body still full of unaccustomed sensation. 'You have . . . I don't know in English . . . Godemiché?'

'What?'

'Godemiché.' She drew the shape of a phallus in the air with her fingers. 'Like this.'

'A dildo?' Stephanie laughed. 'Is that what you want? You're not exactly shy, are you?'

'I want to try. Everything.' Jasmina smiled broadly, her eyes sparkling with pleasure. 'You will teach me?'

'Yes, if that's what you want. You can come and spend the weekend with me – '

'Can't I come tomorrow?'

'Tomorrow?'

'I can take my holiday.'

Stephanie thought for a moment. She could think of no good reason to say no. 'All right, why not?'

'Good. Then we can fuck, yes?'

Stephanie laughed again. Jasmina's enthusiasm was infectious.

'Yes.'

'Very good.'

She did not seem interested in the details, in whether Stephanie was married, or whether she liked men as well as women, in where and how she lived. All that she was prepared to take on trust. She appeared only to want to repeat the experience as soon as possible, whatever that involved.

Stephanie stood up and went over to the window. Standing looking straight across at the two men, she slowly buttoned up her dress. She wanted them to know she had seen them. They immediately turned away, pretending to be doing something else, shuffling rapidly away from the window.

An hour later, having made the arrangements with Jasmina, Stephanie was back in her hotel room. She quickly stripped off her clothes, took a hot shower in the huge, rather antique bathroom of the suite, put the 'Do Not Disturb' notice on the handle of the door, and lay naked in the fresh linen sheets to sleep for an hour.

As soon as she closed her eyes, images of Jasmina, of the strange modelling room, of the other girls parading in the tight leather costumes, of knickers, and basques, and taut stockings, swam into her mind. She felt Jasmina's mouth pressed into her sex.

In no more than a minute she was asleep, a deep and dreamless sleep.

FIVE

The Rolls Royce Silver Wraith glided almost silently to a halt. On Stephanie's instructions, the driver had picked the perfect spot. The shadow from the street lights was deep. Yet, from the back of the car, there was a perfect view of the circular gravel driveway in front of Gianni's Palladian-designed mansion, the ornate bronze fountain, in the middle of the drive, and the large panelled front door, painted red and lit by a brass lantern hanging under the columned portico.

Stephanie sat back in the leather seat and waited, the blacked-out windows of the car affording her perfect anonymity. She had woken after an hour's siesta, feeling relaxed and rested. Her experience with Jasmina had not diverted her from the main reason for her trip to Rome. Her plans were laid. Now all she had to do was wait.

After half-an-hour the front door of the house opened and a woman appeared in the bright aura of light. Stephanie could see her quite clearly. Though she was probably not more than forty-five, her hair was completely white. She was short and podgy. Her knee length skirt revealed thick calves and plump ankles; the short mink jacket she wore did nothing to hide a well-rounded waist and bust. She wore glasses, elaborately decorated black-framed glasses, sparkling with dia-

51

manté. Even from this distance, Stephanie could see jewellery sparkling too, a large diamond ring on each finger, a double string of pearls around her rather flabby neck. She matched the description Devlin had provided. There was no doubt this woman was Signora Gianni.

Taking keys from a small black clutch-bag, the woman strode to a red Ferrari Testarossa that was parked in the driveway, and climbed into the driving seat. Seconds later the engine roared into life. Pumping the accelerator, like a Grand Prix driver on the starting grid, Signora Gianni let in the clutch and, in a squeal of tyres and spray of gravel, swung the car through the squared columns of the entrance and off down the street. In the four seconds it took to reach the T-junction at the end of the road, the car must have touched eighty miles an hour. With a squeal of brakes it halted before turning left and disappearing from view. The noise of its engine passing through the gears lingered, however, shattering the peace of the neighbourhood.

Calmly, Stephanie adjusted her hair in the mirror set in the rear quarter of the Rolls, picked up the heavy leather bag she was carrying – a bag that resembled the type used by doctors – and got out of the car. Purposefully, she walked through the Palladian columns at the entrance to the drive and up to the front door, her boots crunching on the gravel. There was a small illuminated bell to the side of the door, which she pressed.

After a moment, the door opened. A woman dressed entirely in black stood in the doorway. She was in her early fifties, her dark hair scraped into a bun, her face wearing a scowl. She was a big woman – her arms looked strong, her body hard with years of physical work, her legs meaty and trunk-like.

The woman asked a question in Italian.

Whatever it meant, Stephanie ignored her. She walked past her into the house, as though she owned it. Slipping out of the full length wolf-skin fur she was wearing against the chill of the Roman night, she simply let it fall on to the black and white tiled floor of the huge vestibule. She looked around her. A wide, sweeping staircase led up to the first floor. An elaborate chandelier hung in a domed ceiling. There were artifacts everywhere; ancient busts and sculptures stood in every corner.

'Gianni?' Stephanie said to the astonished woman, who still stood by the open front door.

'Là,' she said, indicating a pair of double doors to one side of the vestibule.

'Grazie,' Stephanie said.

'Prego,' the woman in black intoned, the response automatic.

Stephanie strode over to the doors, her high heels clacking on the tiled floor, and threw them both open. Gianni was sitting in front of a huge marble fireplace on one of two matching sofas which were covered in the hide of what had once been a brown and white cow. He was watching football on a large-screened television.

'Gianni!' Stephanie said.

'Stephanie?' His surprise was total.

She stood in front of him, her legs apart, her arms akimbo. She had chosen her outfit with great care. The sleeveless, black Lycra cat-suit fitted her like it had been sprayed on to her body, hugging every curve and line of her figure from her breasts to her waist, from her thighs to her buttocks, even, she knew, following the delicate fold of her sex. The Lycra made the material shiny: it looked slippery, almost wet. The black high-heeled boots were an equally tight fit, so tight they

53

almost seemed to be part of the cat-suit. A pair of elbow-length gloves in the same material as the cat-suit completed the outfit. The only flesh visible below the neck was the flesh of her upper arms above the gloves. Somehow, by contrast to the black, it seemed incredibly white, white and exposed, soft and almost obscenely naked.

Stephanie dropped the leather bag she was carrying on to the sofa. It clanked heavily as it fell.

'What are you doing here?'

'That's not a very nice greeting. Aren't you pleased to see me, darling? I'm very pleased to see you.'

'My wife . . .' He used the remote control to turn off the television.

'I saw your wife leave, don't worry. She won't be back for hours, will she? Plenty of time. You don't seem very happy to see me at all. And I chose this outfit especially for you.' She ran her hands down from her waist to her hips, then up over the shiny black to her breasts, which she squeezed gently.

'You look magnificent,' he said, his eyes watching her hands.

'You really think so?'

She ran one hand down over her navel and between her legs, caressing the hard curve there. Gianni's eyes followed her hand.

'Why have you come?' he said haltingly.

The housekeeper had come to stand in the double doorway, the astonishment on her face replaced by her scowl of disapproval.

'Aren't you going to offer me something to drink?' Stephanie said, looking towards the door.

'Angelina,' Gianni said, 'bring some champagne.'

The woman disappeared immediately. Stephanie slid down on to the sofa next to Gianni.

'It's so good to see you,' she lied, gripping his fore-arm and caressing the front of his shirt.

'What is this?' he said, still not smiling. He could feel her heat pressing into him, and the way the slippery material moved, almost without friction, against his clothes.

'What do you think Gianni? Aren't you glad to see me? Didn't I mean anything to you?'

'You are a very . . .'

The housekeeper appeared with the champagne. She set it on the glass and chrome coffee table that stood between the two sofas, next to a copy of the Salvador Dali pocket watch that melted over the edge of the glass.

'Close the door,' Gianni ordered firmly.

They watched the woman retreat. She swung the heavy doors closed. They were alone.

'Oh Gianni, you don't know how I've wanted to be with you again.' Stephanie squeezed his arm.

'I thought . . .'

'What?'

He was about to say he thought she didn't like him, but stopped himself. That was ridiculous. All women loved him, however he had treated them.

'You're not pleased to see me. Aren't you English crazee anymore?' she said, pouting.

'Of course I am.' He poured the champagne and handed her a glass. He did not take one for himself.

'I just want to know for why you are here,' he said firmly, trying to ignore the warmth of her body and the way she looked.

'For you, you want the truth, Gianni. What happened at the castle. What you did to me. Everything you did to me. I have never been so turned on, so alive, felt so much . . . You understand?'

'Sì.'

She could see his eyes moving over her body.

'I just couldn't forget it. My God, I tried. Really tried. Tried to rid myself of you. But I couldn't. You know how to please a woman. You know how to handle a woman, what makes a woman come alive. I just had to see you again, Gianni. For three weeks I've done nothing else but think about you, what you did to me. I don't just mean fucking me, but everything. The way you had me in the cellars, all bound and helpless. My god, it was so exciting. The way you used the whip on me . . . I'm sorry, it just makes me hot to think about it.'

'I thought . . .'

'Do you remember what you did? God, I'm making a fool of myself, aren't I? I expect you're used to this. Women throwing themselves at you.' Stephanie's hand had unbuttoned the middle of his shirt and was feeling inside for his nipple.

'Yes.'

'Do you remember what you did? I do.' She pinched his nipple, then flicked it with her nail. She moved closer to him, pushing her long sensual body against his, moving it against him. She whispered in his ear now, filling it with her hot breath.

'I remember every detail Gianni, every little thing you did. How you made me suck your cock, how you made me wait for it, teased me, made me beg for it, how you wanked . . . I remember everything Gianni. It's been driving me craz*ee*.'

She could see his penis standing hard in his Armani slacks. He turned towards her, pulling her on to him, his hand on her thigh.

'No,' she said firmly, pushing his hand away and standing up. 'No, Gianni. I've come a long way for this. Tonight we do it my way.'

56

'What way?'

'I've been thinking about it for three weeks, what I'd do when we're alone.'

'What will you do?'

'Send the servants away and I'll tell you.'

'The servants? They won't come in.'

'Send them away. I want to be able to scream. You're going to make me scream. You don't want your wife to find out. Send them away.'

'There's only Angelica and the cook.'

'Do it. Please, Gianni . . .'

For a moment she thought it wasn't going to work, that he'd seen through her pretended ardour.

'Please . . .' she whispered again. She was standing in front of him, her legs apart. He looked into her crotch, up at her strong pubic bone, as wide as a fist, but wonderfully smooth except for a single fold that the slippery material of the cat-suit followed down between her long, powerful thighs. He was flattered. It didn't occur to him to question anything Stephanie said; of course she would want him so urgently. He was a man, a real man. What woman could resist?

He got up from the sofa, and adjusted his erection by putting his hand in his pocket and pulling it to one side.

'I give you what you want,' he said, and slowly started to grin. 'I give you everything you want.' He walked over to the doors and went out.

Stephanie sipped the champagne. Phase one successfully completed. Congratulations were in order. Everything according to plan. And now Phase Two was about to begin . . .

It took fifteen minutes before the two servants, surprised but delighted not to have to prepare and serve the evening meal, were out of the house. Stephanie watched them from the window as they walked out of the driveway, through the imposing columns of the entrance, and off down the road.

'Well, English,' Gianni said, closing the door, his broad grin, back on his face, 'now we are alone.'

He came over to the sofa and sat beside her. He turned his face to kiss her, but she moved away. She fended off the hand that groped for her breast, too.

'No. Not yet. I have something special in mind, Gianni. Very special. I want to give you an experience like the one you gave me. Special. Something you won't forget.' At least that was true.

'First I fuck you.' He groped for her again, but she rolled away.

'Please, Gianni. I've been thinking about this. Let me – '

'What is this so special?'

Stephanie opened the leather bag she had brought with her. From it she extracted a black silk blindfold, shaped to the contours of the face and padded so that not the slightest hint of light could creep behind it.

'Let me put this on.' Stephanie raised the blindfold to his eyes, but just as she was about to slip it on, Gianni caught her by the wrist. He looked her straight in the eyes, staring to try and see what was in her mind. Stephanie held her breath, and tried to make her eyes show nothing more than rabid sexual desire. It worked. Gianni's hand released her wrist. She pulled the elasticated blindfold down over his eyes, and adjusted it so it was properly placed. As if to compensate him for his co-operation, she pressed the length of her body into his, letting him feel her firm breasts crushed against his chest, her flat belly on his navel, her thigh against his.

'Now all you can do is feel, feel all the things I am going to do to you, Gianni. Stand up.' The order was issued with the air of command Stephanie had learnt at the castle. Gianni obeyed, seemingly having decided to trust her, to let her play her harmless sexual game.

Stephanie unbuckled his Gucci belt and unzipped his trousers. His erection immediately forced its way between the jaws of the zip. She pulled his trousers down until they were around his ankles, then pulled his boxer shorts. His penis was poking through the fly of the shorts. As she pulled them down it was pulled down too – she had no intention of freeing it with her hand – until it was pointing at his feet and slipped out of the material trap, springing back up painfully.

'Ah,' Gianni called.

'Don't be a baby,' Stephanie scolded.

Trying to make sure they did not clank, Stephanie extracted a pair of handcuffs from the black leather bag.

'Hold your hands out, darling,' she said, trying to make it sound innocuous.

'Out where?'

'Out in front of you.'

He obeyed hesitantly. Once the handcuffs were on, Stephanie knew she could drop the pretence – he would be relatively helpless. Until then, she had to let him think this was all an elaborately planned sexual frolic. She caressed his wrists.

'Can you feel that?' she said, moving his hands together, running her fingers all round the joint of his wrists as though trying to discover a new erogenous zone.

'Yes . . .'

'And this?' She moved behind him, pressing herself into his body, hoping to distract him.

'You're very hot,' he said, feeling her body undulating against him, moving as though she were fucking him.

59

'And this?' She took the open cuffs and used them to caress his wrists where her fingers had been.

'It's cold.'

'Yes. Hot and cold. And this –'

With a quick, fluid movement she snapped both cuffs simultaneously over his wrists, the metal loops clicking firmly into the non-return ratchet that locked them in place. Doing it so quickly locked the loops much tighter on to the bone of the wrist, making them uncomfortable.

'Hey!' Gianni protested at once, trying to move his hands away and finding them bound together. 'What you do this for?'

He groped with his hands, trying to catch Stephanie, but she had already moved to one side. With one hand, she pushed him hard in the back. He managed to take a half-step forward, but then his leg was caught in his trouser around his ankle and he stumbled, pitching on to the sofa.

'Basta! Basta! What you do?'

Stephanie mounted his back as if he were a horse, her knees either side of his chest, but facing his feet. She pulled a wide leather strap from the leather bag and strapped it quickly around his knees. He was bucking like a rodeo pony trying to get her off, his naked bum pummelling the air. She was going to gag him, but realised there was no point. No one was going to hear him. The nearest neighbour was a thousand yards away.

Climbing off him, she pulled off the blindfold. The rest of the proceedings she definitely wanted him to see. She stood back to admire her handiwork. Gianni's face was beetroot-red with rage. He cursed her in Italian and English. He screamed and shouted and pulled at the handcuffs. He tried to get to the buckle of the belt at his knees, but hard as he tried he couldn't get his fingers in a position where they could undo it. He was sweating with his efforts; his hair, usually so carefully groomed, all over the place; his eyes fiery with anger.

Calmly, Stephanie stepped over him and took a large masonry hammer from the black leather bag. As soon as he saw it in her hand, his struggles stopped and the expression in his eyes turned from anger to fear.

'Oh, don't worry,' Stephanie said, laughing, 'it's not for you. I'm going to punish you for the way you behaved at the castle, but nothing quite so drastic. I think you'll agree the punishment will fit the crime.'

Looking around the room, Stephanie searched for an appropriate wall. To the left of the fireplace was an ornate, gilded mirror. Taking one of the occasional chairs that dotted the room, Stephanie hauled it over to the mirror and stood on it so she could reach and lift the mirror from its hook. Then she examined the hook. The mirror had been heavy, but the hook was too flimsy for her purpose. It didn't matter. She had come prepared.

She walked back to the black leather bag. She could see Gianni's eyes watching her every movement. He had not resumed his attempts to get free, or his cursing. Her plan had worked: Phase Two completed. Gianni was hers now, and she knew exactly what she was going to do with him. Phase Three.

This time, Stephanie extracted from the bag a large masonry nail, to which was attached a metal ring. She walked back to the chair, feeling Gianni's eyes following her, watching her tight round buttocks rise and fall as she walked, the shiny black material clinging to every curve, even the deep cleft of her arse.

She placed the nail in the middle of the wall, where the mirror had been, and hammered it home with the heavy hammer. Plaster and paint flew everywhere as the nail burrowed into the wall. After six or seven strokes, she paused for a breather; it was hard work. Another six strokes, another storm of dust, another pause. Then she tested the nail by pulling on the metal ring. It still felt a little shaky, so she hammered again. Plaster fell from the delicate cornice above, disturbed by the vibration. A rather dreadful abstract oil painting crashed down from the adjoining wall, hit a sculpture mounted on a pedestal and sent that flying too. It crashed to the floor and shattered into hundreds of pieces. Fortunately, the sculpture was not an antique like those that decorated the vestibule.

At last, the hammering stopped. The nail and its metal ring were completely secure. Stephanie dusted herself off and tested the strength of the ring. The nail had cracked the outer skin of plaster on the wall from floor to ceiling, but was now embedded in the brickwork beneath.

Stephanie went back to the champagne. Her glass was full of bits of plaster, so she swilled it out with fresh champagne and poured this over the cowskin sofa. Then she refilled her glass and sat down Gianni to drink.

'Salute,' she said.

Gianni mumbled something in Italian under his breath.

'Well, back to work,' she said, putting the glass back on the table. She took a short length of chain and two strong padlocks from the leather bag. She expected resistance from Gianni, but got none. He hardly moved as she locked the chain, with one of the padlocks, to the handcuffs.

'Up.' She ordered, pulling on the chain. With difficulty, Gianni got to his feet. She pulled the chain again and he shuffled forward, able to take only tiny steps.

It was then that Gianni saw his chance. As he passed the end of the sofa where the black bag lay open, he pulled back on the chain so viciously that it swept Stephanie off balance and on to the floor. He immediately dived into the bag, rifling through it; reasoning, no doubt, that the keys to the cuffs were inside. He found nothing. He rifled again.

Stephanie got to her feet, dusted herself off again, removing the plaster dust that now covered every surface of the room, and watched as Gianni realised he was not going to find his means of escape.

'I didn't bring any keys,' she said.

'You bitch,' he hissed, the anger flaring in his eyes again.

'Get over to the wall, Gianni.'

He stood motionless. She had expected resistance. She had planned for it.

'You choose, Gianni. Either you go and stand over by the wall like a good boy or . . .' She came up behind him in a flash of movement, and grabbed a handful of his hair. 'Or I'll cut off all your hair. All of it. Oh, I wouldn't be able to make a very good job of it. You'll struggle a lot, I expect. But I'll get most of it. That'll be your punishment. It's your choice.'

She let go of his hair and sat on the sofa. She had calculated that a threat to his vanity would have the maximum effect.

'Well? I haven't got all night.'

He shuffled over to the wall and stood under the metal ring.

'Hands above your head,' she ordered.

Again he obeyed. In minutes, the padlock was secured to the ring, his hands chained above his head.

'You not touch my hair?'

'No, Gianni. I've nearly finished.'

From the black bag she produced a short riding crop. It was the whip he had used on her, tipped not with a short loop of leather, but a thin knotted tassel.

'Recognise this?'

Gianni didn't move.

'Do you?' she said.

'Sì.'

'Good. You used it on me four times. Now it is my turn.'

For the first time, she felt a buzz of sexual excitement – she knew it was the thrill she got from power. She had noticed Gianni's penis as she'd produced the whip, pushing out from between his shirt tails.

She pulled his expensive shirt open.

'I still have the marks. Here,' she tapped his chest with the whip, 'and here,' she tapped the top of his thighs.

Without pausing, she sliced the whip across his chest. He moaned. A bright red welt appeared immediately. She aimed low, and hit him twice across his thigh, just under his cock. His cock was fully erect. She could see a tear of moisture at its tip.

She would have liked to deliver the fourth stroke in the same place he had hit her, down between his thighs, but she had to make do with another cut across the top. He moaned again. Three red welts criss-crossed the white flesh. Stephanie threw the whip aside.

'Please . . .' he moaned.

'Please, what?' she asked.

'Oh, come on, you know . . .'

'Know what?'

'This is all a turn on, right? You do this to get me hard, no? Come on. Please. Do it to me. Look at my cock. You can't leave me like this. Fuck me. Suck me. Do it to me.'

Stephanie took the final item from the bag. A red ribbon. She dropped to her knees in front of Gianni and tied a big bow around his cock. The bow made his erection harder, the veins in his cock straining and taut from all the extra blood.

'Oh yes,' he said. 'That's so good.'

'Is it?'

'You're so sexy, Stephanie.'

'And I'm so wet for you. So hot. You should feel how hot I am.'

'Yes . . .'

'Unfortunately, I haven't got time. I've got to be going. Perhaps another time. Please give my regards to your wife. You've got an hour to think up an explanation.'

Gianni looked puzzled as she stepped away.

'Come on . . .' His puzzlement turned to anger again. She really was going to leave him. Him. 'You can't leave me like this.'

She patted him on the cheek. 'Do you really think you're irresistible, Gianni? Sorry to disappoint you. I'm sure your wife will be only too happy to service your needs.'

'No. Get me down.'

He started cursing her in Italian again, pulling at the chains. The metal ring held firm.

Stephanie opened the double doors and then turned to survey the scene of chaos she had created. The room looked like a bomb had hit it. Everything was covered in a thin layer of plaster dust, the wall to which Gianni was chained was cracked badly and, best of all, Gianni stood helpless, four red welts across his body, a red ribbon tied around his cock. She could see the look of absolute hatred that burned in his eyes. There was no escape for him, no way he would be able to explain this away to his wife.

'Bye,' she said, closing the door after her.

He alternated between threats and pleas. The noise followed her out into the vestibule, where she picked up her fur from the floor. It had lain there untouched. Outside the front door, she signalled across the road to her driver, and the Rolls pulled into the drive, its big tyres crunching on the gravel. The driver got out hastily, opened the rear passenger door for her, and then, as she settled into the luxurious interior, cuddling the fur around her, he gunned the engine, turning the big car out of the drive and back towards the hotel.

Stephanie could not stop smiling. She looked back at the house and realised she had left the front door open. Not that it mattered. The next person through the front door would be Signora Gianni. Her revenge was complete.

Or so she thought.

SIX

It was not until she was sitting comfortably cocooned in the leather seat of the Rolls that Stephanie realised quite how turned on she was. Her whole body seemed to be alive; her mind full of images of Gianni – chained, erect, helpless, the red welts from the whip burnt across his soft flesh. It was an excitement generated by power, she knew, by being in control. It was the same feeling that had thrilled her so much at the castle. Her plan had worked perfectly. Apart from one token show of resistance, which she had dealt with as planned, Gianni had been trapped. She had prevailed. She was the ring master in control of the circus.

Her hand, unconsciously at first, had moved into her lap. As she replayed the images, she caressed her labia softly through the clinging slippery material of the cat-suit.

It was only when she saw the driver's eyes in the rearview mirror, watching her, that she became conscious of what she was doing. She realised too, that she had been making little whimpering noises, as her fingers worked on her sex. She didn't stop. Under her fingers she could feel her labia were swollen and hot, her clitoris hard and throbbing. The cat-suit was wet between her legs.

The glass partition in the Silver Wraith, between

passenger and driver, was half raised already. Stephanie pressed the small black button to wind it up the rest of the way. It slid closed with a satisfying clunk.

Her other hand had not stopped working between her legs. Her need was urgent now. There was no way she could get at herself without taking the cat-suit off completely. With her free hand, she clawed at her breasts, finding her nipples and pinching them hard. She moaned. The sound of her own voice surprised her. It sounded deep, so excited, so like the many times she had moaned with exquisite pleasure at the hands of a woman or a man or both.

She shucked herself out of the fur and put it on the seat beside her. Then she pulled the long zip of the cat-suit that ran from her neck to the small of her back. For a second, she hesitated. She could see the driver's eyes beneath the peak of his cap. They stared intensely in the rearview mirror. The back of the car was dark, but passing street lights illuminated the back seat like a spotlight switched on and off in rapid succession.

She decided she didn't care. Her need was too urgent. If they hadn't been winding their way through suburban streets, she might well have got the driver to stop and fuck her. She pulled the cat-suit off her shoulders, levered her backside up off the seat by arching her back, and pulled it down to her knees. Quickly, she unzipped the boots, and pulled them and the cat-suit off her legs. She was naked. The clinging material would have shown the line of even the smallest G-string, so she had worn no underwear.

Her nakedness doubled her excitement. She writhed around on the leather seat enjoying the freedom. With enormous relief, her hand found her uncovered labia. She put one foot up on the seat beside her and let her fingers delve into her cunt. She moaned again as she pushed them home, deep into the silky black cavern of her cunt. It was soaking wet, running with her juices.

Her other hand kneaded her breast almost viciously, wanting to milk it of sensation. She could see the driver's eyes. They were stationary at a traffic light, and the light from a street lamp spilled into the back of the car. She knew he could see her fingers pushing rhythmically between her thick labia, in the middle of her black public hair spread out over her belly like a rug. She wanted him to see. She arched herself off the seat, pointing her cunt at his eyes in the mirror.

The traffic lights changed. She felt the car move forward, then slow and stop. The driver had parked in a side street, directly under a street lamp. He turned the car engine off but did not look round. Looking round was not allowed, he knew. He had to make do with the mirror.

People were walking on the pavements, voices calling to each other, talking in rapid Italian. The driver adjusted the rearview mirror, angling it down. A man and a woman peered in through the blackened windows, trying to see who was inside. They could see nothing but their own reflection, and moved on.

Stephanie was beyond the point of no return. Her body ached for its release, every nerve taut and ready. She stopped using her fingers in imitation of a cock, and moved them up to hold the flesh of her labia open, stretched open so that her clitoris, the little pink bud of her clitoris, was completely exposed. Then, taking her hand from her breast, she snaked it down until the tip of one finger rested on the centre of her passions. For a moment, she teased herself, making no movement. Then she tapped the clitoris with her finger tip, tapped it softly, then harder, then harder still.

She felt herself coming, each blow of the finger producing a shock wave in her body, each shock wave joining with the one before, taking her higher, her whole body raked by sensation. As her orgasm broke, as the taut elastic of her nerves snapped, making her cry out loud with its intensity, her mind was full of images, feeding her orgasm. She saw the driver's eyes silently watching her in the mirror, she saw Gianni's cock weeping its tear of fluid, but most of all, she saw herself, tall and straight, clad in the clinging cat-suit, standing whip in hand next to the helpless Gianni. She saw her revenge. It was that image, she knew, that brought her off again, a final shock wave pulsing through her already tingling nerves, a final moan of pleasure wrested from her lips.

Without a word from her, the driver started the engine and pulled the car out into the traffic. Stephanie lay still for a moment, luxuriating in the aftermath of her orgasm. Both her hands were wet with her own juices; the back of the car reeked of the smell of sex.

They were heading past the Palazzo Barberini, a baroque seventeenth century palace, and were, therefore, very near the hotel.

Stephanie slipped on her boots and climbed back into the fur coat. There was no way she could squeeze herself back into the cat-suit, even if she'd wanted to – which she didn't. The idea of walking through the Excelsior, naked but for her fur, made her smile.

The driver pulled the car into the small colonnade of the hotel. A doorman immediately opened the rear passenger door, and was rewarded by a view of the whole stretch of Stephanie's thigh as she climbed out, and a ten thousand lira note which she pressed into his palm.

'I won't be needing you again tonight,' she said to the driver. He stood impassively by the driver's door, his face giving no indication of what had happened. 'Think of me,' she wanted to say, 'when you're fucking your wife.' But she said nothing, not even smiling at him.

Stephanie felt wild. Her body was tingling, her nerves flaring. As she walked up the steps into the hotel, she felt the cool silk lining of the fur against her naked body, against her rump and her thighs, against her hard nipples.

She was much too excited to sleep, that was certain. She turned into the bar, instead of heading for the lift.

'A very dry Martini,' she said to the smart but diminutive barman, arranging herself on one of the barstools. 'With a twist.'

She watched him make it, shaking it in a silver mixer before pouring it into a triangular cocktail glass.

'Grazie,' she said.

'Prego,' came the automatic response. The barman smiled, revealing two gold teeth.

The bar was almost empty. A middle-aged couple sat in the heavy brocade armchairs, drinking a bottle of French wine. The man had watched Stephanie come in. It was not easy for him to see her from where he was sitting, but he tried his best, twisting around, attracted, no doubt, by the way the fur coat fell away from her crossed legs to reveal a great deal of tanned and shapely thigh – so much it almost looked as if she had nothing else on under the fur. Could it be true? He strained to see.

The martini was just what she needed; a big cold jolt of strong spirit.

'Where is the best night life near here?' she asked the barman.

'Well . . .' He thought for a moment. 'La Sinistra. If you want to dance, is good.'

Dancing was exactly what Stephanie wanted to do.

'Can I walk there?'

'Sì. Is just across the street. Where Harry's Bar is, on that corner.'

'Great.'

She finished the martini.

'You look very happy, signorina. Is nice to see people looking happy.'

'I am.'

'Better than looking sad. Too many people, they look sad all day. Look sad, feel sad.'

'Yes.'

She peeled a ten thousand lira note from her purse and left it on the bar.

'Grazie, signorina.'

'Prego,' she said, smiling.

As she climbed down from the bar-stool, the fur fell away and a naked breast swung into view, as well as a quick flash of dark pubic hair. The man who had been watching her was sipping his wine. He almost choked as his secret suspicion proved to be a reality.

Stephanie walked past him, wrapping the fur around herself and smiling at him sweetly.

Back in her room she had a long bath, towelled herself down then searched through the packages that had been delivered from the shops after her morning shopping expedition. She soon found what she was looking for, a short navy-blue leather skirt she had bought in Trussadi. It came with a matching leather halter top which was really no more than a bra – the sort of bra that was cut to push the breasts upwards and together to form a deep cleavage, its shoulder straps as far apart as possible.

Since her experiences at the castle, Stephanie had hardly worn tights. Tights were associated with work, with the office, with her life as it had been. But the skirt was too short for stockings, so tonight she would need tights again. Fortunately, she had bought two or three pairs for her shorter dresses.

Sitting on the bed, she pointed her toe and fitted the sheer nylon over her foot. Gradually, she played the material she had gathered in her hands, out over her calf, up over her knee, and then watched as it encased her thigh. She repeated the process with the other leg, before standing up so she could pull the hose over her belly and in between her legs, smoothing it on to her flesh. She didn't bother to wear knickers.

As she stood she glimpsed herself in the long mirror on the wardrobe doors, naked but for the sheer black tights. Her breasts looked white in contrast to the dark shiny nylon, but her waist was trim, her legs looked long and strong and firm, shaped by the nylon, and her black hair streamed down over her shoulders. Not bad, she thought to herself smiling. She turned sideways to admire the pertness of her arse and the prominence of her uptilted breasts. Not bad.

She pulled the leather skirt up over her hips and zipped it into place. She hooked the halter top over her breasts and found a pair of high heels to match the blue. She clipped her hair into a long pony tail so it would stay together when she danced. She looked at herself in the mirror again. The halter emphasised the nakedness above the skirt and the ripeness of her breasts. The skirt was short, covering no more than two or three inches of her thighs, leaving her long legs, shining in the black nylon, a definite object of desire.

She looked so sexy as she pirouetted in the heels that she was turning herself on. And that, of course, was her intention. Her whole body still throbbed with a sexuality she could not control, nor had the slightest desire to. Masturbating in the car had temporarily relieved her most intense feelings but it had, in turn, created a new need. Her sexual appetite had been assuaged but not sated. Now she wanted it satisfied. What she badly needed now was cock; hard, hot, spunking cock. She needed to feel it thrusting inside her, taking her, using her. Nothing else would do.

Yes, she wanted to dance. She wanted to dance and use the energy that seemed to be coursing through her like electricity. But dancing was foreplay, a foreplay to sex. She wanted to fuck. Fuck and be fucked. Sate herself with fucking.

And since she had been at the castle, since she had been with Devlin, since her new life had begun, the wonder was that now she always got what she wanted.

She stuck her tongue out at herself in the mirror and laughed out loud. She picked up a small bag to carry her purse, put the fur around her shoulders and walked out of the suite.

'You shall go to the ball,' she said aloud, for no particular reason.

Judging from the admiring – not to say leering – looks she got as she marched through the spacious marble-pillared lobby of the hotel, she was not going to have any trouble satisfying her appetites.

Outside there was a distinct chill in the Roman air.

'Taxi?' It was the doorman she had tipped earlier.

'No. La Sinistra.' She pointed over to Harry's Bar. 'It's there.'

'Sì, signorina. For this you don't need a taxi.'

'That's what I was told. Help me, would you.'

She took the fur from her shoulders and had him hold it for her while she put her arms in the sleeves. She could feel his eyes on her cleavage. Actually, he was not bad looking, she thought; he was tall and looked strong.

'What time do you go home?' she asked.

'Two, signorina.'

'See you later, then.' She pressed another ten thousand lira note into his hand. He was her insurance policy; if there was nothing better at the club well, he would just have to do.

She crossed the road and walked up towards Harry's Bar. As she approached, she could see a bright red and blue neon sign in the side street flashing the name 'LA SINISTRA' with a curved arrow pointing to a small door.

At the door, a short but thick-set man in an evening suit and black tie let her pass without a word. He demanded no payment, despite the fact that the couple in front of her had been charged fifteen thousand lira each.

Stephanie walked down the narrow, red-carpeted staircase, decorated with signed pictures of Italian pop singers. At the bottom there was a cloakroom, where a girl in a red leotard and black fishnet tights took her fur in exchange for a small plastic token in the form of a hand engraved with a number. Beyond the cloakroom was a lozenge-shaped bar in the middle of a large brightly coloured room, from which half-a-dozen staff mixed and served cocktails as colourful as the lights that flashed continuously from the dance floor on the other side of the bar.

The club was not crowded. Stephanie found a table where she could survey both the dance floor and most of the bar area. Almost before she was seated, a waiter, dressed in a black and white striped T-shirt and white trousers, was at her side.

'Signorina?'

'A bottle of champagne. Dom Perignon.'

'Sì, signorina. Presto.'

Stephanie crossed her legs, the nylon rasping on her thighs as she watched the waiter go over to the bar and place the order. She watched the bottle being extracted from the refrigeration, opened, placed in an ice bucket in the shape of a top hat, then on a tray with two glasses – perhaps they thought Stephanie was not alone – and swung over the counter to the waiter. In a minute, he was back, setting the tray down in front of her knees.

He murmured a question.

Stephanie looked puzzled. The waiter indicated the cork on the bottle.

'Sì. Grazie,' she said.

He eased the cork out without a sound and poured the wine into one of the glasses.

'Grazie,' Stephanie repeated.

'Prego,' he said, bowing slightly and hurrying away.

Sipping the champagne, Stephanie looked around. The hard, insistent rhythm of the disco music pounding from the speakers on the dance floor perfectly matched her mood. Her foot tapped to the beat.

There were several groups of men in the bar, some with women in the party, some without. Stephanie had attracted everything from admiring glances to lecherous stares. The fact that, seated, her leather skirt hid little, did nothing to discourage their looks. There were two young men sitting on bar-stools that she particularly noticed, however. One was tall, slim but athletic, with black curly hair and an open face with strong features and a firm chin. He looked like he might be a long distance runner for the Italian Olympic Team. His friend was shorter, but with equally curly dark hair. He looked fit too, but was much broader in the shoulders, looking as though he had considerable upper-body strength. His face was puckish, his eyes glinting with mischief. Neither was more than twenty years old.

Both men had glanced at Stephanie with admiration, their eyes lingering on her long legs. The next time the taller of the two looked round, Stephanie caught his eye. She beckoned him over with a crooked finger. He pointed at himself as if to say, 'What, me?' then nudged his friend before walking over to her table.

'Buone sera,' he said cheerily, smiling his best smile.

'You speak English?' she asked.

He shook his head and shrugged. Not that it mattered. For what she had in mind sign language would be quite enough. She patted the seat next to her and poured a glass of champagne. Handing it to him, she clinked the side of her own glass against his.

'Cheers,' she said.

'Salute,' he replied, sipping the champagne.

'No English at all?'

He shrugged again.

'You'll dance?' She indicated the dance floor.

'Danzare? Sì, sì.'

He stood up, looking down into her cleavage and at her long legs. 'Bella,' he said, almost to himself. He held out his hand to help her up from the rather low seats. He did not let go of her hand when she was up, but instead used it to lead her on to the dance floor. She saw him exchange looks with his friend.

It was not difficult to be carried away by the throbbing beat of the disco music. The DJ was good at his job. He increased the pace of the music gradually but continually, each song a little bit more upbeat, requiring a little bit more effort. Stephanie had always loved to dance. She let her body move with the music, let it take her over until she felt her pulse rate rising, her heart pumping, and a sort of euphoria overtaking her;

nothing left in her mind but the pounding beat.

The DJ changed the mood with Chris de Burgh and *Lady in Red*. Her Italian caught her hand and pulled her to him, both his hands snaking behind her back to hold her tightly against him. That was what she wanted, too. She suddenly felt seventeen again, dancing at school balls, remembering how all the girls had teased the boys, trying to see if they could give them an erection by stroking their necks, biting and blowing in their ears, pushing themselves against their groins. She remembered how it had felt as their penises unfurled, nosing up against her navel, hot and hard. In those days, the boy would often blush and break away. Or not. Those that didn't were the experienced ones, the ones that knew. They pushed their erections rhythmically into her navel, up and down, while their hands worked their way over the cheeks of her arse . . .

The music stopped, and a more aggressive number blared out again to start another sequence. Her Italian started to dance again, but she caught his hand and pulled him towards the bar.

At the table, most of the ice in the bucket had melted and the Dom Perignon was now very cold. The Italian refilled both their glasses. Using sign language, Stephanie indicated the glass and then the Italian's friend, who still sat on the bar-stool all alone. The Italian, catching on quickly, beckoned his friend over.

'Would you like a drink?' Stephanie said when he arrived.

'Sì, grazie.'

He glanced at his friend, uncertain as to what was going on. The friend shrugged his shoulders, equally puzzled. Stephanie attracted the waiter's attention and asked him to bring another glass and another bottle.

'Stephanie,' she said, pointing at herself.

'Angelo,' the Italian she had danced with said, smiling.

'Carlo,' the new arrival added.

'Well boys, here's to a wonderful evening.'

'Salute.'

'Salute.'

'You speak English, Carlo? Parla l'inglese?'

Carlo smiled, his mischievous face radiating pleasure, his eyes darting over Stephanie's body.

'A little,' he said haltingly.

'Come on, let's dance some more.'

Stephanie got up and took Carlo's hand. Angelo looked crestfallen until she extended her other hand to him. Then his puzzlement returned.

She pulled them both to the dance floor and danced with them both. She aimed her body subtly at each in turn, moving her hips in time to the music, making circles in the air, looking into their eyes to tell them what she was thinking as she was dancing: that dancing was a form of sex, a rehearsal, a movement class in sexual gyration. She held her breast, she caressed her sides, she shimmied and shook, and let the music and the excitement she was creating in both men's eyes carry her away with the pounding rhythm.

When the slow number came this time she pulled them both to her, dancing with them in a little triangle, until Carlo broke away, not liking what she was making them do. She immediately closed up on Angelo, pushing her belly into him, holding him tightly in her arms, whispering into his ear.

'Are you going to fuck me, Angelo?' she breathed. 'Are you good at fucking? I need to be fucked.'

She knew he didn't understand a word she said, but her tone must have meant something. She felt his erection grow. She pushed her thigh hard between his

79

legs and bit the lobe of his ear. She ran her hand down over his buttocks. His cock hardened.

'Sì?' she questioned. 'Bene?'

'Così?' he said, pushing his growing erection against her.

'Sì. Sì.' Now it was not a question.

She kissed him on the mouth, a hard, penetrating kiss, her hand holding the back of his head so she could push her lips up against his. She broke the kiss, looked straight into his eyes, then kissed him again. His erection felt like a bone now, sticking up between their bodies.

'Bello,' she said, looking at him again. 'That's what I want, Angelo.'

She led him off the dance floor in the middle of the song. Carlo was sitting on a stool, at the table. She came up behind him and pushed herself into his back, the hem of the leather skirt, because the stool was so low, brushing the nape of his neck. Her hands massaged his shoulders. Then she pulled him to his feet and on to the dance floor.

It was Angelo's turn to look sulky. He sat and poured himself more champagne.

Stephanie felt Carlo's body against her. It was different from Angelo's. Angelo was slim, skinny, bony. Carlo was muscled, plump but hard. Even his hands were rough and calloused. She hugged him to her. But none of her tricks had his penis unfurl, not the ear biting, not the hand between his buttocks, not the seductive words she whispered to him, which, even in another language, must have been clear in their tone.

The evening continued in the same vein. More champagne was consumed. More dancing. More sulky looks from the one consigned to sit it out at the table, to watch the object of his affection dancing with another.

It was the perfect evening for Stephanie. The dancing made her body feel energised and alive. The tension between the two men amused her, the champagne relaxed her, and the music reached inside her to the rhythms and tempos that, she had recently discovered, were now essential to her life. The lack of conversation, the need to make small talk removed, was curiously refreshing. It was a silent movie, a ballet of seduction.

She played with them like a cat, teasing them with her paws, giving them a little nudge, a little scratch with her claw.

At two she decided she had drunk enough champagne and paid the bill, giving the waiter a generous tip. Both her male companions looked embarrassed as she counted out the money, but neither attempted to offer to pay. Dom Perignon is expensive in any language. What the men thought she was, or did, to be able to afford such luxuries, she did not know or care.

For a final dance she took Angelo's hand and smooched with him around the dance floor. The DJ was playing mostly moody music now, and the many couples on the dance floor were stuck to each other, their hands caressing arms and backs, their lips pressed to shoulder, neck or cheek.

'We go home now,' Stephanie said. 'Casa . . .' she remembered the word.

'Sì.' He smiled. 'Sì.'

In the bar again, Angelo looked distinctly pleased with himself. He said something to Carlo, who shrugged his shoulders in a gesture of acceptance. They followed Stephanie to the cloakroom, where she exchanged the plastic token and a ten thousand lira note for her fur coat. Angelo held it for her while she slipped her arms into the sleeves.

'Bella,' he said. She was not sure whether he meant her or the coat.

Carlo led the way up the stairs. They walked out into the clear and chilly night. Several people were leaving too, and a series of taxis had arrived in the narrow street to pick them up. Stephanie looked round. Suddenly, Carlo had disappeared.

'Carlo? Where's he going?' she said to Angelo, who immediately looked sulky again.

She had seen Carlo getting into a taxi, the last in the line in the street. Taking Angelo's hand firmly in hers, she ran to the taxi, which was unable to pull away because of the others in front, and got in, pulling a reluctant Angelo in beside her.

'Carlo! Where are you going?' She desperately needed some Italian. How could she explain what she wanted. 'I want you both,' she said. 'Both.'

The taxi driver started to laugh, a deep, throaty, dirty laugh. He turned round to look at Stephanie. The fur coat was open. He looked up her long legs, admired her tight cleavage, and laughed more. 'English, yes?' he said.

'Yes. You speak English?'

'I worked in London, two years, Terrazza Restaurant – '

'Take us to the Excelsior. I know it's only across the street.' She extracted a fifty thousand lira note from her bag.

'Anything you want, lady.'

'I want you to translate.'

'Both?' He laughed. 'You want both, yes?'

She saw no point being embarrassed. She had drunk too much champagne to be embarrassed. 'Yes, I'm a very greedy girl.'

'You wouldn't like to make it three, would you?'

'I don't think you could stand the pace.' The driver was sixty. His huge pasta belly almost rested against the bottom of the steering wheel. He looked as though he had never taken a day's exercise in his life.

'You're right.' He burst into laughter again, the road ahead still blocked by other taxis and people climbing into them.

Angelo snapped a question at the driver, obviously irritated by his exclusion from the conversation.

The driver spoke in rapid Italian with what seemed to Stephanie to be obvious passion. Neither Carlo nor Angelo made any reply. As he delivered his diatribe, the road ahead cleared and he drove the taxi into the Via Veneto, turned right and then left into the hotel colonnade, no more than a thousand yards away.

The doorman opened the rear door of the taxi. Angelo and Carlo remained silent. Nobody moved. Then the taxi-driver burst into another lilting passage of Italian in which the only word Stephanie recognised was 'presto'.

'What did you tell them?'

'That they should be so lucky. That the honour of the whole of Italy was on their shoulders.'

Now it was Stephanie's turn to laugh. 'Ask them how old they are?'

He did. 'The tall one's eighteen and his brother's twenty.'

'They're brothers?' she said, astonished.

'Sì, signorina. It makes a difference?'

'No.'

Angelo got out and helped Stephanie. Carlo slid along the seat and got out of the same door. Stephanie bent down to the window of the taxi.

'Grazie,' she said, smiling.

'Prego,' the driver said, grinning broadly to reveal gums which had more gaps than teeth.

SEVEN

The mini-bar in the sitting room of the suite was stocked with champagne. Stephanie gave it to Angelo, signed that he should open it, and went into the bathroom. She contemplated stripping her clothes off but decided against it.

Angelo poured the champagne and handed her a glass. He had only poured one glass. Before she took it, she reached behind her back and unhooked the leather halter top. She slid it off her shoulders and dropped it on to one of the armchairs. Her breasts trembled at their freedom, her nipples flat. She took the glass of champagne, already covered with condensation, and held it against each nipple in turn. As if by magic both nipples sprung up from her breasts, like mushrooms maturing in time-lapse photography, round and swollen. Both men's eyes were watching her.

She didn't really want any more champagne, and handed the glass to Carlo, who sipped at it without taking his eyes from her breasts. He handed it to his younger brother, who did not drink.

Stephanie walked around the huge sitting room of the suite with its rather ancient reproduction furniture, her high heels clacking on the parquet floor where it was not covered with rugs, her firm breasts bouncing slightly as she moved. A delicious sense of anticipation was coursing through her body. So much potential for pleasure, her pleasure, so many possibilities, so many things she could do, so many things she could think of doing.

'Who's going to unzip me, then?'

Both men stood together looking uncomfortable and uneasy, as if they didn't know where to put their hands, how to stand, or what to do. They shifted from one foot to another, looking at Stephanie as she prowled the room like some big cat.

Stephanie pointed to the short zip at the side of the skirt and mimed the action of unzipping it. She was closest to Angelo, who moved towards the zip as if approaching a poisonous snake. The skirt fell to the floor. Stephanie stepped out of it but did not pick it up. She took the champagne glass from Angelo and sipped from it.

The brothers were staring at her legs in the shiny black tights clinging to every contour, revealing and yet, at the same time, not revealing. They could see the shadow of her pubic hair but not the detail. They could see what all evening their fevered imaginations had strained to see under the skirt. This was the vision in the mirror Stephanie had seen earlier as she had dressed. With her high heels shaping her calves and tipping her arse into a distinct pout, she walked some more, letting them watch her, turning so they could examine every angle of her body – front, side, back – the black nylon cutting her into two halves, black and white; soft sensual white, shiny slippery black.

'Where shall we start, then?' The words hung in the air. She stopped walking and stood facing both men, her legs apart, one arm on her hip the other holding the champagne glass to her lips. She licked the edge of the glass with her tongue.

She put the glass down and came over to Angelo. 'You first,' she said, with a slight tone of menace in her voice.

She stood directly in front of him. He looked down at her naked breasts, so round and plump, the nipples corrugated by the cold of the glass. Stephanie unbuttoned his shirt slowly. There was no hurry. She wanted to be fucked, but there was plenty of time. Her mood was teasing, quizzical, adventurous. She unbuckled his belt and pulled down his zip. The trousers fell from his skinny hips.

Stephanie dropped to her knees. He wore small black briefs in cotton. His cock was only just beginning to engorge. She pulled the tight elastic of his briefs until they were down to his knees, then circled his cock with her hand. She felt it growing. Wanting to feel it grow in her mouth, she moved her head to gobble it up. Wetting it all over with her tongue, she sucked hard and felt it swell at an alarming rate, thrusting out and burying itself in her throat. She sucked again, and this time felt no increase in size. It was fully grown.

Carlo moved to his brother's side. She saw his eyes watching her. She saw him pulling off his shirt.

She concentrated on Angelo. She pulled away from his cock to look at it, holding it in her hand. It was long and thin. A perfect match for Angelo's figure. The foreskin was already back and she used her hand to retract it fully. Angelo groaned. She sucked on the tip, using her tongue to probe the little slit while her hand grasped first one ball and then, reeling it in by the scrotum, the other. She felt him tense as she cupped his balls in her hand, but then, as she pulled them gently downward, away from his body while her mouth went back to his cock, plunging down on it as far as she could go, his tension became pleasure.

87

She took him deep in her throat, thinking how good this cock would feel in her cunt. It would skewer her, pierce her, go so deep. Unconsciously, she wriggled her arse.

It was all too much for him – what she was doing to his balls, how she looked, his cock so deep in her mouth. Too much for his eighteen years.

She felt his cock begin to spasm and before she could do anything she felt him come, his hot spunk jetting out of him just as she was about to pull him back from her throat. He made a sound of anguish, a throaty moan, as he lost control.

Stephanie swallowed, but there was so much, some escaped from the sides of her mouth. She used her hand to milk his balls, to get every last drop. She felt his cock beginning to shrink. Too much excitement, she thought. But at eighteen, recovery time was meant to be short.

She had no time to feel disappointment however. As Angelo's cock slipped from her mouth she felt Carlo's naked thighs pressing into her shoulders. She turned and was confronted by a hard, circumcised cock, not as long as Angelo's but much thicker. Eagerly, she sucked it into her mouth, taking it all in until she could feel the coarse curls of pubic hair on her lips. Carlo's hands were on the back of her head. He found the elastic that held her hair in the pony tail and pulled it free, letting Stephanie's long black hair cascade over her naked shoulders. Then he held her head and began to control her rhythm, pushing her down on to him, then pulling her back.

Instead of reaching for his balls, as she had done with his brother, Stephanie moved her hands round to his muscular buttocks. She could feel them contract as he drove his cock forward to meet her mouth. She worked her hand down into the cleft of his arse, searching for the opening to his anus. As soon as she found it, she pushed a finger in. He groaned and stopped his movement. For a moment she thought he was going to come. She pushed her finger deeper and moved it around, reaming his arse like she had reamed Jasmina's cunt.

He started his rhythm again. She'd nearly made him come but he was in control now. He took his cock almost all the way out, until his glans was poised at her lips, then plunged back down again, all the way.

Stephanie looked up, as best she could without moving her head, and saw Angelo, naked now, standing at their side, his hand gently wanking his cock. It was already semi-erect again.

Pulling away from Carlo's cock, Stephanie stood up. Without looking at either man she walked slowly into the bedroom, aware of their eyes on her back, on the movement of her buttocks in the tights. Nylon rasping on nylon, her high heels clacked on the wooden floor.

In the bedroom, she kicked off her shoes and threw herself on the bed. She felt wild, hungry for sex. She waited until Carlo and Angelo came into the room, then raised her buttocks off the bed and pulled the tights down over her hips and thighs. Finally she pulled them from her ankles. She picked them up and threw them at Angelo. They hit his chest, then fell to hook on his hand where it held his long, thin cock. It was fully erect now, as erect as its brother.

'Carlo,' she said, wanting Carlo first. She wanted to talk dirty – to tell Carlo to fuck her arse off, to stuff his cock up her cunt – but it was pointless. Instead she pushed her fingers into her own cunt and was not surprised to find it running with her juices. Carlo knelt on the bed. He pulled her hand away from her cunt and sucked on her wet fingers greedily. Then he pinned her hands back on the bed, slid on top of her and bucked his cock into her, all in one movement as though they had practised the manoeuvre a thousand times. He pushed deep, right up to the hilt, then stopped as his arm slid around the back of her neck. He kissed her on the lips, his tongue probing her mouth, thick and fat like his cock. His other hand moved down between their navels until his finger, the tip of his middle finger, found the bud of her clitoris and started to rub it, circle it, pull it, to and fro, up and down, as he started to pump his cock into her.

It was an exquisite feeling. Stephanie was alight with pleasure. She looked over at Angelo. His eyes were riveted to her cunt, watching it fucked, watching her cunt lips stretched and pursed on Carlo's thick sword of flesh.

Carlo's finger was making her come. It was expert. It knew when to push, when to circle, when to pull. It was like being wanked by a woman while being fucked by a man. Stephanie felt herself drowning in sensation from this man, his finger, his hard body on top of her, his hard cock inside her. She started moaning, loud moans that were almost the words 'Oh yes, yes, do it,' but not quite. She felt her juices running out of her, over his cock, down over his balls, as her orgasm jolted through her and she hugged this man to her, the feel of his muscled body giving her an extra kick of pleasure.

But Carlo did not come. He pulled out of her as soon as he felt her orgasm subside, and spoke in rapid fire Italian to his brother. Stephanie lay on the bed naked, her legs open, her thick pubic hair plastered down with her own wetness, her labia exposed. The brothers were talking. Whatever the words, the intonation was a question; Angelo asking questions, Carlo reassuring, persuading, asserting authority.

The conversation ended, presumably with Angelo appeased, as he lay next to Stephanie on the bed, his long cock sticking up into the air. Carlo nudged Stephanie, miming that she should get on top of Angelo. She was only too happy to oblige. She climbed over his thin frame and positioned herself with her knees either side of his hips, her labia poised above the tip of his cock. She reached back between her legs and held the long slim shaft, as hard now as it had been in her mouth, while she lowered herself on to it. It went deep. Very deep. So deep it took her breath away. It was deep and sharp, a feeling she had never had before. She rocked forward to ease it a little, her nipples grazing Angelo's hairless chest. He lifted his head and kissed her mouth before taking both her nipples into his mouth in turn – sucking them, licking them, flicking them with his tongue, biting them gently and not so gently.

She squirmed on his cock, responding to the feelings from her breasts. She allowed his cock deeper again, experimenting to see where it felt best.

She felt a hand at her cunt, fingers either side of her labia, either side of Angelo's cock, and she knew instantly what Carlo had said in Italian. His fingers were stroking her wetness upward, up towards her arse, making it wet with the juices from her cunt. She knew what was going to happen. The thought made her come. She pushed down on Angelo's cock, and felt an orgasm break in her, felt an arc of pleasure between her cunt and the nipple between his teeth join with the sudden realisation of what Carlo was going to do to her.

Carlo felt the shudder of pleasure. 'Sì, sì, bella.'

He knelt on the bed behind her, his penis immediately pushing into the small of her back. He stroked her long black hair, pulling it all back, back

91

until it was long pony tail again held by his hand.

His penis nosed lower. She could feel it at her arse. She could not stop herself from trembling with excitement. The orgasm she had had refused to go away; it lingered in her body waiting to be renewed, redoubled. Carlo caressed her back with his free hand and then moved it on to her breast. He squeezed her nipple. The other nipple was in Angelo's mouth.

'Sì, sì, sì . . .' he was saying in the tone of voice that would sooth a skittish horse.

Suddenly, he pushed forward with his cock. It went in no more than an inch but felt as though it were filling her to overflowing. That did not stop her body. Her body wanted it. Her nipples were tortured with pleasure, her cunt invaded, and now she wanted this.

'Sì, sì,' he said gently, and then 'sì,' much harder, as a statement. At the same time he pushed his cock deep into her arse.

Stephanie screamed, but not with pain. Her orgasm took her body over, moving her on the two cocks, moving her body, every erotic zone flooded with sensation. She could not tell where she came, in her cunt, her arse, her nipples or her mind. Her orgasm was everywhere at once.

'Yes . . .' she shouted, pushing down, bucking to meet the two men as they thrust into her, every movement an inducement to greater feeling.

Angelo was fucking her, moving his cock and wanting to come. Carlo was buggering her with equal urgency. In her mind she heard a voice, her voice, repeating, over and over again, 'Two cocks inside her, two cocks inside her.'

Another orgasm broke in her. Her whole body shuddered. She concentrated on the feelings they were giving her, on Angelo's long cock embedded in her, on his brother's cock deep in her arse, the two separated only by the thin membranes of her body. She was impaled on cock, full of cock, hard urgent hot cock.

There was nothing she could do now. She could hear a voice moaning, trembling with every thrust and knew it was her own. Her body was climaxing continuously, pumping waves of crystal pure pleasure through every nerve.

Carlo was hammering faster now, all gentleness gone, his cock wanting only its completion. Stephanie knew he was coming. She felt his cock swell as it spasmed, then exploded its spunk in her arse. It was only then that she realised she had further to go, that what she had experienced before was only the prelude to the orgasm that the feeling of his hot spunk jetting into her arse would produce. Now she was plunging into a long blackness where there was nothing but ecstasy.

The blackness did not last long. Angelo's cock demanded her attention. As she felt Carlo soften and slip from her arse, as she felt him stroking her back and her hair, Angelo's thrusts became more insistent. He bucked his hips to drive up into her. He reached up and cupped both her breasts in his hands.

As Angelo worked himself to a climax, Stephanie felt Carlo's spunk oozing out of her arse.

Angelo's body tensed under her. His cock poked her like a sword. It did not fill her cunt but probed it like a finger. He hammered into her twice more before he found his place and stopped, letting the momentum of his spunking take over, feeling his cock pulse and heave his spunk out into the place he had found, the silky wet walls of her sex. Stephanie came too, not the plunging blackness of before, but a melting orgasm, melting over him as Carlo's hand stroked her hair, ordering it neatly

93

in a long stream down the middle of her back.

She rolled over Angelo and on to her back to wallow in the sensations coming from her body. Her arse felt sore and so did her nipples, but it was a delicious, sensual soreness. Her body was full of spunk. She had it in her mouth, her arse and her cunt. She congratulated herself on her choice. They may not have been able to speak English but they knew the most important language.

Carlo walked through into the sitting room, naked, and returned with the champagne and two glasses. He poured and offered her a glass. Sitting up, she took the champagne and sipped it. The two brothers shared the other glass.

Stephanie looked at Carlo's body. His muscles were hard and well defined. It was now she most missed the ability to talk to him. Instead, she reached out and circled his cock with her hand. Almost immediately she felt it swell slightly. She wanked it gently just to see what would happen, rubbing her finger along the rim of the glans. She wondered why one brother was circumcised and the other not. Another question she would never be able to ask.

Carlo's cock grew in her hand. He put down the glass on the bedside table.

Stephanie reached out with her other hand to find Angelo's cock, not because she wanted him to get erect too, but just to have the feeling of a cock in each hand. Angelo was lying next to her on the bed while Carlo remained standing. The three bodies formed a chain, Stephanie's hands on their cocks, the links binding them together. A chain of three. A prelude to passion, or an epilogue.

Almost as soon as Stephanie's fingers wrapped themselves around it, Angelo's cock began to swell. The powers of recovery of an eighteen-year-old were remarkable. Two erect cocks. She wanked them together, idly, gently, with no passion, almost absent-mindedly.

Pulling on his cock, she indicated to Carlo that he should kneel on the bed. With a combination of signing and manoeuvring she got Angelo up on his knees too, got them kneeling side by side, their erections, of unequal size, sticking out in front of them. Then she rolled over on to her back and planted her head under Carlo's cock. With one hand she wanked Angelo while, with the other, she fed Carlo's balls into her mouth. She heard Carlo groan. She sucked on his balls, then on the thick tube of flesh under his balls.

She opened her legs and bent her knees. She wanted them to be able to see her, open, her legs splayed, her dark pubic hair matted and wet.

Moving her head she reached up to Angelo's cock, sucked on his balls, licked the thick tube of flesh under his cock, repeated exactly what she had done to Carlo, while she wanked Carlo with her hand.

A drop of moisture had appeared on each cock, a tear of their excitement. With no way to explain what she wanted (What was the Italian for wank? It would hardly be in the phrase books.) she took Carlo's hand and wrapped it around his cock. Then, using her own hand on top of his, she moved it up and down. She repeated the process with Angelo. The demonstration worked; they continued to wank as she took her hands away.

'Bene,' she said. 'Very good. Ora osservare.' That was in the phrase book. She hoped it meant, 'Watch me.'

There was no need to ask them to watch. Their eyes were rooted to her body. She turned round so that her cunt was facing them and opened her legs again. With the toes of one foot, she reached up between their legs, feeling their balls, each one in turn. She saw their eyes on her swollen labia.

'Wank for me. I want to see you come,' she said. Perhaps they'd understand.

Her hands fell to her cunt. With one hand she held open her cunt lips while, with the other, she plunged two fingers deep into the hot, sticky depths. Quite suddenly, her mood changed. Up to now this post-coital exercise had all been a languid experiment, a game of 'what if' and 'just suppose' (just suppose she could make them come again). But now it had changed to need. She needed to come. The sight of the cocks, wanking almost in time, wet, hot, ready, was too much to contemplate in the abstract. She plunged her fingers in and out of her cunt while her other hand pulled viciously at her clitoris. This was not the moment for subtlety. She had to reach through the veil of sensation she had already experienced, to make herself feel more. She felt the first sign, the first shudder as her body prepared for another onslaught, like the first trickle of water through a breeched dam. But she didn't want to come quickly. She eased up, trying to control herself. She wanted to wait, to hold it at bay until she saw the men coming, until she saw their cocks jerking spunk out on to her thighs.

'Do it, do it,' she cried.

They needed no translation. Their fists worked faster, their eyes locked on her body, on the way her fingers worked on her cunt, on her tits, on her pink clitoris pummelled by the tip of her finger.

Stephanie saw Carlo's muscles lock. His fist stopped pumping and squeezed instead. She saw his cock spasm and the white hot spunk jet out from the little black slit,

96

spitting on to her thighs, hot as tar. Then she let herself come, or could not stop herself any longer, whichever; her orgasm breaking the dam, flooding over her, reminding her of all the sensation she had had already that night. As she closed her eyes to sink into the darkness behind them, she felt a hot splash of spunk on her other thigh, like acid burning her soft flesh, as Angelo spunked too. Her orgasm rolled on, this last sensation feeding its flow, as she forced her eyes open to see the last drops of white spunk erupt from Angelo's cock.

She hugged her cunt with both hands, pressing it hard, then not moving, just holding it, feeling it, feeling her orgasm die away on her own hard fingers.

When she opened her eyes again, she was alone on the bed.

She heard a shuffling of clothes in the sitting room and some whispered conversation. She would have liked to get up and go and say goodbye. But she did not have the energy and she didn't want to end the little aftershocks of pleasure that still ran through her body.

She heard the outer door of the suite close quietly, as though they imagined she had gone to sleep.

In her mind, she determined to get up and shower, but her body did not want to respond. She felt something running down her thigh and realised it was spunk. She shuddered with a jolt of pleasure, a pale imitation of the pleasure she had just experienced, but pleasure nevertheless.

It was a night worthy of Rome, she thought. A Roman night, her Roman night.

EIGHT

It was no more than a ten minute flight from Rome to
Devlin's private airfield alongside the shore of Lake
Trasimeno. It wouldn't have taken much longer to
drive, but Stephanie had not yet got over the novelty of
having a private plane more or less at her disposal, and
was determined to take advantage of it at every oppor-
tunity. On the plane, Susie the Malaysian flight attendant had served her coffee and, by the time she had
finished the cup, the captain was announcing that she
would be able to see the lake from the left side of the
aircraft.

As the plane banked to make its approach, the lake
lay in the sun beneath her. The castle, on its island, was
virtually in the centre of the irregularly-shaped stretch
of water. A power-boat was cutting a wake across the
lake, no doubt on its way to the jetty to pick Stephanie
up. Its wake curved through the almost still water,
creating waves that rippled out for thousands of feet
before dying away entirely. The castle looked, for all
the world, like the site of a fairy tale, where the Prince
would come to wake a sleeping beauty from a hundred
years of sleep. And in a way that was near the truth.
Her life had become sort of fairy tale, though she was,
and would remain, very firmly awake.

Down on the ground Stephanie could see little

figures working in the orchards, vineyards and gardens behind the castle. At the landing strip she could see the black Mercedes waiting to take her to the castle, its driver leaning on the bonnet reading a newspaper.

As soon as they had landed, Susie unbuckled herself from her seat in the front cabin and came through to open the pressurised door.

'You're going to London now, to pick up Devlin?' Stephanie asked, in case there had been a change of plan.

'Yes, miss,' Susie replied. 'Back tomorrow morning.'

'Tell him I'll be waiting.'

'Yes, miss.' Susie's Malaysian accent struggled with the 'ss'.

The results of Stephanie's shopping spree had been packed away in the empty suitcases, most still in their shop bags. The cases were transferred to the Mercedes. After a short five minutes' drive the car arrived at the jetty where the power-boat, its wood varnish and polished brass shining in the sun, waited for her. The boatmen helped her abroad, cast off and drifted a little way from the jetty before gunning the big engines of the boat out across the lake.

Sitting in the transom, Stephanie enjoyed the sensation of wind in her hair as the boat sped over the water, cutting through the almost mirror-like calm of the lake. The sun, not as high in the sky as it had been when Stephanie first came to the castle, was shaded by a few white, fluffy clouds. But to the west she could see the leading edge of a bank of cloud, broken ragged cloud, mackerel cloud, the first precursor of a storm, she thought.

At the castle jetty she told the boatmen to be ready to pick up a guest that evening. She had arranged with Jasmina that the Rolls would pick her up and drive her to the castle, as the plane had to go to London.

A servant helped her ashore. She climbed the narrow stone steps, worn in the centre by four centuries of use, and draped in a canopy of climbing flowers. Her cases were unloaded, the boatmen and the servant making a stack on the wooden jetty.

Inside the castle she ordered lunch. She was hungry. She had drunk a great deal of champagne last night but had not eaten anything. The morning croissant had not slaked her appetite. In sudden glee she thought of Gianni, chained to his living room wall. She imagined his wife coming home, finding the front door open, the servants gone, calling out her husband's name, wandering into the living room and finding him there, the pretty red ribbon decorating his cock. It wouldn't be easy to unchain him either. She's left no keys to the heavy padlocks. She giggled to herself as she danced upstairs. That's what you get if you mess with me, she thought.

She determined to swim before lunch. In her bedroom, she pulled on a black, one-piece bathing suit – of a very practical design, except perhaps that it was cut high on the hips – a black chiffon wrap, and a pair of high-heeled sandals. She wrapped her hair into a chignon at the back of her head and pinned it there.

As she came downstairs, one of the servants was bringing the first of her cases up to her room.

There was a duty to perform before her swim and lunch, however. She pulled aside the corner of the large modern tapestry that decorated one of the walls at the bottom of the staircase, to reveal the thick wooden door that led to the cellars. As she stepped inside, she felt a cool rush of air.

Stephanie picked her way carefully down the stone steps, worn by the passage of time just as the jetty steps were. She walked across the brick-vaulted cellar used for storing Devlin's extensive collection of wine, to the heavy door that was the entrance to the more unusual feature of the castle.

Bruno, the keeper of the keys, answered her double knock immediately, swinging the door open. Here the brick-vaulted cellar – once a dungeon for the enemies of the duke who had built this impressive fortress – had been divided into cells, each with its own thick wooden door.

'Any problems while I've been away?' Stephanie asked.

Bruno answered by shaking his head. Dressed like a mediaevel executioner, with a black tunic and breeches, and a ring of keys and a sturdy whip hanging from a wide leather belt at his thick waist, Bruno's face betrayed no other emotion. As he had, apparently, suffered an accident which had deprived him of his masculine attributes, he was ideal for his job in the cellars.

Most of the slaves were out in the fields working. There were only two in the cellars, both women. One was cleaning the suite of rooms at the far end of the corridor, a set of rooms lavishly decorated and comfortably furnished. Devlin's guests could take the slaves there, or to what was called the bondage room, where those with more active imaginations could indulge their whims for more unusual sexual tastes. Everything, in fact, the heart might desire.

The other slave was chained, naked, to the corridor wall where all punishments were carried out. Though all the slaves were at the castle as an alternative to prison sentences, and therefore rarely caused discipline problems, occasionally they forgot their situation and rebelled. If the rebellion persisted, they were returned to the mainland and prosecuted for whatever crime against Devlin's empire they had committed originally, but generally it did not. Generally, they realised that life at the castle was a great deal better than life in prison.

Stephanie walked over to the woman for a closer look. Bruno followed.

'What exactly have you done?' she asked. The women had short fair hair and, though not fat, was distinctly plump around her waist and her hips. She had heavy, sagging tits. In two weeks, Stephanie thought, she wouldn't recognise herself; a controlled diet and regular exercise would do wonders for her figure. She hadn't been at the castle long.

The woman's arms had been chained to a metal ring above her head. Her legs were spread and chained apart and she was facing the wall, her over-weight arse bearing the marks of Bruno's whip.

She did not answer Stephanie's question. Stephanie pulled the chain that hung around her neck. The disc bearing her name was jammed between her ample breasts and the stone wall. Stephanie pulled until it was up by her throat and she could swing it round her neck and read 'FRAN' inscribed on the metal.

'Answer my question, Fran.'

Fran turned her head and looked Stephanie in the eyes. The expression on her face was surprising; it was quite clearly an expression of lust.

'You're very tasty,' the woman said.

'Answer my question.'

'If I don't will it get me whipped again? I can still feel my arse. It's still hot. Why don't you feel it?'

'Answer my question,' was all Stephanie could think to say, trying to ignore her own nascent sexual excitement.

'I refused to dig the bloody garden.'

103

Almost without thinking what she was doing, as a reaction to the woman's insolence, Stephanie slapped her hand across her wide buttocks. There was a resounding 'thwack' of flesh on flesh. The woman's eyes flared with excitement.

'Couldn't you use the whip?' Fran said, still looking straight into Stephanie's eyes. 'What do I have to do to get you to use the whip on me?'

Stephanie, again almost without thinking, pulled the whip, a short crop, from Bruno's belt, and slashed it down on the white flesh of the woman's arse. A red welt appeared. The woman moaned, but it was not a moan of pain.

'I never knew it would turn me on . . .' she said, almost to herself.

Stephanie ran her hand along the woman's spine and round her plump arse. She was astonished at how much heat it seemed to be generating.

'Feel how wet you've made me,' Fran said. 'Feel it.'

Stephanie's hand dipped between the woman's legs. Her pubic hair was wispy and sparse. Her labia were wet. She moaned at Stephanie's touch.

'Do it to me. You know you want to, I can see it in your eyes. Please . . .'

The woman's words hung in the air. Bruno stood impassively, his arms folded over his chest. With an effort of self-control, Stephanie pulled her hand away. In her mind she could see herself pressing into this woman's soft body, feeling it envelope her, her fingers finding no resistance in the pliable, plasticene flesh . . .

'If you dig the garden when you are told to dig the garden, then you might get what you want,' she said. Discipline was a mixture of the carrot and the stick. The stick had patently failed with this woman; perhaps the carrot would work.

'I want it now,' the slave replied.

'Good.'

This time her movement was deliberate. She ran her hand down between the woman's legs again, found her labia and then her clitoris. She caressed it wantonly, provoking a moan of delight from Fran, her body arching with pleasure.

'Do as you're told and you get more,' Stephanie whispered, taking her hand away, denying the woman what she so obviously wanted.

'You bitch,' the woman shouted, as Stephanie walked away. 'Come back here. Don't leave me like this . . .'

Walking away was against all her instincts. Her excitement was intense. It was the excitement she had felt the first weekend at the castle, the excitement of power. In the castle, down here in the cellars, she was the mistress of all she surveyed; she could do anything, have anything. Last night had been a marvellous sexual experience for her and had proved, had she really needed proof, that she didn't *need* the pleasures of power to enhance her sexuality. Power was an extra, an optional extra. It was the same as her realisation that she could get pleasure from women as well as men. Being able to enjoy sex with a woman didn't mean she never wanted a man again. On the contrary, it made her feelings for men that much stronger. So it was with the feelings she got from being in a dominant role. It didn't mean she couldn't lose herself in the sort of sex she had experienced last night, couldn't resume her traditional submissiveness, the role she had played before she had discovered the other worlds of sex. It was different, that was all. The two were not mutually exclusive. And they fed on each other: being spread and used as she had been last night was exciting now because she knew how it felt to play the other role, to spread and use in return.

Man or woman, dominant or submissive, in the end, it was all sex. The more she experienced the more she wanted to experience, the stronger and more pleasurable her sexual feelings were. A wonderful world of sex, she thought to herself, parodying the title of a television programme she had watched regularly as a child. The more she knew the more she wanted to know; the more she felt the more, it seemed, she was capable of feeling.

But not now. Now she walked purposefully out of the cellars, ignoring the appetites the slave had created, and up into the light. Out in the sun on the jetty, she plunged into the warm waters of the lake. She would swim and eat and have a siesta before Jasmina arrived.

The waters of the lake were silky and smooth against her skin. She swam strongly, stretching all her muscles, wanting to work, to feel the strain. Then, some distance from the island, she trod water and relaxed. The lake was full of fish. None seemed inhibited by the presence of a large mammal in their territory and, as she floated lazily, they swam up to investigate this strange phenomenon.

She swam back to the jetty as energetically as she had swum out. Pulling herself from the water, she lay on the wooden boards to dry off in the sun. The clouds were still threatening to the west but as yet were a long way off. At the moment, the sun blazed down unobstructed. Turning herself like a steak on a griddle, she was soon completely dry.

She thought about going upstairs to change for lunch but hunger overcame her, and she pulled on the chiffon wrap instead and walked up to the terrace where the servants had laid the table for her lunch. A crisp, pink linen tablecloth matched the pink and white crockery and the tiny flower arrangement of pink and dark red flowers that she did not recognise but that were, no doubt, grown in the greenhouses behind the castle.

She had ordered fillet steak, bleu. She wanted red meat. And a salad, a green salad fresh from the gardens, tossed in virgin olive oil. She drank two glasses of Barolo 1983 with the meat and gazed out over the lake watching the inexorable approach of the leading edge of cloud as it gradually advanced from the horizon. The servants, in their crisply laundered white linen jackets, served her without a word. After the main course she asked for a small portion of melon ice cream that was one of the specialities of the castle chef. She didn't have coffee, wanting to be sure she slept for a while this afternoon.

Upstairs in the bedroom, the maid had already closed the shutters and curtains on the windows to keep out the midday sun, and the room was pleasantly cool. Stephanie stripped off the swimsuit and lay naked on the bed. She pulled a single sheet over her body and settled her head on to the goose-down pillow. After the strong Barolo she felt delightfully relaxed, her eyes heavy, her body unstrung. She knew she would sleep deeply after the rigours of last night, and she was right.

She was licking Devlin's body. His body was as misshapen as his face. His torso was short and compacted, his shoulders badly rounded, his legs scrawny and bowed. Every inch of his flesh was covered in thick wiry hair – once black, now grey and white. His back was hairy too, dense clumps of hair covering his kidneys. Stephanie found it exciting. His extreme ugliness was exciting, as exciting as extreme beauty.

She licked his face, his grotesque bulbous nose, his

107

pock-marked cheeks, his ears, from which great tufts of hair grew. She kissed and licked his neck and his chest and bit his nipples, teasing them with her teeth, watching the effect this had on his penis, his huge erect penis. It twitched with each bite like the rod of a water diviner. She worked her mouth over his navel while her hand took his penis by its root.

His penis was like an ageing tree trunk circled and bound by fronds of ivy. Blue and purple veins, distended and swollen, ran up and round it in a chaos of directions, apparently at random and to no purpose. Each vein was a different shape, some long and twisting following the whole length of his stem, others short and wide, rising from his tumescence only to disappear again. Some looked so gnarled as to be varicose, an angry purple red; others were veins on veins, hitching a ride on the back of a bigger cousin. Devlin's cock could be mapped, a road map of a strange new planet.

Stephanie licked and nibbled at its base, then worked her mouth higher while her hand played with his balls. Devlin groaned, a large tear of fluid leaking from the slit of his penis to further signal his excitement. With the tip of her tongue Stephanie licked it off greedily, then plunged her mouth down on to him as far as she could go. His penis filled her cheeks, down into her throat. She was gagged with flesh.

Without moving her head she could see Gianni. He was struggling against his chains, rattling them against the wall. His cock was erect, swathed in red ribbon and erect, his whole body tensed.

'Let me help,' Signora Gianni said. She was smiling at Stephanie, still wearing the little mink jacket, the elaborate spectacles with diamante inlay. She knelt on the other side of Devlin and started to use her mouth on the base of his penis. There was plenty of room for both their mouths.

'Oh, it's good,' she said, licking and sucking until her mouth met Stephanie's lips. 'Let me take it,' she whispered.

Reluctantly, Stephanie pulled away and watched as the white-haired woman sunk her mouth down on to Devlin's monstrous cock. She watched as her lips engulfed the rim of his glans, then another inch, and another, until the whole cock was buried deep in her mouth and her lips were hard up against his thick, wiry pubic hair. It was impossible, Stephanie knew. How could she take so much. The white hair bobbed up and Devlin's cock slid out glistening with salvia. Then it disappeared again, devoured in her mouth.

Stephanie felt jealous. She wanted Devlin, she wanted his spunk.

There was a crack like thunder. The wall holding the nail to which Gianni was chained split in two, the whole wall tearing like a piece of paper. There was dust and plaster everywhere. It was difficult to see. Gianni appeared, striding towards them, pulling free of his chains, the metal links snapping like elastic bands. Gianni was free.

'Stop that,' he said to his wife. He pulled her off Devlin's cock, but it was too late. Devlin's spunk jetted out into the air, landing on the black mink jacket, great white gobs of spunk catching in the fur.

'She's got to be punished,' Gianni said, advancing towards Stephanie.

'Oh yes, she's got to be punished,' his wife said, ignoring the spunk and getting up.

Stephanie backed away across the room, her feet leaving a trail of footsteps in the white plaster dust that covered everything. Gianni was covered in it, covered as though he had walked through a vast vat of talcum powder. Stephanie backed away until she felt the wall, the torn wall. It crumbled at her touch, filling the air with more dust and plaster and brick.

Devlin had not moved. He lay covered in the white powder. She cried out for him to help her. She could hardly see him now through the fog of dust. She couldn't see Gianni now. Only his wife. She was nearest to her now, untouched by the powder, her mink jacket still black.

'She's got to be punished,' she said.

Stephanie turned and ran. She ran through the crumbling wall and was almost free. But then something caught her by the wrist, a hand caught her by the wrist, a grip like steel. She tried to pull away but it was useless. The hand pulled her closer. Through the dust she couldn't see anything, just the fingers locked on to her wrist.

She felt a soft, warm body next to hers. She felt arms wrapping round her, hugging her. She felt lips licking and sucking at her body. She felt her thighs being opened, her labia being opened, her sex being opened . . .

'She's got to be punished,' a voice said. Not Signora Gianni. Another voice. Stephanie could see who was holding her now. It was Fran, her naked body plump and pliant, pressing into her . . .

Stephanie woke with a start. She looked around to check that there was no one else in the room, and couldn't think what had woken her so suddenly. The room was full of shadows. It was almost dark. She switched on the bedside light. The bedroom was empty.

Getting up, Stephanie went over to the terrace doors and threw back the curtains and shutters to reveal a torrent of rain outside. It splattered up off the terracotta tiling, the drops bouncing more than a foot, they were so hard and heavy. They battered the orange trees in their pots and rustled through the thatch of climbing plants that clung to the castle wall. The sky was black and a clap of thunder followed a startling streak of fork lightning that hit the mainland to the east.

It must have been the thunder that woke her, Stephanie thought. And that probably accounted for a curious sense of foreboding that seemed to have rooted itself in the back of her mind like a persistent dull headache. She felt cold too, an unusual experience at the castle.

A hot shower dispelled the chill but not the emotion. After she'd washed her hair, dried it with a hair dryer – previously it had always dried in the sun – and applied her make-up, it was still there, a nagging premonition.

Since it was, as far as she could tell, completely without foundation, she tried to put it to one side. She glanced at her watch. It was six o'clock. She had plenty of time before Jasmina's arrival. She went to the phone and dialled Devlin's number, sure that the sound of his voice would make her feel better. The ringing was answered almost immediately.

'727 1800.'

'Venetia, it's Stephanie.' She'd recognised Venetia's voice.

'Hi. Devlin's right here.' Stephanie heard Venetia telling him who was on the phone.

'Stephanie!' he said, sounding genuinely glad to hear from her.

'Devlin, how's it going?'

'All on schedule. But what about you? You've got the big news. How is our Roman friend?'

'It went like clockwork. Perfect. Not a hitch.' She found herself smiling broadly.

'I want to hear all the details.'

'Are you coming back in the morning?' After the shower, she had not bothered to put on a robe. She stared down at her naked body. As she spoke to Devlin she saw her nipples begin to pucker.

'Yes. Can't wait.'

'I've invited a guest. Someone I met in Rome.'

'Man or woman?'

'Woman. A very beautiful black woman.' Stephanie would tell him about the two Italian brothers too, tell him in detail everything they had done to her, but that would have to wait.

'If you say she's beautiful, I think she must be extra-ordinary.'

'She is. She's arriving tonight.'

'And what will you do with her?'

'Need you ask?'

'Is she . . . co-operative?'

'She wants to learn. She is very enthusiastic. She's never had an experience with a woman.'

'But you've changed that?'

'I gave her a taste, that's all. She appeared eager to have the whole meal.'

'Tell me about it.'

'I'll tell you tomorrow, Devlin.'

'Please . . .'

'You want to wank again?'

'Please . . .'

'No, Devlin.' She made her voice stern. 'You're to wait, is that understood?'

He noticed the change in tone immediately. If he wasn't hard already that would provoke his erection.

'Yes, mistress,' he said, the word 'mistress' clearly lingering in his mind.

'You come only when I say, don't you?'

'Yes, mistress.'

Stephanie smiled to herself, knowing what Devlin's reaction would be, knowing how much he would want her in the morning when he got home. Well, if he was lucky, he would have an extra bonus – he would have Jasmina to watch and maybe even join in.

'Can't wait,' he said, as if he would be scolded for saying it.

'Neither can I,' she replied with no sternness.

They exchanged goodbyes and Stephanie hung up. The rain outside had let up and the terrace was awash with water. Lightning still forked down on the mainland, closely followed by thunder, but the sky was not quite as dark. However, Stephanie's feeling of foreboding had not abated.

For half-an-hour she idly unwrapped some of the parcels from her shopping expedition, but was in no mood to try things on. She hung them in the wardrobe or stacked them, unwrapped, on the floor. Tomorrow she would go over everything with Jasmina's help. They could play with all her new toys.

She dressed carefully, wanting to resume her relationship with Jasmina just where it had been left, in a tangle of desire. The teddy she chose was black, black silk with fine lace at the bust and panels of lace at each hip. She found a pair of black, sheer, hold-up stockings, with a band of black lace holding them in place on her thigh. The stockings were much higher then usual, the lace welt reaching almost to the feathers of pubic hair from the lush growth between her legs.

The dress she wore was red: the bodice a single slash of ruckled organza from shoulder to waist, in contrast to the absolutely plain A-line skirt which reached to just above her knee. It was not too obvious. Not too vampy. If Jasmina's enthusiasm had started to wane

113

she didn't want to suggest she was the wicked witch of the sex castle waiting to draw her into the lair.

Downstairs, Stephanie had the servants lay a table for two at one end of the enormous plate-glass dining table that could actually seat twenty or more people. The fire in the wide, gothic-style fireplace had already been lit. Even in the height of summer the evenings were always chill in this part of the castle, the sun not penetrating the thick stone walls.

Remembering what had been said in Rome, and imagining that after dinner they might not get as far as the bedroom, Stephanie had tried to think of everything. She tucked the little black velvet bag out of sight by the side of the hearth.

The power-boat had gone out at seven. The chauffeur had rung from the Rolls to say they would be at the jetty by seven-thirty, and that they had been delayed by the torrential rain. Stephanie sat by the fire gazing into the flames, the foreboding she had felt displaced, though not replaced, by her growing sense of excitement.

It was eight o'clock before she heard the power-boat's engines. She went into the hall and called for a servant to bring a golfing umbrella, taking one herself before heading down to the jetty. The stone steps were slippery in the wet. The rain was heavy again now, the calm lake boiling with tiny ripples as the raindrops poured down.

Jasmina sat next to the boatman, crunched up under the small canopy of the boat. The boat was not designed for wet weather. Skilfully, the boat was manoeuvred alongside the jetty. As soon as it was secured fore and aft, the servant jumped aboard with the umbrella and sheltered Jasmina as she came ashore. Stephanie held out her hand to help her.

'You made it.'

'Mais oui. It is terrible. Il tombe des cordes.'

'Translate.'

'It rains, you say cats and dogs.'

'Come on, there's a fire inside. Mind the steps, they're very slippery.'

Jasmina was wearing a grey, snake-skin pattern leotard and a short black skirt. Her legs were bare. She wore a man's hat, a large black fedora that suited the bold outlines of her face. Stephanie watched her long legs pick their way up the steps. The servant followed with her small weekend case.

They dashed across the courtyard in front of the castle doors which Stephanie had left open.

'Wow!' Jasmina said, looking around. 'It is beautiful!'

'Come through here. Or do you want to change?'

'No.'

Jasmina took off the hat. Her short, black hair emphasised her long, elegant neck. Here eyes were smiling as was her mouth.

'D'abord,' she said, then translated, 'first.'

She moved close to Stephanie, hooked her hand around the back of her neck and pulled her into a kiss. She kissed hard, wrapping her other arm around Stephanie and hugging her hard too.

'So now you know,' she said. 'I have not changed my mind.'

'You certainly haven't,' Stephanie said.

They walked through to the fireplace hand in hand. Jasmina asked for a Scotch, neat and Stephanie decided to have the same. They clinked the big crystal tumblers.

'To us.'

'Oui. To us both.'

Jasmina's eyes sparkled in the firelight. Stephanie felt a surge of raw desire. The woman was more beautiful than she remembered. It was not only the way she looked. She had a natural grace and elegance, an economy of movement that made even a small inclination of the head seem like a ballet motion. Stephanie put out her hand to touch Jasmina's cheek as if wanting to reassure herself that she was real. Immediately Jasmina put her own hand on Stephanie's, holding it to her cheek, then she moved her head and pressed the palm of Stephanie's hand to her lips. It seemed like a long time before she let Stephanie's hand fall.

The servant announced that dinner was ready. Stephanie led Jasmina to the table. A broccoli soup was welcome against the chill of the rain, and the sea bass that followed was grilled with fennel. They drunk Frascati from a vineyard not more than sixty miles away. There was fruit and an almond cake and a plate of tiny *dolci*.

Jasmina ate voraciously, constantly finding things in the room to comment on: the huge flower arrangement in the centre of the table, the gothic wood-carvings decorating the fireplace, the modern rugs strewn over the marble floor.

She continually broke into French. 'Je peux . . . Pardon. I speak to someone who is not Italian and it makes me want to speak French.'

'You speak Italian too?'

'Yes. And Spanish. I seem to have an ability with language. I am not fluent in all, but enough to get by, I think.'

'Your English is good.'

'I will get better. There are many things I would like to ask you, that I have thought . . .'

'Ask away.'

'I looked up the word in my dictionary. You are lesbian?'

Stephanie laughed at her directness. 'No.'

'But – '

'I like men too. I like men a lot. But recently I've discovered that I like women.'

'Me too, I think. This is very new for me.'

'Jasmina,' Stephanie considered her words carefully, 'this castle can offer many experiences, new experiences, if that's what you want.'

'I think it is.'

'You are very beautiful.'

'Stephanie.' Jasmina pronounced it in French, emphasising each syllable equally, ste/phan/ie. It sounded so sexy. 'What you did to me. So suddenly, so unexpected. You make me quiver, tremble. You understand?'

'It's what you make me feel, too.'

'How can this be? You are so experienced.'

'You are very exciting.'

'I want to learn, Stephanie. Everything. You will teach me?'

'If that's what you want.'

'Oh yes.'

They drank coffee by the fire. The storm had abated slightly during the dinner, but now appeared to have circled back over the lake. The forks of lightning and cracks of thunder were, if anything, more violent than before.

They decided to leave the guided tour of the castle until the morning. If Jasmina wanted to know everything, Stephanie would certainly take her into the cellars, but not tonight.

'So how does a black, French girl come to be working in Rome?' Stephanie asked, genuinely curious.

'I was born in Chad. It was, I think you say, the arsehole of the world. I had not family. They put me in, in . . .'

'An orphanage?'

'Yes. A French missionary, he helped me. I worked for him. Then, when he went back to France, he took me with him. Back to Angouleme. There I was like a side-show. The first black they had seen. The man was kind to me. I was very young. But as I grew up he changed. His wife died. Just the two of us left in the house. Alone together, it was not good. So I went to Paris. Then I went around Europe. Amsterdam. Munich. Madrid. I learn languages. I work in all kinds of places. I learn many things. I come to Rome. I get this job as a model – '

'Have you been to London?'

'No. London next.'

Jasmina put down her coffee. They had been sitting on chairs opposite each other in front of the fireplace. Jasmina slid to her knees on the thick rug in front of Stephanie and looked up at her.

'No more talking. I want to make love. I want you. You know what I am saying?'

'Yes.'

'You can do what you want with me. Anything you want.'

Stephanie felt a surge of desire. Jasmina had a directness that was disarming.

They kissed, a long, inquisitive kiss, Jasmina's head tilted backward, her throat one long stretch of dark, sinewy flesh. Stephanie felt her heart racing, her whole body alive with anticipation. Jasmina was so open, so willing, so fresh, like the pages of a diary waiting to be written on. She seemed to have no inhibitions, no taboos. She wanted only to learn. She had no idea what her limits were, where she would draw the line. She wanted only to discover the new world Stephanie had transported her to.

Stephanie broke the kiss.

'Shall we go upstairs?'

'Non,' Jasmina said. 'Ici. By the fire.'

'I thought you might say that.'

Stephanie stood up. She ran her fingers into Jasmina's short curls and pressed her head into her lap.

'I feel your heat.'

Stephanie did not move, savouring the anticipation. Then she stepped away and pulled the red dress off over her head.

'Oh, so sexy,' Jasmina said, looking at the black teddy, its lace panels tantalising in what they revealed, the black hold-ups making Stephanie's legs seem even longer, the thin band of naked thigh between the lacy tops of the stocking and the silk teddy, a magnet for the eye.

Stephanie had left her hair loose. She shook her head to straighten it again, the hair streaming down her back.

'Take your skirt off.' A note of command crept into her voice. Still kneeling, Jasmina unzipped the garment and let it fall to her knees. She rocked back to sit on her bottom and kicked the skirt away.

'Now lie on your back.'

Jasmina obeyed again. The rug in front of the fire was thick cream wool, its pile so deep a whole hand could disappear into it. Jasmina lay on it, one leg flat, one leg bent at the knee. She began to massage her right breast with her left hand under the leotard. In this prone position her breasts were no more than the faintest swelling on her chest but her nipples, Stephanie could see, were already fat and swollen like the knobs of a cupboard door.

119

'Come.' Jasmina held out her hand. 'Please . . .'

Stephanie took three steps forward until she was standing over Jasmina, the toe of her red high heel shoe grazing her waist. Jasmina caressed her slim ankle, feeling the sheer nylon, looking up her stockinged legs. She could see where the silk of the teddy was stretched by Stephanie's pubic bone, where it curved down between her thighs; she could see the mass of thick black curly hair escaping from underneath the tight silk.

'Please . . .' Jasmina said again, arching her back off the floor, the evidence of her eyes fuelling her lust.

Stephanie knelt at her feet. She took Jasmina's calves in her hands and parted them, moving forward until she knelt between her open legs. Reaching forward she cupped the full curve of Jasmina's pubis in her hand, feeling its heat. Jasmina whimpered at her touch. Stephanie found the three fasteners that held the crotch of the leotard in place and worked each open in turn, having to press each popper hard into Jasmina's soft labia to get it undone. As soon as the last was free the material sprang back, Jasmina's cunt lips blatantly revealed. Against the chocolate brown of her skin her cunt appeared pink, like the centre of some exotic fruit. It was glistening too, wet with her own juices.

'Now it's my turn,' Stephanie said.

She dipped her head down to the pink, moist fruit. It was no more pink than her own sex, but the dark thighs and belly made it look much more so, made it look somehow more exposed, more precious, more virginal. Stephanie licked it first, like a child licking an ice cream, long wet licks with the whole breadth of her tongue, relishing the taste of Jasmina's juices.

'Mon dieu . . .' Jasmina sighed.

Stephanie's tongue worked up the whole length of

her sex, from the little rosette of her arse to the very top of her clitoris. Jasmina had never had a woman do this to her, never felt the roughness of a woman's tongue and the softness of her cheeks on her thighs. It was making her come, an orgasm so sharp and sudden she could not help herself from screaming and scissoring her legs together to catch Stephanie's head, clamping it fast to her sex.

Stephanie could feel her come. She felt her sex contract. She felt a rush of juices, like a man spunking, in her mouth.

Jasmina's thighs relaxed, allowing Stephanie's head to move again. But Stephanie had no intention of leaving it at that. This time she concentrated on Jasmina's clitoris, nudging it with the tip of her tongue, drawing little circles around it. As she did she reached out with her hand to the black velvet bag she had hidden at the corner of the hearth. Without losing contact with Jasmina's sex she managed to snag the velvet with the tips of her fingers, pulling it towards her across the thick rug.

Jasmina's eyes were closed; she did not see what Stephanie was doing. She was too busy coping with the sensations from her body.

As Stephanie played with the engorged clitoris, using her tongue to manipulate it from side to side now, rhythmically, and feeling Jasmina's body respond with the same beat, she groped inside the bag and drew out the dildo.

She brought the rigid plastic phallus up to the entrance of Jasmina's cunt and positioned herself to thrust it forward. Then she sucked Jasmina's clitoris into her mouth, gobbling it up as, at that instant, she drove the dildo home, right up into the depths of Jasmina's wet, open cunt, right up until only an inch

121

remained in view. There was not the slightest resistance.

Jasmina moaned, opened her eyes in astonishment, but had to close them again as her body swamped her with feeling. Somewhere, a long way in the back of her mind, she remembered the conversation she had had with Stephanie, remembered asking her if she had a dildo . .

Without pause Stephanie pulled the long, thick dildo out again, seeing it glistening wet, then pushed it back up, all the way up. Jasmina groaned again. She started to groan in time with Stephanie's strokes. Her body began to shake, her voice shaking too, unable to do anything but surrender to her second orgasm as it broke over the head of the hard plastic dildo. Or did it start at her clitoris, still sucked into Stephanie's mouth? She could not tell. It did not matter. All that mattered was the feeling rocking through her body, making her whimper and moan, tremble and quiver, her body not under her control, her nerves dancing their own tune to extract the greatest feeling from the sexual circumstance, her mind joining in the conspiracy to rob her of control, telling her this was a woman on her body, a woman's mouth, a woman's hand fucking her with a great plastic dildo.

Stephanie released her clitoris and held the dildo deep, no longer moving it in and out. She watched as Jasmina arched herself off the rug, her whole body taut like a long-bow, supported on her shoulders and the heels of her feet, her cunt uppermost, the dildo buried to the hilt.

It was a long time before she lowered herself with a sigh of utter contentment. Stephanie let the dildo go, and it slipped of its own accord from the pink lips of Jasmina's cunt.

Jasmina raised herself on one elbow and looked down at the dildo between her legs.

'You remembered,' she said.

'I planted one down here just in case we didn't make it upstairs. What did you call it in French?'

'Godemiché. C'était extra. It was very good.' She sat up further and pulled the leotard, which was bunched around her waist, up over her head. She smiled broadly. 'That is one expression in French you will know now, I think.'

Stephanie couldn't help staring at Jasmina's body. It was the first time she had seen it at her leisure. Her body was superb. It was more muscled than other women's, long cord of muscle on her thighs and arms. It looked like the body of a black athlete, a body seen on running tracks in skimpy shorts and vest. Experimentally, she squeezed Jasmina's thigh and felt a knot of muscle.

'I train with weights.'

'It looks marvellous.'

'Pumping iron.' She laughed. 'You like this?'

'Yes.'

'You speak any French?'

'Not much.'

Jasmina grinned broadly. 'But you know soixante-neuf?'

Before she could answer, Jasmina reached forward and kissed Stephanie hungrily on the mouth, pressing her naked body against the black silk teddy. She reached behind Stephanie and stroked her long hair as her tongue probed into her hot mouth. Then she pushed her down on to the rug, breaking the kiss and letting her lips move down from Stephanie's mouth to her neck, her lace-covered breasts, kissing her flat silk-covered navel, and then the precipice of her pubic triangle, falling away between her legs like a steep cliff. As Stephanie had done to her, now it was her turn to unfasten the catches between her legs and pull the silk clear. In the modelling room in Rome neither had seen much of each other's body. Now she was able to see Stephanie's labia emerge from her black, pubic curls as she teased them out with her fingers. Now she could see the pink knot of her clitoris, seemingly so exposed and vulnerable. Now she could see the contrast as her dark brown fingers probed the white flesh of Stephanie's thighs and the pink of her cunt.

Jasmina lowered her lips to the slit of Stephanie's sex. She repeated what Stephanie had done to her, long tonguing licks as she reached up to Stephanie's breast to knead and squeeze the soft flesh – so different from her own breasts – and the hard nipple. It felt so good. It thrilled her. She had no idea a women could feel this good. She licked hard, roughly, almost wanting to make Stephanie feel her excitement. With her other hand she slipped two fingers between Stephanie's labia, and felt herself swamped in another new sensation as the silky wet walls of Stephanie's cunt wrapped themselves around her fingers. She took her mouth away and probed deeper with her hand, astonished at the wetness and the heat. She found she could get another finger inside the elastic flesh. Stephanie moaned. Almost by accident a fourth finger slipped into the little hole of Stephanie's arse. It was so wet there was no resistance. Stephanie moaned again. Jasmina had no experience with a women, had never done this with a woman. She relied on her instinct, thought of what she liked men to do to her. She wanked both holes slowly, moving her thumb to Stephanie's clitoris. The gentleness began to disappear as she saw Stephanie's body respond to her thrusts and heard her moan, 'Harder.' Her rhythm increased; she pounded into Stephanie's cunt, faster, harder, deeper. She wanked Stephanie like men had wanked her, unremittingly, until she had come on their hands.

Stephanie managed to lift her head from the floor to look down at Jasmina kneeling by her side, her mouth open, her tongue between her teeth, her delight at what she was doing like that of a child who had discovered some new dexterity. Stephanie could not keep her head up for long. Her body was too full of sensation. There was no energy left for anything else. She rested back on the rug and closed her eyes. She let Jasmina take over, let her do it, wank her, wrest the orgasm out of her with hand, fingers and her relentless thumb strumming on her clitoris as though it were the string of her guitar. She was rough. She was too rough, too hard, too relentless. She was untutored but she was having a shattering effect on Stephanie's body.

Stephanie felt herself coming. It was like riding a bronco in a rodeo. She wanted to get off, stop Jasmina hammering at her body, but at the same time knowing she would stay on, see it through, come to her climax in the saddle. And she did – a rough, unceremonious climax, almost painful, though it was only the pain of extremes of pleasure.

'Stop!' she had to say in the end, as soon as her orgasm let her speak. 'Stop,' she said a second time, quietly. Jasmina obeyed and Stephanie relaxed, allowing her body to wallow in the aftermath of sensation.

Jasmina pulled her fingers from Stephanie body.

'Lick me,' Stephanie said. 'Lick me gently.'

'Was I too rough?'

'No. Just lick me.'

'I want to learn.'

Jasmina's mouth descended to Stephanie's distended

labia. By contrast now it seemed incredibly soft, her fleshly lips and hot tongue melting over Stephanie's sex, like a hot sticky glue. She made it even wetter with her own saliva, so wet Stephanie could feel it running down between her legs, down into the cleft of her arse.

'Better?' Jasmina asked, without taking her lips away.

'Don't stop . . .' Stephanie managed to say, raising her head again momentarily. This was so much better, so good, what only a woman can do for another woman. 'Soixante-neuf,' she had said. That's what Stephanie wanted now to make her pleasure complete.

But Jasmina was ahead of her. As if by some telepathic signal, she was swinging herself over Stephanie's body so her knees rested either side of Stephanie's head and the slit of her sex was poised above Stephanie's face.

'Soixante-neuf,' she said, the words vibrating against the lips of Stephanie's cunt.

Stephanie reached up, hooking her hands around Jasmina's thighs and pulling her down on to her mouth. As soon as she tasted the sweet wetness of Jasmina's cunt, she felt the first frisson of orgasm. She opened her eyes to look at the angular curves of Jasmina's arse – not plump and soft, but bony and tight, her own white arms stretching around it like alabaster against the dark brown flesh. Coffee and cream, salt and pepper, white and black.

She began to shudder. This time her orgasm was long, reaching back to gather in all her nerves, making them all feel the great waves that began to rise and fall in her body, pulling them into harmony. The waves got higher, the troughs of the waves deeper. She was coming in Jasmina's mouth, right in her wet, clinging, sucking, melting mouth, glued to her nether lips while she, in turn, lapped and tasted Jasmina. No woman had ever done this to Jasmina before. Was that the thought that made her finally abandon control, lose track of what she was doing, of the difference between doing and being done to, and feel the explosion of pleasure rake through her perfectly tuned body.

They lay next to each other for a long time. Jasmina naked, Stephanie still in her stockings, the teddy rucked up around her waist. They lay end to end, Stephanie's arm wrapped around Jasmina's thigh and vice versa. The flames of the fire were all but embers now, with no new wood to consume. Outside, the storm had subsided too, no more than a gentle patter of rain echoing from the terrace.

'I have a lot to learn,' Jasmina said without moving.

'Not necessarily . . .'

'This means?'

'You only have to exploit your natural talent.'

Jasmina laughed. 'C'est en forgeant qu'on devient forgeron.'

'That you will have to translate.'

'It is a country expression. Only by forging do you become a blacksmith.'

Now it was Stephanie's turn to laugh. 'Practice makes perfect.'

'Exactement. Is that what you mean?'

'Yes.'

'Good. I would like to practise. But you want to tell me something else?'

'Tomorrow. I'll tell you about Devlin. He's coming back in the morning.'

'Tell me now. A little.'

'Well.' She thought of how to put it best. 'He is a very extraordinary man.'

'You want me to fuck him?' Her directness had a way of making everything simple.

'Not if you don't want to.'

'I would like to fuck. After all these feelings with you. Après les doigts et la bouche j'ai besoin d'un zob. You too, you say. Can we fuck him together?'

'He would like that.'

Jasmina smiled. 'But he must be good. Not coming quickly.'

'That he does not do.'

'Marvellous.'

'You wouldn't mind?'

'Stephanie.' She pronounced it again ste/phan/ie. 'I love what we do here. But I have told you, I want to learn. This is the beginning. I feel so good, so alive. Tomorrow I learn more. You are a good teacher.'

'Am I?'

'And we fuck this Devlin. But now we sleep.'

They picked themselves up off the floor, Stephanie careful not to leave the dildo lying on the rug, and walked up to Stephanie's bedroom.

While Jasmina showered, Stephanie wandered out on to the terrace, pulling on a towelling robe and slippers. The rain had stopped completely now and a big white moon had suddenly appeared through the clouds, lighting the water of the lake with an eerie luminescence that made the water look like molten silver. The rain had renewed the scent of the flowers and, apart from the odd drop of rainwater falling from the leaves, there was complete silence. Nothing moved. Or so it seemed.

Stephanie slipped back inside, closing the terrace doors but leaving the curtains open so they could see the moon.

Jasmina dried herself and slipped between the silk sheets. Stephanie showered. She thought about Jasmina – how open and direct she was, how she appeared to have no inhibitions, none of the social taboos that had so overlaid her own attitudes to sex. Tomorrow Devlin was going to have another experience he was unlikely to forget.

Drying herself off, she came back into the bedroom and got into bed. She had taken her watch off and put it on the bedside table, but now didn't have the energy to reach over and put it back on.

'Tomorrow,' was all that Jasmina said.

Stephanie stroked her arm, and in no more than two or three minutes they were sound asleep.

NINE

She was not dreaming. As far as she could tell it was not
a dream that had startled her awake. It was a noise. She
opened her eyes and looked around the room, trying to
remember the sound. What sort of noise? The room,
still bathed in moonlight, was perfectly silent now.
Jasmina had not moved; she slept soundlessly at her
side. She closed her eyes again, the adrenaline rush
caused by her shock suddenly draining away. Her eyes
felt heavy with sleep again. Just as the edges of con-
sciousness began to soften, she realised the terrace door
was open. She could have sworn she'd closed it when
she came in to shower. But what did it matter? It wasn't
cold and she usually slept with the doors open anyway.

The sharp edges blurred again. She felt herself falling
back into the blackness of sleep as she heard Jasmina's
regular breathing beside her.

She woke again, jerked awake with a much bigger
rush of adrenaline, her heart pumping blood, violently
reacting to whatever unconscious alarm signal her
mind had heard. She looked around the room. Whether
it was a minute or an hour since she had woken before
she could not tell. She could see nothing but the familiar objects in the room and dark shadows where the
moonlight could not reach. She tried to look into the
shadows, but they were too deep. But something was

wrong. She couldn't tell what, but something was wrong.

As quietly as she could, not wanting to disturb Jasmina, she pulled away the sheet –

Everything happened at once. A man sprang from the floor alongside the bed, caught Stephanie by the shoulders, pushed her back on to the bed, and jumped on top of her to hold her down with his body. A thick leather glove over her mouth gagged her scream. At the same time, a second man leapt from the shadows and, in the instant Jasmina awoke, stifled her screams with his hand, jumping up on the bed too, kneeling over her to hold her down.

Stephanie's heart was beating like a wild bird trapped in a cage. What did they want, who were they, how did they get in? They must be robbers. The castle had immensely valuable furniture, antiques, paintings. Even in her panic she found herself wondering how on earth they would get the stuff off the island. They'd need a huge boat.

Jasmina started to buck her powerful muscles, pushing at the man. Fortunately for him, her arms and legs were trapped under the sheet. She tried to roll her head to get his hand off her mouth, but it held firm.

A third man stepped into the pool of moonlight. He held a small black case, like the case of a geometry set.

The man on Jasmina hissed a question in Italian to his companion. Jasmina had wrestled a long black arm from the bedclothes. The man caught it by the wrist, but Jasmina twisted it out of his grip and, in a flash, raked his cheek with her blood-red fingernails. Real blood appeared instantly from three parallel scratches on his face, as though he had been mauled by a tiger.

'Lupa!' he snarled, catching her wrist again before she could repeat the treatment.

132

Stephanie did not struggle. There was no point. Whatever these men had come for they were going to get it, no matter what. They would not care if they left casualties. Stephanie had read about the Italian *banditos*, and cursed Devlin for not taking better precautions. If she could have spoken she would have told Jasmina to stop her struggles.

The third man had put the little case down on the bedside table and opened it. He drew out a large hypodermic syringe and filled it from a vial of colourless fluid. He put the vial back in the bag and pushed the plunger of the syringe until fluid jetted out from its tip. Then he moved to Jasmina's side.

'Lupa!' the man on top of her repeated.

Jasmina saw the man coming and redoubled her efforts. The bedsheets had worked down to her waist and her naked breasts quivered with her efforts. The arm that was not trapped in the man's hand was under his knee. She concentrated on trying to worm it free.

'Do not move,' the third man hissed. The needle was inches from the top of Jasmina's arm. 'If it breaks, is bad for you,' he whispered, in a heavy Italian accent. Jasmina's eyes filled with fear and she stopped struggling. The needle jabbed into her arm.

'Uno, due, tre, quattro, cinque . . .' the third man counted quietly. By 'cinque' Jasmina's eyes had rolled up and her body went completely loose.

The man climbed off her. He pulled the sheet off the rest of the body and looked down at her long-limbed nakedness. The third man came round to Stephanie's side of the bed.

'You are more sensible,' he said, still whispering.

Stephanie looked away as she saw the needle approach her arm. The gloved hand over her mouth would not let her head turn far, but she could see

Jasmina's naked body and see, to her relief, that she was still breathing normally. The man who had sat on top of her was running his hand over her navel and into her sparse pubic hair. He started to open her thighs. He wants to see what she looks like between her legs, Stephanie thought. Never seen a black woman's cunt. It was at that moment the needle went in. She could feel fluid pumped under her skin.

How were they going to get away with it? How were they going to deal with the servants, how were they going to get the stuff in their boat . . .

'Une, due, tre, quattro, cinque . . .'

Stephanie did not hear the word 'cinque'. The moonlight disappeared, everything disappeared: images, thoughts, sounds. There was only blackness, a blackness so profound, so perfect, it had no seams, no corners, no edges and no end.

The feeling was like being steam-rollered by cotton wool clouds. The blackness cleared a little, enough to allow billowing whiteness to roll in, and pass over, as if it was going to suffocate her underneath it. Then more blackness. Gradually longer periods of white cotton moving like clouds, almost rolling in and over her, knocking her down as she struggled to come round, every effort her mind made to grip on to something that wasn't black or white, defeated by the clouds that pulled her down again into the numbing edgeless void.

Eventually, after hours, or minutes, or days, the whiteness turned to grey. Only at the edges at first. But now there were edges. There were shapes, even straight lines for a few minutes, before the clouds returned and whited everything out. With the greyness came nausea. Something, somewhere in her mind, told her nausea must be a good sign. She felt her gorge rising hot and acid in her throat. Then she was back in the downy whiteness again.

It was the nausea that woke her up. The clouds cleared and she sat up, convinced she was going to vomit. The feeling passed, replaced by a dizziness caused by sitting up too quickly. She had a pounding headache, its rhythm in time with her pulse. She opened her eyes and closed them again, not believing what she saw. She must still be dreaming.

She took a deep breath and felt a little better. She opened her eyes again. Her first thought was to wonder how on earth they had managed to change her bedroom so drastically and completely in such a short time. It took quite an effort of mental reasoning before she worked out that this was not, and never had been, her bedroom. Her mind took it on from there, normal thought restored. The men had not come to the castle to rob it. They had come for her.

She looked around slowly, not wanting to make any sudden movements to exacerbate the hammer that appeared to be driving a nail into her forehead. The room was small, not much bigger than a double bed. The walls were of unplastered brick, two looking as though they had been recently built, two looking old, the mortar crumbling. There was a heavy wooden door but no window. The floor was paved in large flagstones. She was sitting on a wooden-framed single bed, covered with a thin mattress. There were no sheets, no pillow, no bedding of any sort. The room was lit by a single light bulb hanging from the wood beamed ceiling. In one corner of the room there was a bucket. Beside the bed, incongruously, was an English Windsor chair. On the seat of the chair was a glass of water.

Seeing the water, Stephanie realised she was desperately thirsty. It was probably the drug they had given

135

her. Slowly, she swung her legs off the bed and tried to take the two steps to the chair. She only managed one before her legs buckled and she sank to the floor. But at least she could reach the glass now. She took it in her hand and drank the whole glass.

She felt nauseous again, as the cold water drained into her system. She also felt cold. The room was damp and chilled. Getting back on to the mattress she tucked her legs up to her chest for warmth. There was absolutely nothing else she could use to cover herself. They had left her as naked as they'd found her.

Examining her body, she found a small, sensitive bruise where the needle had been injected into her upper arm. Otherwise, she appeared to be untouched.

Her feeling of disorientation was beginning to lessen. Her mind formed questions. How long had she been here? Where was Jasmina? What time was it? Automatically she looked for her watch and, as she stared at her bare wrist, remembered it was sitting on the bedside table back at the castle. Where was this room?

One thing she didn't have to question. There was only one person who could be responsible for this: Gianni. It had to be Gianni. It was the only explanation; his vengeance for what she had done to him. She cursed herself. She should have known better, she should have been on her guard, she should have realised that a man as powerful and egotistical as Gianni wouldn't simply ignore the humiliation she had meted out to him. How stupid not to have taken precautions . . .

And he'd probably taken Jasmina too. Taking her was one thing, in a sense she accepted she was fair game. But not Jasmina. Jasmina had nothing to do with it.

She rolled herself into a foetal position, more for

warmth than anything else, and closed her eyes. The headache was pounding less and, curiously, she began to feel a sense of euphoria. She felt light-headed, the feeling of having had just a little too much to drink. Despite her situation the world began to look rosy, she was smiling to herself. She felt good. It was puzzling, but her mood meant she had no desire to question it. She lay back on the bed, grinning.

She heard the key turn in the lock and saw the door open. Gianni walked into the cell, his face creased in a grin that matched her own.

Stephanie tried to pull herself off the bed, tried to summon up her anger, fly at him in rage, claw at his eyes, knee him in the balls. But nothing worked. Her body would not respond, nor would her mind. Her muscles refused to work, her anger would not rise. She couldn't even wipe the foolish grin from her face.

'Come on then, English,' he said. 'You don't want to beat me again, eh?'

She wanted to say that he had got what he deserved, but instead she continued to grin.

'No? Well, that is good.' He sat down in the Windsor chair, pulling at the knees of his trousers so as not to spoil the crease in his Gucci slacks. The tone of his voice changed. 'You really think I let you get away with it? Ah? You think you can do that to me? Lupa! Bitch! Well, now I teach you the lesson. A longer lesson. I learn quick. I learn from Devlin. From your castle. I think I start my castle here. All my friends come here. You will entertain them, no? Give them a show. Like at the castle. They can have what they want, my friends, like at the castle. Anything they want. And you are my star attraction, I think. You'll be very popular.'

Stephanie tried to say something, she wasn't at all sure what, but couldn't form the words.

'You think this is good? I teach you, Giancarlo Gianni cannot be treated like a piece of meat, hung up like a piece of meat.' He was getting angry. He stood up. She thought he was going to hit her, but instead he reached into his pocket and tossed a ball of material on to the bed. 'Here, these will keep you warm.'

He slammed the cell door and Stephanie heard the key turn in the lock. It was a long time before her muscles would respond to her commands again. As the strange feeling of euphoria wore off, so her muscles allowed her to move again. She didn't try to get off the bed, but reached down to the balled material Gianni had thrown at her feet. Unravelling it, she found a thin black satin suspender belt and a pair of sheer black stockings. As quickly as she could, she put them on. It may have been Gianni's idea of a cruel joke, but the stockings did give her some warmth.

After a while she ventured off the bed and managed to get her legs to support her. She tottered around the room like a child learning to walk.

One thing was certain. There was going to be no escape from this room. The door was thick and moved not at all when she put her shoulder against it. There was a ventilator grill set high up in the wall above the bed, but there was no way she could reach it, and anyway it was only six inches wide and three inches deep. She couldn't reach the light in the ceiling either and there was no switch in the room.

She walked around the tiny room like a caged animal. In the door she noticed a peep-hole, the kind people have on their front doors to inspect visitors, but she could see nothing through it.

There was no way of knowing how long it was before a small section at the bottom of the door opened – an arrangement like a cat-flap, the hinges for which she hadn't noticed – and a tray of food was pushed into the room. It was no more than a bowl of soup and a piece of bread. There was another glass of water.

Stephanie realised she was starving hungry. Not wanting to repeat her nausea however, she tried to eat slowly. Judging from her hunger, it must have been some time since she had eaten. How long had she been in this room? And what the hell was she going to do?

It was not more than five minutes after she had finished the soup, a concoction of beans and vegetables, that the light went out. The room was plunged into total darkness, or almost total. As her eyes became accustomed to the gloom, a weak line of light appeared around the frame of the door. But after two or three minutes that too clicked out.

Stephanie had no choice but to close her eyes and try to sleep. She curled herself into a ball and, surprisingly, was asleep in minutes.

The light woke her. For half a second she thought it was daylight, that she had been having a nightmare, that she would open her eyes and turn to Jasmina and walk out on to the terrace and into the warm sun. She opened her eyes to find a bare brick wall. It was not a dream.

The tray she had eaten from was gone. On the Windsor chair was another glass of water. She drank it, once again having woken with a ferocious thirst. There was something else different this morning if, of course, she could take it that the light being turned on meant it was morning. It was warm. The room was warm. It did not take long to track down the source of the warmth. Heat was flooding out of the ventilator duct above the bed, a steady flow of warm air.

She experienced an immediate euphoria. The warmth crept into her bones. She lay back, not having to curl up, being able to stretch out on the bed. It was some minutes before she realised the euphoria was not just caused by the heat. It was the same feeling she had had before, a light-headedness, turning the world to rights.

The key ground in the lock and the door opened. A middle-aged man shuffled uncertainly into the room. He was wearing a business suit. In his fifties, he was flabby and unhealthy looking. He smoked an untipped cigarette. He had scraped what was left of his hair over the top of his bald pate, as though trying to disguise his hair loss.

Stephanie tried to cover herself but found she could not move. Anyway, there was no need, the euphoria she felt made it unnecessary. Let him look. Let his little piggy eyes look at her if he wanted. She didn't care.

The balding man appeared reluctant, uncertain. The cell door had closed behind him. Stephanie had the impression he wasn't at all sure what he should do. He was looking at her body, looking at her legs and the band of flesh above the black welts of the stockings, looking down into her thick black pubic hair.

Stephanie felt warm and relaxed. She liked the little man, the way he looked at her, so desiring. She wanted to tell him he could have her, do what he wanted to her, but the words would just not come out.

He was nervous. Very nervous. He didn't trust Gianni at first. He was convinced it was a set-up.

He checked the walls of the cell, the ceiling; peered into the ventilator grill, anywhere a camera lens could be hidden. There was nowhere. He was reassured. If Gianni had told the truth about that, he had probably told the truth about the girl. Or so he reasoned. He'd told him she was not a whore, that she loved men, craved them, liked to be used, liked to be handled.

And, after all, she was smiling at him. A big smile. And she was relaxed, so relaxed. Any doubts he might have had disappeared when he looked at her. She was beautiful. Long dark hair, plump breasts with hard nipples, her legs wrapped in sheer nylon, thin black suspenders snaking down over her hips. She was beautiful. He believed Gianni. He wanted to believe him so badly.

Still looking around, he took off his clothes, folding them neatly on the chair. He saw the woman's eyes following what he was doing. She was still smiling. He extracted the leather belt from his trousers. Tentatively, he stretched his hand out to stroke the curves of her breast. He felt his penis harden immediately. She made no objection. Taking her arm he pulled her over on to her side, then stroked the subtle curve of her arse, feeling the black satin suspender under his hand. His penis hardened more. He pulled her over on to her stomach. Her perfect arse was framed like a picture by the suspender belt at her waist, the suspenders at her sides, and the black tops of the stockings underneath. A few stray hairs from her forest of pubic hair escaped from the junction of her thighs. The cleft of her arse was deep and full, her buttocks round and firm. He used two hands now, circling her buttocks with them, feeling their heat and their weight, their softness and, under that, the strong muscle. His erection nudged against her hip.

He used his hands to push her ankles apart, and knelt on the thin mattress between them. He was not a strong man, not muscled or fit, but he could feel his strength increasing with his lust as he looked down at this near naked woman. He moved his knees forward, pushing

141

her legs further apart. He could see the bush of her pubic hair now, spreading out from the long slit of her sex, like a plant that needed to be trimmed back into its original shape.

He took the belt and wound it around the knuckle of his right hand. The first stroke was tentative, but there was a satisfying 'whack' as it landed on her superb white flesh. He had never done this before except in his dreams. In his dreams he had done it a thousand times, a hundred thousand times. The second blow was firmer, the third perfect. A perfect stroke, a perfect hit. The thin belt landed in the middle of the woman's rump, cutting across both cheeks. The woman moaned. It was a moan of pleasure. She wanted more. Gianni had been right, he hadn't lied about her. The woman wanted more. He would hear her asking him for more, like the woman in his dreams, wanting, begging. Wasn't she?

His left hand was clutching his penis, squeezing it in his fist. He had never felt it so hard. It was made of steel. He pulled the belt back again. He heard the 'whack' and saw the soft flesh tremble.

He couldn't manage another stroke. His cock demanded all his attention. He let the belt drop to the floor. With both his hands he pulled the cheeks of the woman's arse apart. The little rosebud of her arse winked at him, just as it always did in his dreams. He touched it with the tip of his finger, gently, as though it were the most delicate piece of porcelain. Then he pushed his finger inside. All around he could feel the heat of her reddened flesh from where he had used his belt. He knelt closer, bending his head so he could watch his finger fucking her arse, in and out like a tiny cock. And see how she loved it, how she moaned with pleasure, wriggled and squirmed with pleasure, just like the women in his dreams always had. Didn't she?

Suddenly the arse lifted off the bed, no more than two or three inches, but pointed up at him. He knew what it meant. He knew what she was doing. She wanted him. He took his finger away and pushed his cock forward between her thighs, up between her legs, feeling her wiry hair on his steel-hard cock, then the heat, the incredible heat he had created in her. She wanted it, Gianni hadn't lied. She wanted it and he was going to give it to her, bugger her, bugger her like he'd buggered so many women in his dreams.

As he grasped his cock in his hand, guided it down to the tight corona of her arse, he came. Spunk lashed out between his fingers. It was propelled further than he could ever remember, right up over her arse, splashing her back and the black satin strap of the suspender belt, gobs of his white spunk.

He got up quickly. Using a handkerchief from his jacket pocket he wiped his hand clean and then dabbed ineffectively at the spunk on the woman's back. When he touched her buttocks she moaned. He knew what that meant. She'd come too. She'd had a good time and wanted more. Well he'd give her more all right. He'd ask Gianni. Gianni wanted a discount on his order, a big discount. The size of his order didn't justify it, but he'd give him the discount. They'd been discussing it before Gianni brought him here. Well, he'd give Gianni the discount, he'd tell him right now. But there was a condition. He had to have this woman again, this wonderful woman, this woman of his dreams. Tomorrow. The day after tomorrow. He *had* to. She wanted it. He wanted it. Tomorrow he'd really do it. He'd only come so quickly today because he wasn't ready, wasn't expecting it. Tomorrow he'd be ready. He'd give her what she wanted tomorrow.

He dressed without looking at the woman. He left his spunk-stained handkerchief on the bed and knocked on the cell door as he'd been told to do. It was opened and locked again after he'd left.

Stephanie felt it all at second hand, numbed by the euphoria. She felt everything he'd done, but almost as if it were being done to someone else. She felt the strokes of his belt; she felt the heat it created in her. She wanted to respond. But her body was already so high, so contented, so filled with sensation it was impossible, or so it seemed, to do anything but lay and enjoy the feelings.

It was like looking down the wrong end of a telescope. He looked and felt so far away.

She felt him push her legs apart. She wanted him. She wanted to tell him to give it to her, to use her, to take her. She felt his fingers too, prying fingers.

Why didn't he do it to her? Couldn't he see she wanted it? She wanted to push her arse up at him and, to her surprise, her muscles responded. But only once. She tried to move again, undulate her hips, but nothing happened. She sank back on to the bed.

The euphoria was wearing off. Irritation took over. What was he doing there? He'd made her all wet. And now when he touched her with his handkerchief, right on the spot where he'd beaten her, she winced.

She heard the man go. As she came down from the high, she felt the pain in her buttocks. She tried to move her hand and it responded. Gradually her ability to move returned.

Slowly, very slowly, she got up. Her arse was red and sore. She cursed Gianni aloud, shouting more because she wanted to hear her voice than from any hope that he would hear her.

'You bastard, Gianni. Get me out of here.'

She paced the room again, then stopped when she heard the key turning in the lock. The door opened and a woman entered. Stephanie recognised her at once. It was the woman who had answered the door to her, Angelina. The scowl still set on her face, a look that suggested she regarded Stephanie as little more than an annoyance; her black dress and lisle stockings also remained unchanged.

She indicated that Stephanie should follow her, turning back down the corridor outside the cell door.

It did not occur to Stephanie for a moment that she was being released. She knew Gianni better than that. His vengeance wouldn't be satisfied by keeping her just one night. Outside the cell door she stepped into a short corridor, in the same new brick as the two outer walls of the cell, at the end of which was another stout wooden door. To the left the only other door was open.

The woman in black grasped Stephanie by the wrist, dissatisfied at her slowness, and pulled her through the open door. Inside was a bathtub and a toilet. The bathtub was already full of water.

'Clean,' the woman said. There was a small wooden stool in the corner of the room. The woman rested her ample weight on it. 'Quickly, quickly,' she said angrily.

Stephanie sat on the loo . . .

Back in the cell it was cold again. The heating from the overhead vent had been turned off. The woman in black had taken Stephanie's stockings and the suspender belt away; only the spunk-stained handkerchief remained, and that was hardly going to keep her warm. Stephanie curled herself into a ball on the bed to keep warm.

A meal arrived through the door flap, soup and bread as before. She ate it all, scraping the bowl with the bread to get every last drop, wiping the plate clean.

She had no idea how long after the meal it was when she felt the heat flooding through the vent again. Just as before, this event was followed by a glass of water being pushed through the flap in the door. Stephanie had been thirsty the whole time she had been in the cell. When she'd been taken to the bathroom she had been so desperate to drink she'd used her hand to scoop up some of the bathwater before she used the soap.

She had thought at first it was due to the injection, a strange side effect. But the combination of the turning on of heat and the arrival of water was too much of a coincidence. Twice she'd been given water and twice she'd felt a wonderful euphoria and relaxation. Twice she'd been unable to move. The water she'd been given with the meal had had no effect. But now the room was being heated, just like this morning (if it was morning, she had no way of knowing) when the bald man had come in. Heat for a visitor and a drug to keep her quiet. It must be, she thought. The water was drugged, with an after effect of making her thirsty. The more she drank the more she would want to drink.

She picked up the water and sniffed it. There was no odour. She held it up to the light but could see no coloration. The trouble was her thirst. Perhaps if she just took a sip. She sipped experimentally, but the water tasted of nothing other than water and the sip did not quench her thirst. She drank more and more. She wanted to stop herself but she was just so thirsty. She drank three quarters of a glass. She wanted to drink the rest desperately, but she had to test her theory. If it was drugged and she drank less the effects would wear off sooner. Well, that was the theory. She looked around the room for somewhere to dump the remaining water. In one corner of the cell the floor stones were badly joined and there was a gap of a couple of inches between

146

them. Carefully, she poured the water into the crack. It disappeared immediately. She spilt a little but mopped it up with the handkerchief. She put the empty glass down.

Her suspicions evaporated. She sat on the bed. What did it matter? She just felt so good, so relaxed, so wonderfully unworried. She lay back on the bed and looked up at the ceiling. It was like a wave at the beach had knocked her off her feet, knocked her down into a world of contentment. The heat from the overheat vent above the bed began to warm her body, making her sense of well-being complete.

She heard the key turn in the lock and managed to turn her head to watch the woman come into the cell. She tried to smile at her. The woman did not smile back.

Gina had known Gianni a long time. They had done business together for a long time. He had tried to seduce her many times. She was a very attractive woman, a redhead, a flaming redhead, tall and strong. He had tried so many times that, in the end, she had told him the truth – that she was not interested in men, other than the fact that she would have liked to be one. That had made him give up the chase.

They continued to do business, good business. A lot of business. Gianni had called her this morning. He said he had something interesting for her, something she would especially like, something classy and English . . .

He was right. She sat on the thin mattress of the bed and looked down at the naked woman. She was beautiful, her long, black hair spread around her head like a garland, her firm breasts, narrow waist, the fullness of her hips and her long subtle legs. Gorgeous. Best of all,

Gina thought, the triangle of her belly, the thick hair. Gina loved thick pubic hair. She brushed it with the palm of her hand and felt a jolt of excitement.

She stood up and stripped off her plain, white dress, her cotton bra and panties. Her body was a great disappointment to her. Her breasts sagged, she had no waist and her hips were too fat. She should have been a man. On a man her figure would have been acceptable. Not that the woman on the bed seemed to mind. She smiled. Smiled her approval.

Bending over the bed, she ran her fingers along the woman's lips, then kissed them with her own while her hand squeezed at the firm mound of her breast.

'You English,' she said. 'Gianni tells me what you like. I give you.'

She picked up her bag and took out the double dildo. It looked like a misshapen boomerang. She heard the woman moan when she saw it. Gianni had been right. Using a jar of cream she oiled it, both ends, greasing it, then wiping the excess cream on the woman's breasts, making them greasy and slippery too.

Still standing, she bent her legs slightly and inserted one end of the double phallus into her own sex. She had done this a thousand times and it never ceased to thrill her – feeling it invade her and then, looking down, seeing herself transformed, a huge erection growing from between her legs, just like a man. Just like a man. Her other partners hardly ever let her use this toy: they said it was too big, that she was too brutal with it, that she got carried away. It may have been true. It was the nearest she ever got to fucking like a man, taking a woman like a man. With this buried inside her she would feel like a man too, every thrust producing a feeling in her to match what it was doing to the woman underneath her.

And this woman understood. Gianni had told her she would. She could see her smiling, wanting, eyeing the phallus.

She pulled her legs apart, Gina felt like a man, the erection sticking out as she lay on the woman.

'I fuck you,' she said, the words thrilling her.

The woman moaned, 'Yes.'

Gina worked the cock – it was a cock, her cock – between the lips of the woman's cunt. This was the moment she loved. She thrust her hips forward and felt the cock slide home with no resistance. At the same time it levered down in her own cunt. The woman under her moaned.

Gina reached between their bodies and found the woman's breasts. She squeezed them, kneaded them, caressed them as she bucked her hips in and out. She squeezed her cunt around the dildo, holding it firm as it pumped in and out of the woman. She pressed her mouth on to the woman's mouth and plunged her tongue inside her lips as far as it would go, wanting to fill her here too.

She felt herself coming. The dildo moved so beautifully inside her as she bucked her hips. The pressure of pushing into the other woman made her end lever into her cunt, finding new places, new deeps, new darknesses. It gave her feelings she could not control. The base of the dildo, where it bent outward, rubbed at her clitoris too, exactly at the right place. She had to break the kiss because she had to scream with pleasure. Her body quivered with excitement as her orgasm exploded. In her mind she spunked, spunked into the soft wet depths of the cunt underneath her. She felt like a man.

Finally she stopped bucking her hips, pushing one last time with all her might and then stopping, pressing up into the woman, feeling their two cunts joined together by a cock, a cock that was hers, that she controlled, that belonged to her.

The woman moaned again and used her hand to push at her shoulder. It was a gentle push. Gina eased the dildo out from between them and knelt on her haunches. The dildo was glistening wet, still erect, still sprouting from the red hair of her pubis. She looked down at the woman, who had crossed her arms over her breasts. She was trying to say something too, but Gina could not understand what it was. It sounded like 'bitch' but she didn't know what that meant in English.

Gina got up from the bed and reluctantly pulled the phallus from her body. She knew when it finally came out it would almost make her come again – it always did – so she pulled very, very slowly, teasing herself, enjoying the sight of the woman on the bed, well fucked, trying to imagine what it would be like to have really fucked her like a man, with a real cock. Her fingers worked at her clitoris as the other hand extracted the dildo. As she finally felt its tip break out of her labia she came again, as she hoped she would, pressing her finger on her clit and holding it down hard, until all the passion was squeezed out of her body.

'You like to be fucked, I think. Gianni says this.'

Gina dressed. Her body was still tingling, her mind full of images that would be with her for a long time. She packed the dildo back into her bag. The jar of cream was empty and she dropped it on the bed. She knocked twice on the cell door.

'Bella,' she said as she left.

She'd been right. She could move. She'd been able to move. Not very much, but she'd moved, tried to push the woman off. She had felt more, too. In different circumstances she would have enjoyed the experience, but the woman had been unsubtle, carried away with her own feelings, strong and harsh. The feeling of euphoria had evaporated much more quickly, and she was left with her real feelings. So she had been right. The water was drugged.

If she could resist drinking the water, she might be able to do something, to escape. Exactly how, she couldn't imagine, but at least she'd have the element of surprise, at least she'd have all her faculties. Perhaps Angelina would make a mistake.

The problem was resisting the water. Soon she would be thirsty again. Her eyes lighted on the empty cold-cream jar. She picked it up and immediately had an idea. The water they gave her with meals was not drugged. If she could save some of that and drink it instead of the drugged water . . .

She wiped the excess cream out of the jar with her fingers. She used it to soothe the soreness the dildo had created.

She would have to hide it somewhere. Under the bed? But that wasn't very hidden. She lifted the mattress. The wooden bed had a slated frame. If she could make a cradle with the handkerchief tied between two slats it would hold the jar and be very unlikely to be seen. She worked quickly, the handkerchief just big enough to form a hammock into which the jar would fit. All she had to do now was fill it with water.

It was a feeble plot, but her own. At least it gave her hope, though hope of what she was not entirely sure.

TEN

The light woke her. Or it might have been the cold. Or her thirst. As she had no way of telling the time she had no means of telling how long it had been before her raging thirst had returned. They had not given her a drink before the light had gone out, so now her thirst was savage.

'Breakfast' consisted of bread and water passed through the flap. She grabbed the beaker of water, and was about to down it all at once when she remembered the jar. She finished half the glass, but her thirst was hardly quenched. She took the jar from its hiding place and filled it with water. It took the whole half glass. She screwed the top back on and put it in the handkerchief cradle. Her thirst was still terrible.

If she took just another sip? She sat on the bed and tried to think of something else. She ate the bread and put her knees up to her chin to keep warm.

She heard the key turning in the lock and Angelina entered to take her for her bath. She managed to swig a few mouthfuls of the bathwater, but on the third mouthful Angelina saw what she was doing, slapped her hand down from her mouth and shouted 'Basta!' For the rest of the time her eyes never left Stephanie's as she cleaned herself and used the toilet.

Back in the cell, Angelina threw a red basque on to

the bed and a pair of grey stockings. Stephanie put them on immediately. It was the most she had been given to wear since her arrival in the cell. And she knew what it meant. She knew she was going to be getting another visitor.

As she sat trying to forget her thirst, the optimism her little plan had created began to seep away and be replaced by depression. The cold depressed her too, the thin basque and stockings providing little warmth. What good would it do her? Even if she got free of the drug she could never overpower Gianni or whoever it was. If she got out of the cell, the outer door was bound to be locked. She was trapped.

She thought of life at the castle, the brief weeks of absolute luxury she had passed there. It seemed so far away now. Well, she only had herself to blame; she had been hoist by her own petard. She had played a danger-ous game and lost, well and truly lost. If she hadn't reacted to what Gianni had done to her at the castle none of this would have happened. It wasn't as though she hadn't enjoyed it. She had. In the end she begged him to take her. Why hadn't she just left it at that? Why did she have to teach him a lesson?

The vent began to blow heat. On schedule, a few minutes later, the flap in the door opened and a glass of water appeared. The same pattern. Stephanie stared at the water as if it were a complicated puzzle she had to solve. Her thirst immediately raged, made worse by the water, her mouth salivating, her whole body begging her to drink. She reached out and took the glass in her hand. It was trembling, making little waves on the surface of the water. Why didn't she just drink it all, lay on the bed in a haze of euphoria, let them do what they wanted with her? Did it matter?

Quickly, before she lost her willpower, she poured

the water into the crack in the floor. She flipped up the mattress, opened the jar, and downed all the water in it. She wanted to save some, but she couldn't. The water tasted of cold-cream. Screwing back the top, she replaced the jar in its cradle and lay flat out on the bed.

She waited, her thirst not slaked but bearable.

The key turned in the lock. Gianni strode in. With him was another man or, more accurately, a boy.

'Well, my dear,' he said, grinning. 'I hope you enjoy your stay with us. This is my nephew, Paulo. Tomorrow is his eighteenth birthday. His father has given him his own flat. So I think what I can give.' He started to laugh. 'I think I give him you.'

Since he had shuffled uneasily into the cell, the boy's eyes had not left Stephanie's body.

Stephanie did not move.

'Bene?' Gianni asked.

'Meraviglioso . . .' the boy replied, almost under his breath.

'Happy birthday!' Gianni said in English, slapping his shoulder and closing the cell door as he left.

The boy continued to stare at first, hardly registering that his uncle had left. Then he began unbuttoning his shirt and pulled it off. His chest was almost concave, the ribs showing on either side. He stepped out of his shoes and socks and pulled down his trousers and pants together. His penis was already sticking out from his adolescent body. It didn't match the rest of him at all: it was a man's penis, thick and mature.

Paulo bent over Stephanie as she lay playing doggo on the bed and, as though expecting to receive an electric shock, touched the top of her breast. When she did not react, he moved his hand down under the lace of the basque and on to her nipple. He used his other hand

155

to do the same with the other breast, sitting down beside her on the mattress.

Stephanie saw his erection bobbing out from his lap. A tear of moisture indicated his excitement. Whatever he intended to do with her was not going to last long, she guessed. If this wasn't his first time, it was certainly the first time with a mature women dressed like something out of one of the men's magazines he undoubtedly read and wanked over in secret. The expression on his face said it all: birthday and Christmas all wrapped into one.

He moved his hand down the satin of the basque until he reached her navel. She moaned. His hand dropped into her pubic hair. She moaned again, parting her legs slightly.

Experimentally, he pushed down between her legs with the tips of his fingers. Very softly, hardly moving her lips, she whispered 'Do it to me.'

He'd only done this once before and that hadn't been very successful. It had been in his bedroom in his parents' house and he hadn't been at all sure what he was doing. Neither had the girl. They'd groped and fumbled at each other's clothing and he'd come. He hadn't even been sure he'd penetrated her and hadn't liked to ask. She had been as nervous and scared as him. Good Catholic girls in Italy are expected to stay virgins. Her father would have killed him if he'd known he'd deflowered his daughter: any father would.

This wasn't a girl. It was a woman. A gorgeous, mature, sexy woman. He pushed his hands down between her legs and she co-operated by opening them more. He felt her heat. He parted her pubic hair and, ignoring her clitoris, found the opening to her cunt. He pushed his finger inside and felt it engulfed in wetness.

She wanted it. His uncle had been right. Wanted it and wanted him.

He felt his heart pounding with excitement. He didn't quite know what to do next. There were so many possibilities. She felt so wet and hot and sticky. She felt like all the descriptions in all the books he had read. He pushed his finger higher, feeling it parting the fleshy walls of her cunt. Oh my god, what a feeling . . .

In his lap, his cock pulsed and hot white spunk jetted out over his thighs. Without being touched his cock had come.

Paulo blushed beetroot red. He stood up and immediately grabbed for his pants. Stephanie saw what had happened. And she saw a chance. A slim one, but a chance. She would have to get him to trust her.

'Don't go,' she said quietly. The boy ignored her, pulling his pants up over his rapidly diminishing penis. 'Do you speak English?'

'Yes,' he said. 'We learn at school.'

'Don't go then, stay with me.'

'I go.'

'But I want you, Paulo. Don't you understand. That was so sexy. So exciting.'

'No.' He refused to look into her eyes.

'It made me feel so good. I mean, that I got you that excited. It's such a compliment. Do you know how that makes me feel?'

'How?'

'So sexy. Just come here for a minute.'

Paulo did nothing. Then, with obvious reluctance, he took the two steps back to the bed. Stephanie reached up and took his hand. 'Feel me again. You almost made me come the first time. You have such a marvellous touch,' she lied.

She pulled his hand down between her legs and held it there, pressing it hard into her sex, then relaxing, then pressing again.

'Oh, so good.'

'Is it?' He looked into her eyes. She took her hand away. He pressed down between her labia, his finger sliding between the wet lips.

'You have such a good touch,' she panted breathily. Reaching up, she caught the front of his pants in her hand and pulled them down to his ankles. She circled his cock with her hand and felt it swell again. She rubbed the sensitive rim of his glans and he moaned, his penis swelling rapidly. 'See, aren't you glad you didn't go?' As she had discovered with Angelo, eighteen-year-olds have remarkable powers of recovery given the right circumstances.

She wanked him gently with her hand, hoping this wouldn't make him come again, while his fingers investigated her sex. He explored her clitoris, her labia, her vagina – all as though he were examining a new pet hamster, brusquely, with little feeling. Not that Stephanie intended to tell him that.

'Oh, darling,' she said instead, 'so good . . .' She sighed too, as though he were giving her untold pleasure.'Why don't you let me give you a treat?'

'What sort of treat?'

'I'll take you in my mouth. I love to do that.' She felt his cock twitch in her hand as she said it. He'd read about it. It was the stuff of his fantasies.

'Would you?'

'I love it. Lay down here.' She patted the mattress. He obeyed.

His penis stood erect. Her plan was gradually taking shape in her mind. She had to make him feel good. She mustn't make him come too quickly again, or he'd really run away and never want to come back.

She kissed his thighs, slow wet kisses, then worked her tongue on to his balls, while she held his cock in her hand. It was a handsome cock: the glans a perfect acorn shape; the stem, as yet not sprouting hair, smooth and thick. There was little hair on his balls either. Stephanie probed them with her tongue and felt an immediate spasm of excitement in his cock. She pulled away quickly. That was too much for him. Instead she started licking his cock, long wet licks, her hand still circling the stem. This he seemed able to take. She licked and licked, moaning too and mouthing 'So good' between mouthfuls.

He made no attempt to touch her. He was as rigid as an ironing board. She knew the moment she put him in her mouth he would come, so she tried to delay it as long as possible. She stroked his chest and kissed his nipples, which immediately produced another spasm in his cock.

She knew he was going to come. She could feel it. She had to take him in her mouth now or forget her plan.

'Give it to me darling,' she whispered. 'Please. Now, now . . .'

She plunged her mouth down over the perfect acorn, expecting his spunk to jet out into her throat. But it didn't.

Paulo expected it to as much as she had. He felt a surge of pleasure as her wet mouth sucked him in, a surge he thought would take him over the top. But instead the pleasure continued; the rising spunk in his cock stopped rising and stayed, for the moment, where it was. He was in control.

Stephanie pulled her mouth back, using her tongue to probe the opening of his urethra. He wriggled in pleasure. She felt him relax. She sucked him deep into her throat.

'Yes,' he said, more to himself than to her. 'Yes.'

She moved up and down on him, her black hair falling on his groin as her head bobbed. She reached behind her to try and collect it in her hand, but he put out his arm to stop her.

'I like it.'

The hair fell back, sweeping over his navel.

She could do more adventurous things now. She slipped her hand under his cock, down to his buttocks, feeling for the eyelet of his arse, while her other hand reached up to pinch at his nipple, all while she sucked on his cock.

He moaned as her finger probed his arse, but was still under control. He began to buck his hips, enjoying himself now, feeling like a man. He was in control. And he wanted more.

'I want to fuck you,' he said, with a new authority in his voice, mentally thanking his schoolfriend who had brought back a copy of *Lady Chatterley's Lover* from England. He'd learnt the right word.

'Oh, yes . . .' Stephanie said.

'From behind.' He'd never thought learning English would prove so valuable.

Stephanie pulled herself up on to all fours and pointed her perfect arse at him, the tight waist of the basque emphasising the fullness of her hips, the rich curves of her buttocks. And there, between the half moons, he could see the whole of the slit of her sex, its thick hair plastered down with her juices.

'Give it to me, Stephanie hissed.

And he did. He took his cock in his hand and pushed forward, watching it disappear between her buttocks. He pulled it out again and could see it shining with her juices. In all his dreams, he'd never imagined this.

He bucked his hips, bucked his cock in and out of her

cunt and heard her moan. He bucked faster, feeling his spunk rising. But he could control it. He was a man now. He could control it. He'd come when he was ready. He bucked faster and faster, watching his cock pummelling in and out of her like a piston. He reached forward with one hand to squeeze at her breast. Her long, black hair was tipped forward like a black cloak over her head. She thrust her buttocks back at him.

'Give it to me,' she screamed. 'I want your spunk.'

And she did. He had created her need. He was hard. Her play-acting was over. Her cunt was running wet. She could feel his heat and urgency, feel his spunk. She wanted it badly. She pushed back at him, his trusts stronger, harder, faster. She reached down between her legs and found his balls. They were soaking wet. She didn't know any more whether she was doing it as part of her plan, or because she needed his spunk to make her come. It didn't matter. She took his balls in her hand and pulled them down, away from his body. He could resist no longer. He pushed forward for the last time, pushed deeper and deeper until he found a place, a dark cavern of sticky, wet walls and, in his mind's eye, saw his cock shooting spunk out into her, as he had seen it do so many times in his own hand.

Stephanie exploded too. She gasped. She could swear she felt the spunk splashing into her. It was as though it had hit the centre of her sex, the secret place that released all her feeling. Her body rocked and trembled.

She didn't move for a long time. Neither did he. They wanted to hold on to the feelings for as long as they lasted, every second.

When his penis finally slipped from her cunt she rolled on to her back. Her senses, and priorities, were restored.

'God, you're so good . . .' she said, and this time it was not a lie.

He sat on the edge of the bed. 'It's you. You do just the right things.' He touched her cheek with his hand. 'You make me into a man.'

'You are a man. A real man. Any women would love what you've just done.'

'Really?'

'You have to promise me something, Paulo,' she said seriously.

'Anything.'

'You mustn't tell your uncle what happened.' If Paulo described their activities to Gianni, he would soon realise she had somehow evaded the drug.

'What?'

'You promise?'

'I won't.' He blushed. 'I won't tell anyone.'

'Not a thing.'

'No.'

'Will you do something else. Another promise?'

'I'll do anything.'

'Come and see me again. Please. Soon.'

'Oh yes . . .'

'What did your uncle tell you about me, Paulo?'

'Nothing. I thought . . .' He blushed an even deeper red.

'You thought what? That I was a prostitute?'

'Yes.'

'Paulo, you've got to help me.' Stephanie mentally took a deep breath. It was a slim chance, but it was the only one she had. There was nothing to do but take it. 'Will you help me? Your uncle's got me locked up down here. I did something stupid to him and he's very angry with me. He keeps me prisoner down here. He drugs me and brings people down here . . .'

162

'You are not drugged now.'

'I managed to trick him. Will you help me? It's just that it was so good with you, Paulo. I'd love to be with you. I'd do anything if you'll help me. I could come and be with you. You could do whatever you wanted with me. I'd never leave you. Oh, just imagine what we could do. This would just be the beginning. I could teach you so much. We could do everything.'

Stephanie could see his mind working, making calculations. His eyes were unfocused as he tried to sort out what she had said. Then she felt sure she'd failed, that he'd seen through it, that he was going to walk out and tell his uncle everything. I should have waited, she thought, worked out what I was going to say. But then he might not have come back at all.

'I have my own flat now,' he said, almost to himself.

'Yes.' Hope returned in a flood. 'Yes, take me there, Paulo. Take me to your flat. We could have such a good time.'

Paulo stood up and started to pull his clothes on. Stephanie's heart sank again.

'Paulo, please,' she begged.

'I come back tomorrow.'

'Will you help me?'

'I come back tomorrow.'

'Please . . .'

'What's your name?'

'Stephanie.'

'Stephanie,' he repeated. 'Stephanie.'

He knocked twice on the cell door. It seemed like a long time before the door was opened and he was gone.

The next day, if it was a day every time the light came on, the pattern continued. Woken by the light. Given breakfast. Taken to the bathroom. The clothes taken

163

away. Led back to the cold cell by Angelina. At least she wasn't thirsty. Not having taken the drug had meant the water with breakfast and the soup at what she took to be lunchtime, were sufficient. She filled the cold cream jar just in case.

When the heat started to flow from the overhead vent, and the glass of water appeared through the flap in the door, Stephanie could quite calmly pour it through the crack in the paving stones and lay back on the bed to wait for her next visitor.

She heard the key turn in the lock, a grating, rusty sound, and the door creaked open. It was Paulo. She had never imagined she would be so glad to see anyone.

'Oh, Paulo . . .' she said, immediately the door was closed. 'It's so good to see you.'

'I told you I'd come back.' He looked uneasy and unsure of himself. He came over to the bed and sat down beside her.

'What's the matter?'

'I've been thinking so much about you, Stephanie.'

'Paulo, that's good.'

'My uncle, he shouldn't do this. It's wrong. I am going to tell him it's wrong.'

'No!'

'Why not?'

'Because he won't listen. That's not the way to help me.'

'What is the way, then?'

'You have to try and get me out of here. I don't even know where I am.'

'In the cellar of his house.'

'In Rome?'

'Yes.'

'What about his wife?'

'She's gone away on a holiday, I think.'

Stephanie smiled inwardly at that. I bet she's gone away, she thought, and for a very long holiday, after finding her husband chained to the living room wall.

'So there's only the servants and Gianni. If you came when he was out one night . . .'

He was looking at her naked body. 'You are so beautiful, Stephanie. I have never seen anyone as beautiful as you.'

'Oh Paulo, I want us to be together. Could you imagine what it would be like. The two of us.' She ran her hand into his lap to help his imagination along, and quickly unzipped his trousers. His cock was already hardening. She grasped it firmly. 'Lay back here.'

She made room for him on the narrow bed. He lay back, his cock poking up through his trousers, while she lay next to him on her side, her hand wanking his erection.

'Can you imagine, Paulo?' she whispered. 'My breasts, my mouth, my cunt . . . Whenever you wanted, whatever you wanted. Have you ever watched a woman wank herself, Paulo? I'd love to do that for you. And I'd wank you, and suck you and swallow all your spunk. Oh, it would be so good. And you'd fuck me like you did yesterday.' She felt his cock pulsing in her hand. 'Please, Paulo, spunk for me now. Will you, if I beg you to come in my mouth?'

She knelt up by the side of him and bent her head down to suck him deep into her mouth. At the same time, she found his nipple and pinched it hard under his shirt, so hard he winced. But the momentary pain took his spunk to the top of his cock and, as she sucked, sucked his cock as though literally trying to suck the spunk out of him, he came, his cock spasming in her mouth, his spunk hitting the back of her throat. She swallowed all she could.

'See, Paulo, just like that. Whatever you wanted. Oh God, you make me feel so sexy.' She lay beside him and pushed her hand down between her legs. She was giving a performance, but the performance was exciting her. Her clitoris was already hard. She stabbed at it, using no subtlety, wanking only for instant gratification, to satisfy a need she had created in herself. She saw Paulo's eyes watching her. She pulled, hammered and squeezed her clit, doing all these things quickly. And she came quickly too, muffling her moan of pleasure by pressing her face into Paulo's chest, feeling his clothes against her nakedness, trembling as her orgasm pierced her body.

'See how you turn me on,' she said.

'I get you out of here somehow.'

Paulo turned on to his side, allowing Stephanie to lie on her back. He ran his hand down her neck and between the channel of her breasts. He was just about to go lower when they both heard the key turning in the lock. They looked at each other in panic. The cell door opened and Gianni strode in.

Stephanie made her body go limp and hoped Paulo would realise why. Thank God he hadn't come in a few minutes earlier, she thought.

'Well, boy,' he said in English, looking at Paulo's flaccid cock hanging out of the front of his trousers. 'Been practising your English? His English very good, bitch. Top of the class. He's been to the best school. He tell you this?'

Gianni was drunk. His words were slurred and he lurched as he moved towards the wooden bed. Paulo quickly zipped himself back into his trousers and stood up.

'He takes after me. English crazee.'

The boy went to the cell door, which was still open.

166

'Don't go, Paulo. I show you how to fuck. You watch how a real man fucks. You learn, ah?'

Paulo blushed beetroot red, glanced at Stephanie and fled, slamming the cell door after him.

Gianni laughed. 'Just a boy. You need a man.' He fumbled with his trouser belt and, with difficulty, managed to free it. His trousers dropped to his ankles. He knelt at the foot of the bed, playing with his flaccid cock. 'I have a plan now. I decided I keep you. My friends were very pleased. They like you. The woman, Gina, she thought you are so sexy. Very good business. Devlin is right. That's how he uses his castle, no? For business. Well, now I do the same. Find a place.'

His cock was erect. He lay on top of her and started pushing it down between her thighs. He pumped it up and down, but it was only grazing the wetness of her nether lips. He was too drunk to notice the difference.

'Not here. A place somewhere in the country,' he said into her ear, as his buttocks rose and fell lazily, with no urgency. 'Get some more girls. Oh yes. I think will be good for me. And you'll be the star attraction.'

He bucked his hips three or four more times and then moaned. Stephanie felt a wetness spreading between her legs. He's come without penetrating her. Then he lay on her, inert, his weight bearing down on her body. She desperately wanted to push him off. For a second, she thought of running. The cell door was ajar. Paulo had slammed it, but it had bounced open again. Paulo might still be in the house –

She thought better of it. The corridor was probably locked. Angelina was probably out there doing her duty. Not only would she not escape, but he would know she was not drugged.

She allowed herself a moan, and the slightest of movements, to indicate her discomfort. Gianni took the hint, thinking, no doubt, that the drug was beginning to wear off. He climbed off her and got unsteadily to his feet.

'I have been meaning to tell you, English,' he said, pulling his trousers up from his ankles. 'Your plan. Your little plan. What you intended for me. It didn't work. My secretary came for to give me papers I have to sign. Fortunatementa, you left the front door open. She found me.' He laughed. 'You wanted it to be my wife, no? But I had the luck.She got me down in time. It cost me a very large bonus. And then I tell my wife how terrible. The house, it has cracked. These old buildings. Is lucky I am not killed, I tell her. She is very sympathetic. Very. She even says she'll cancel her holidays. But I say no. I am brave. She must go. so she goes. Convenient, eh? All the luck.'

He opened the cell doors. 'Tomorrow my friends come again,' he said, closing the door after him, the key grating in the lock.

She was alone again. The heating stopped. She felt miserable and depressed, the lowest she had felt since she had been kidnapped. Her plans had all gone wrong. Gianni had almost certainly scared off Paulo. She had seen the look of disgust in his face. She had tried to create the illusion that she would be his alone. Gianni had shattered that. Now, in Paulo's eyes, she was used goods, no more than a whore.

And, to make matters worse, she didn't even have the satisfaction of knowing that, at least, Gianni had suffered too. His wife was blithely unaware that anything had happened.

Stephanie curled herself up into a ball and cursed. 'Damn you,' she said aloud.

ELEVEN

She had been dreaming. She was back in London, back at her office in the advertising agency. Her boss, Norman Hughes, was standing by her desk, welcoming her back, telling her how glad they were she'd accepted his offer, how they'd missed her, how he'd always known she'd come back in the end. His huge paunch had gone. His height and rugged features were now complimented by an iron flat stomach. To Stephanie he looked strong and handsome. She wanted to remind him what had happened when she left, but there were too many people about.

Come into the conference room, he told her. You'll be needed on a new campaign for a new client, he told her. The conference room was already full of people, all sitting around a massive oval table. Stephanie couldn't find anywhere to sit.

'Come and sit here,' Norman Hughes said.

He was sitting at the top of the table. Stephanie walked the length of the room. She realised there was no one at the table she knew other than her boss.

She sat next to him. He put his hand on her knee and then slid it up till it was on her thigh. She looked down into her lap. His hand had revealed her stocking tops, the white suspender and white stocking in contrast to the tanned flesh of her thigh. She pulled her skirt down over his hand.

169

Norman started to speak. He was speaking Italian. She had never heard him speak Italian before. He spoke it fluently, the phrases rolling off his tongue as his hand worked further up her thigh, until his fingertips were at the side of her panties. Stephanie noticed every seat at the table had a glossy, purple box in front of it. Norman, and everyone else at the table, opened their boxes and took out the product, a U-shaped double dildo.

Stephanie could hear Gina's voice, but she couldn't see her. She searched all the faces at the table but none of them belonged to Gina. Suddenly she saw her. She was standing at the far end of the conference table wearing a man's pin-striped suit, a shirt and tie, her flaming red hair cut short like a man's hair and parted. She climbed up on to the table and started to walk down to Stephanie, over the opened purple boxes.

'Stephanie will help me demonstrate the product. It has tremendous advantages over the traditional equipment, enabling both parties to reach mutual orgasm. We are currently working on an ejaculation system.'

Gina held out her hand to help Stephanie up on to the table. As Stephanie got up, everyone applauded.

'Another advantage is that fellatio can also produce an excellent orgasm. Stephanie is familiar with the product and will help me demonstrate the suitable positions.' Gina's English was perfect. She took off the jacket of the suit, stripped off the tie and unbuttoned the shirt. Her sagging breasts had gone. She had a man's chest.

'Stephanie can vouch for the effectiveness of the product, as you will see. Kneel please, Stephanie.' Stephanie obeyed.

Gina unzipped her trousers and they fell to her ankles. She wore no pants, male or female. In front of

Stephanie's face was not one end of the double dildo but a cock, a tiny, flaccid cock. Gina pulled Stephanie's head forward. She kissed it reluctantly then took it in her mouth. She saw everyone at the table leaning forward to get a better view. The cock was growing erect, but it felt strange. She pulled back and saw that now it was hard plastic. She could see the other end arching out of Gina's cunt.

'Lie down, Stephanie,' Norman said.

'Lie down, Stephanie,' Gina said.

'No,' Stephanie screamed. She wanted to go. Coming back to work had been a mistake. She wanted to go back to the castle.

She started to climb off the table, but as she got down Norman pushed her back and Gina grabbed her by the hand and pulled her on to her back, in the centre of the table. She held her down with the strength of a man. Another man got up and pulled at her skirt. Stephanie recognised him, his hair combed over his bald pate. She was naked now. She begged them to let her go, but no sound came out. She tried to struggle but she couldn't move a muscle. She felt her thighs spread apart. Everyone was on the table now, all the men with erections bobbing out of their flies, all the women with the double dildos inserted between their legs, all the phalluses pointing at Stephanie.

'Now if you'd like to try the product for yourselves Stephanie will be only too pleased to co-operate . . .'

Gina smiled down at her, as Stephanie felt hands parting her thighs –

The noise woke her with a start. It was the noise of the key turning in the lock. But how could that be? The dream had momentarily disorientated her. It was pitch black. The light hadn't come on. The door had never been opened without the light coming on.

As the door was pushed open she saw the beam of a torch. It shone into the cell. She couldn't see behind the torch. She heard the door being closed again.

'Stephanie.' It was Paulo's voice.

'Paulo,' she said with relief. Her naked breast brushed against his hand as he groped in the semi-darkness.

'I've come for you.'

'What?'

'I've come to take you away.'

'Really?' An enormous rush of hope dispelled the remnants of sleep.

'My uncle is drunk. I hid until he went to bed. I thought it was a good time.'

'Oh yes, yes. You're wonderful,' she said, hugging him to her. She kissed his face, his cheeks, his neck. 'Oh thank you, Paulo.' It had worked. She could hardly believe it, but it had worked.

'We have to be careful.'

'Yes. How did you get the keys?'

'He hangs them on a hook outside the main cellar door. That wasn't difficult. But his housekeeper. She sleeps by the entrance. We have to be very quiet or she'll wake up.'

'What time is it?'

'Two in the morning. Here, I brought this for you.'

He shone the torch down on to a plastic shopping bag. Inside was a black track suit.

'It's Uncle Gianni's. It's all I could find.'

Stephanie quickly slipped it on. Her joy knew no bounds. For the first time in she had no idea how long, she was actually wearing proper clothes. The effect on her spirits was remarkable. But she wasn't free yet, she told herself. She still had to get out of the house. She still had to deal with Paulo too.

172

'Stephanie,' he said earnestly.

'Yes?'

'What you said. You meant those things?'

'About us? Of course, Paulo.'

'You'd be with me? We'd do what we've done here?'
Paulo's altruism was flawed. He wanted reassurance
that she would be his chattel.

'Oh Paulo, you silly boy,' she said, taking his hands
in hers. 'I've thought of nothing else. You're such a
wonderful lover, such a man. My God, it makes me wet
just to think about what you did to me. I don't want to
have anyone else, ever.' She hoped she was not over-
doing it. 'Paulo, darling, I want you so much . . .' She
whispered this in his ear, running her hand down to his
fly. 'Get me out of here and we'll make love all night. I'll
give you experiences you've never even imagined.'

'Stephanie . . .' He was about to say something but
changed his mind. 'We have to be very quiet.'

The light from the torch moved around to the
doorway. Paulo led the way out of the cell and down the
short corridor where Angelina had taken Stephanie to
bathe. At the end, the wooden door was open. Stephanie
felt a surge of excitement as she stepped through it.

With the single, narrow beam of light from the torch
it was difficult to get her bearings, but it looked as
though they were now in a much larger open space.
Stephanie glimpsed brick pillars every so often and she
saw packing cases and bric-a-brac and discarded furniture and bank boxes full of files. A distinct path had
been cleared through all this mess.

Paulo slowed as the torch picked up the outlines of a
wooden staircase.

'The housekeeper sleeps the other side of the door,'
he whispered, flicking the torch beam upwards to show
her the door at the top of the stairs.

They mounted the stairs slowly, but the bare boards creaked as though they were being climbed by a herd of elephants. Each time Stephanie transferred her weight from one foot to another the wood protested with a shriek that she thought must wake the dead. However slowly, however lightly she tried to tread, the next step produced another creak, louder, longer, more insistent. Then Paulo's footfalls behind her produced another rondo of noise echoing through the vast cellars.

At any moment Stephanie expected the door at the top of the stairs to be thrown open and the lights to be snapped on. At any moment Angelina would appear.

They reached the small wooden landing in front of the door without incident.

Paulo shone the torch on the door to find the handle. He gripped it and turned it. The handle rotated, making a noise like a rasp grating on metal. Paulo pushed the door. Nothing happened. He pushed the door again. Nothing.

'It's stuck,' he whispered.

'Let me try.' Stephanie grasped the handle, but as Paulo's hand gave way to hers the handle sprung back. A click as loud as a rifle shot echoed through the cellars. As it died down they listened intently. Had they woken the housekeeper? Stephanie heard a sound and her heart stopped. It sounded like a rustle of clothing. But then there was silence.

After minutes of silence she dared to try the handle again. Again the terrible rasping noise of unoiled metal on metal. As soon as it was fully rotated she pushed. Nothing. Not the slightest movement. She pushed again with all her might. The door didn't move a fraction of an inch.

She almost started to cry. She was so close to escape. So close. And now this. If they forced the door it would undoubtedly wake the housekeeper and they'd be back where they started, or she would. And Gianni would see his nephew never got another chance to free his prisoner.

There had to be a way. This was her chance and it might be the only one she got. There had to be a way.

'Why did you close it?'

'I had to. What if she'd woken up and found it open?'

That was true. 'There's only one thing to do. Force the door and grab her before she can get up. The two of us can overpower her. She'll be drowsy. There must be something we can tie her up with.'

Paulo didn't hesitate. 'Stay here, I'll look.' The stairs creaked again. Stephanie watched the beam of light darting to and fro across the cellar floor. After what seemed to be ages it started back up the stairs, the noise reverberating again.

Paulo shone the torch on his hand. He had some curtain cord from an old set of curtains and a pair of old woollen socks, moth-eaten and ragged.

'Good,' Stephanie whispered. 'Where is she, exactly?'

'On the left of the door.'

'You hold her down. I'll stuff these in her mouth.' Stephanie took the socks from his hand and balled them up.

They took a deep breath. Paulo turned the handle and held it, then they both stood shoulder to shoulder and slammed into the door with every ounce of energy they could muster. The door budged half an inch but still didn't move. They shouldered it again and it burst open.

The first thump had woken the housekeeper, the second had made her start to sit up. Fortunately, Stephanie could see her clearly in the gloom of the room, her eyes dilated by the darkness of the cellar. She dived for the woman's head, catching her around the neck and pulling her down on the bed again. The woman's mouth was opened to scream but the sound was muffled by the woollen sock, as Stephanie stuffed it in. Paulo had dived too and was holding the woman's legs down.

Together they tied her wrists and ankles and knotted a piece of cord around her head to hold the socks in place. She struggled, but was soon helpless.

'Well done,' Stephanie said, grinning like a schoolgirl who'd just defeated the school bully.

'I'm not going to be welcome in this house again.'

But they were still not out of the house. They listened to see if the commotion had woken anyone else. Apparently it had not. Apart from the distant tick of a clock the house was still completely quiet. Paulo went to the door that led out into the hallway behind the main staircase. This door opened easily without a sound, and they stole out into the hall. Stephanie soon got her bearings. Paulo led her out into the vast vestibule of the house where she had been what, to her at least, seemed to be weeks before.

Without saying a word they tiptoed to the front door. It was bolted at the top and bottom with two massive steel bolts. Paulo carefully slid them back, the top first, then the bottom, and then pulled the latch back and opened the door.

At that moment, everything happened at once. First, an ear-splitting siren started to wail and every light in the house went on. It was the burglar alarm. Paulo had hidden in the house, forgetting the housekeeper would set the alarm even if his uncle was too drunk to remember it.

Almost immediately, Gianni appeared on the balcony of the staircase, naked but for a pair of boxer shorts.

176

'Paulo!' he screamed, starting down the stairs at the same moment as Angelina appeared from the cellar door, free of her ankle bonds but still tethered by her wrists and gagged.

Paulo and Stephanie stood frozen, like rabbits in the headlights of a car. Then Stephanie started to run, out into the drive, run as fast as she could. The gravel of the driveway cut her feet but she couldn't care about that. This was her only chance.

By the time she was at the entrance columns with Paulo right behind her – somewhere in the back of her mind she thanked God there were no gates – Gianni was at the front door. He too ignored the gravel under his feet and started off across the drive.

Out in the road Stephanie had no idea which way to go. She turned left, but her ankle gave way as her foot hit the edge of the pavement and she sprawled into the road. Paulo helped her up just as she heard a car coming down the road towards her. Gianni was cursing, she could hear, running across the drive and cursing at every painful step.

They ran down the road, the car she had heard coming up behind her, its headlights on. But instead of accelerating past, the car drew up alongside her. Stephanie, concentrating on running, her ankle aching where she had sprained it, her feet sore from the gravel, only looked at it when she heard the voice.

'Stephanie.'

She stopped dead. The car stopped too, its window open. It was the Rolls Royce, and the voice belonged to Devlin. She had never been so surprised to see anyone in her entire life. She could do nothing but stand open-mouthed and stare. The car door opened and he pulled her inside.

'Stephanie,' Paulo called, trying to catch her hand,

then clutching at the handle of the car door. The car accelerated, pulling Paulo's hand off the chrome handle. He ran after it, running harder and harder until he had no hope of catching it. Then he stood in the middle of the road.

Gianni had run too, after Paulo and after the car. Now they stood watching the car brake at the distant T-junction and turn left before it disappeared from view. Then Paulo turned to face his uncle . . .

TWELVE

Matching Stephanie's desires perfectly, the Rolls Royce sped away from the house and then turned north, its big engine effortlessly speeding back to Umbria, Lake Trasimeno and the castle.

Stephanie had let Devlin hold her in his arms for at least an hour before she had said anything, and Devlin, for his part, made no attempt to question her. He was content to let her tell her story in her own time. She did not cry. She remembered the conclusion she had reached in the cellars. What had happened to her was not the result of a quirk of fate; she had played with fire and got burnt. It was as simple as that. If she had not gone to Rome in the first place none of it would have happened. And she had been lucky. Her 'burns' might have been a lot worse. She had managed to escape and evade Gianni's long-term plans.

Her energy and strength returned in direct proportion to her feelings of well-being and, perhaps more importantly, to the warmth inside the car. It was the first time she had felt properly warm for days – the heating in the cell had never lasted long enough to get through to the chill in her bones. She finally started to think calmly and rationally. Firstly, she was going to make sure it never happened again. The castle was going to get a security system. And secondly? Well, secondly would wait. Secondly was a question of what she was going to do about Gianni. That would have to wait until she had eaten some decent food, taken some exercise, and pampered and cosseted herself a little.

Finally, as the powerful headlights of the Rolls picked out the long country road ahead, Stephanie levered herself up from Devlin's arms. She looked in the mirror in the rear quarter of the car with the help of the angled interior light. She switched off the light almost instantly.

'I look a mess,' she said. 'What day is it?'

'Sunday morning.'

'Three days!' She'd lost all sense of time. It had felt more like three weeks. 'I'm a bit confused. How did you come to be outside. Did Paulo – '

'Paulo?'

'Gianni's nephew. He helped me escape.'

'I've been outside since Friday night. We did it in shifts. When Jasmina told us what had happened, I knew there was only one man who could have been responsible. We came to Rome. I got the plans of the house from the City Architect. When I saw the cellars I knew you had to be there. But I couldn't just knock at the door. I was planning a raid, getting some of my people in. Meantime, we always had either Jasmina or Venetia or me outside. Just in case. Just in case what happened, happened . . .'

'Oh thank you.'

'Did he hurt you?'

'Not really hurt. But what about Jasmina?' Stephanie had forgotten about Jasmina since the first day. 'They didn't take her too, then?'

'No, she woke up with a headache. They'd come in through the terrace window. We found the grappling hooks.'

'We're going to get a security system.'

'We certainly are.'

'Have some of this.' Devlin handed her a flask of brandy and Stephanie sipped tentatively at the smooth liquor. It made her feel warm inside, and relaxed.

Nothing else much was said. It was not long before the car pulled up to the jetty where the boat was waiting. It was only when she started to get out of the car that Stephanie felt the cuts in her feet. The deep wool rugs in the Rolls had protected them but now, on the grass, she winced in pain.

Devlin saw the problem and solved it simply. He picked her off her feet and carried her to the boat like a baby in his arms. The image of the short-legged, stout Devlin carrying the tall, slim Stephanie was unexpected enough to make Stephanie laugh. By the time she was seated in the boat, wrapped in a blanket from the car for warmth, she was giggling helplessly. It was the first time she'd laughed in days.

On the castle jetty, illuminated by big floodlights, Venetia and Jasmina, alerted by the sound of the engines, waited impatiently as the boat came alongside. As soon as it was secured they leapt aboard to greet Stephanie with kisses and hugs.

Venetia lent her the shoes she was wearing, and they helped her up the narrow stone steps into the castle, where a big fire was burning in the grate. More than anything, she told them, she was hungry. The cook was woken and a huge breakfast prepared which Stephanie eat ravenously, though careful not to have too much, for fear her stomach would revolt after three days of little more than bread and gruel.

Then, after cleaning up the cuts on her feet and applying plasters, and making sure the sprain in her ankle was not at all serious, they took her up to her bedroom, where, at Stephanie's request, Venetia ran her a hot bath. On Devlin's orders they all left then.

'Just in case you're worried, I hired a security firm. The island's being patrolled. Next week we get electronic security.'

Stephanie was glad to be alone. She bathed quickly in the hottest water she could take without scalding herself and towelled herself dry in warm towels from the heated towel rail. Through the terrace windows she could see the dawn beginning to break across the lake. She went over to the windows, watching the lake for a moment before, despite what Devlin had said, checking that they were firmly bolted. She drew the thick curtains and shutters and found extra blankets for the bed. Piling the blankets on top of her she let the warmth seep into her body. This was one Sunday, she had a feeling, she was not going to see much of.

And she was right. She slept dreamlessly, almost without moving her position, and woke slowly, coming to gradually with a series of little naps and half-sleeps before finally waking completely and feeling, once again, ravenously hungry. Light was seeping through the edges of the curtains. She got up and threw the curtains back. It was a beautiful, hot, sunny morning. She looked around for her watch. It was still where she had left it on Wednesday evening. She put it on her wrist before looking at the time. It was ten o'clock. She had slept for twenty-eight hours.

She picked up the phone and ordered her breakfast. While she waited she showered, a hot, hot shower. Even after such a short period of imprisonment it felt wonderful to be able to bathe and shower freely, without the presence of the sour-faced Angelina watching her every move.

Wrapping herself in a towelling robe she unbolted the terrace windows and sat in the sun, enjoying its warmth. It was not as hot as it had been when she'd first come to the castle but, by English standards, it was still very warm. Stephanie kept the robe on. The cold of the cell had buried itself inside her. It was going to take a lot of real heat before it was gone.

Venetia carried in the breakfast tray. There were scrambled eggs, bacon (specially flown in from England), croissants, fruit, orange juice and coffee. Stephanie fell on it like a starving wolf.

'Do you want to be left alone?' Venetia asked tentatively.

'No.' Stephanie indicated for Venetia to sit.

Venetia was wearing a pair of white slacks and a simple black blouse tucked in at the waist. Her long fair hair had been brushed out and hung, unfettered, on her shoulders.

'Do you want to talk about it?' Venetia asked. 'That bastard.' Venetia had suffered at Gianni's hands too. She knew better than anyone what he was capable of. 'I know what I'd like to do to him.'

'Don't worry. We'll work something out. He's not going to get away with it. And this time there are going to be no mistakes. He's not going to be in a position to do anything about it,' Stephanie said, pausing between mouthfuls of food.

'So how do you feel?'

'I'll be all right. My feet are better already. My ankle's fine. I just feel cold all the time.'

'Cold?'

As she started to explain why, she heard a knock at the bedroom door. Venetia got up to answer it.

'Voilà!' It was Jasmina. 'I heard you were up. Are you alright? You feel better?'

Jasmina bent and kissed Stephanie full on the mouth. She was wearing a silky, white teddy over a negligée in the same material. It hid little of her body: not the crowns of her nipples nor the fold of her sex.

Stephanie felt a rush of desire.

'I'm feeling better by the minute,' she said.

She told them everything that had happened. They listened intently, sitting around the table. The warmth of the sun increased, but Stephanie still kept the robe wrapped firmly around her body right up to her neck. She enjoyed the feeling of sweat dripping from her face.

'So what have you been doing?' she asked, when her story was finished.

'We took it in turns to watch the house with Devlin, the three of us,' Venetia explained. 'He sent us back here on Saturday night. I think he was planning some sort of raid. Then you came out.'

Stephanie looked at the two women at the table. There could not have been a bigger contrast between them. Jasmina's short-cut, jet-black, curly hair, against Venetia's long, straight, fair mane; Jasmina's dark brown, almost black eyes, Venetia's crystal green; Jasmina's small, almost masculine breasts against the full voluptuousness of Venetia's bust. Only their long legs were similar and the fact that, between these, they had little pubic hair. Stephanie felt another pang of desire. She was definitely feeling better.

'So, have you seen the rest of the castle yet?' she asked Jasmina.

'There hasn't been time,' Venetia answered for her.

'And I wanted to wait for you,' Jasmina said.

'So we can pick up where we left off?'

'Yes please if you want.' Jasmina leant over and kissed Stephanie on the cheek. 'We were worried.'

'When do you have to be back in Rome?'

'In another week. I took my holiday.'

'Wonderful.' Stephanie felt her heart quicken. She remembered how much she had wanted to show Jasmina the castle and its secrets, how she had wanted to introduce her to Devlin and show her how to please him. There had been so many things she'd wanted to do with her before they had been so rudely interrupted. Now it appeared there was still time. And now, after her long sleep, and the food, and the heat of the sun, she appeared to have the inclination.

'Where's Devlin?'

'If you woke up, he told me to tell you he'd be back by twelve.'

'It's eleven now. Ring down and tell them he's to come straight up when he gets back. Where's he gone?'

'I don't know. To see someone on the mainland, I think.' Venetia said, getting up to go into the bedroom and use the phone.

'So what do you think of Devlin?' Stephanie asked Jasmina.

'Très intéressant . . .'

'Do you find him attractive?'

'He makes me feel strange.'

'You still want to fuck him?'

'Mais oui. It will be an experience, I think.'

'You still want to fuck me?'

'Oh yes.'

'I'd really like it, right now.'

'Now,' Jasmina said enthusiastically. 'But you are well enough?'

'It will make me feel better.'

'Moi aussi,' Jasmina said, laughing.

Stephanie got up and took Jasmina's hand, leading her into the bedroom. Venetia had just finished on the phone. It was not difficult for her to read the situation

185

between Stephanie and Jasmina, especially when Jasmina peeled off her negligée.

'I'd better go,' Venetia said, walking to the bedroom door.

'Do we want her to go, Jasmina? You wanted to learn, you wanted new experiences, didn't you?' Stephanie said.

Jasmina looked momentarily astonished. So far she had seen Venetia only as Devlin's efficient secretary. She had to adjust to a new perspective. 'Oui,' she said.

'Well, then,' Stephanie continued, 'you'd better come back here, Venetia, hadn't you?' She let a note of authority creep back into her voice.

Venetia came back to stand in front of her. Stephanie touched her cheek with the back of her hand.

'So well behaved. Venetia and I have a very special relationship. She is given privileges the others are not. Aren't you, Venetia?'

'Yes.'

'What others?' Jasmina asked.

'You'll see. One thing at a time. Do you think she is beautiful?'

'Very.'

'Then we'll let her stay. You'd like that, wouldn't you?'

'Very much,' Venetia said. 'It's been a long time.'

It had. It had been a long time since their limbs were intertwined, since they had brought each other to exquisite heights of sexual pleasure. Venetia was not Stephanie's first experience with a woman – that had been when she had known Martin, so long ago it felt like years but was actually only months – but it was her first alone, the first without a man, the first where she couldn't pretend she was doing it for the man's sake and not her own.

186

Stephanie slipped out of her robe. The sun was streaming into the bedroom, but she ordered Venetia to turn the heating on. She didn't want the slightest hint of cold.

'Venetia is a lesbian,' she said to Jasmina. 'She doesn't like cock at all.' She lay on her back on the bed and indicated for Jasmina to lie next to her. 'Take your clothes off, Venetia. Let Jasmina see you.'

A tone had crept into Stephanie's voice that Jasmina did not understand – a hardness, a note of command. 'You order her like this?'

'Yes.'

'But why?'

'Oh, it's a long story. I'll explain it all later.' Stephanie didn't want to explain about the cellars, about Devlin's slaves, that Venetia was a slave too, caught embezzling from Devlin's company, but a slave who enjoyed a special status. Jasmina would have to wait for her explanation. There were other priorities now.

Venetia stood by the foot of the bed and unbuttoned her blouse. Under it she wore a black lace bra. She reached behind her and unclipped it, then pulled it over her shoulders and off her large breasts. They quivered in reaction to their new-found freedom.

'Mon dieu,' Jasmina said, under her breath.

Quickly Venetia shucked her tight slacks and a pair of white knickers. Stephanie patted the bed on her free side and Venetia came to lie beside her.

Stephanie pulled the two women against her body until they rested at her sides. She could feel the weight of Venetia's heavy breasts on one side, and the hardness of Jasmina's large nipples under the silk of her teddy on the other. Both women had curled their thighs over hers, and at her hip she could feel the faint tickle of pubic hair, one bush wiry and coarse, the other soft and downy.

187

There was no need to move. She wallowed in the feeling of their bodies against hers, their contrasts and similarities, a sensation of excitement and anticipation coursing through her body as her heartbeat increased. Soon she would be plunged into a *mélange* of bodies, of feelings, of possibilities. She enjoyed their heat too, her body seemingly feeding off heat, turned, by her experience in the cell, into a heat vampire.

Stephanie turned to Jasmina first. She kissed her willing mouth and pressed her body into hers. Venetia immediately pushed over to press into Stephanie's back, making her the filling in a sandwich of bodies, crushed gently between the two women. She had never realised before how sensitive her back was. At her shoulders she could feel every contour of Venetia's heavy breasts, their nipples as hard as stones, feel them so graphically it was almost as if she had never felt them before. A shiver of delight rippled through her body. She felt Venetia's navel too, pressed hard against the curve of her arse. She shivered again. The two women took it for cold. They pressed in closer, huddling for warmth, trying to cover every inch of her naked flesh with their own.

It was a wonderful feeling, being smothered in flesh. She rocked herself in their arms as they rocked with her. All her instincts, all the sexual dynamism that she had felt since she first came to the castle, were beginning to flood back, as the chill in her body thawed away.

Stephanie ran her hand down the black rump of Jasmina's buttock. It always astonished her how white her tanned arm looked against Jasmina's skin. Her fingertips pushed down into the cleft of her arse and found her fleshy labia under the crotch of the teddy. She pushed deeper until two fingers were inside her sex and, with the other, she could just reach her clitoris.

'I adore . . .' Jasmina whispered in her ear. 'You have taught me to adore this.'

When Venetia saw what Stephanie was doing, she aped her actions, running her hand down into Stephanie's cleft, using her fingertips in exactly the same way. Venetia could hear the rhythm Stephanie was using on Jasmina; every time she pushed, Jasmina moaned slightly, just the faintest of sounds. Venetia used this to match her rhythm on Stephanie.

There was no urgency, no hurry, no pitiless pummelling to meet an overwhelming need, but Stephanie could feel herself coming and had no intention of holding back. She found Jasmina's mouth and kissed it hard, pushing her fingers as deep as they would go, just as she pushed her tongue deep too. It was a bit like masturbation. Whatever she did to Jasmina was, in turn, done to her. And now she could feel Jasmina coming just as she felt her orgasm build, that subtle line between sensual pleasure and sensual need crossed. Once crossed there was no going back. She felt Jasmina's mouth on hers. It was fluttering, trying to make little sounds, her body trembling, her cunt awash with wetness, her big nipples hard against Stephanie's own breasts.

Jasmina came, breaking the kiss through the need to cry out, her whole body vibrating in Stephanie's arms. But Stephanie was so close to her, so much in tune, her climax so near, that feeling Jasmina come made her come too. Venetia's probing fingers, working away between the silky, wet walls of her cunt, had brought her to the edge, and Jasmina had taken her over it. Over it and down the other side, her mind full of images of their three bodies pressed together, twined into each other. They clung to each other, all the little tremors and aftershocks of orgasm felt in each other, multiplied and magnified by being shared.

The room was hot now. With the morning sun streaming through the windows and the heating pumping out from the radiators it was hot and getting hotter. Jasmina and Venetia were sweating. But not Stephanie. Her body was still absorbing heat.

Jasmina unfastened the poppers of the teddy and pulled it over her head. Stephanie turned on to her back again. Venetia immediately cupped Stephanie's breast in her hand and leant over her to take her nipple in her teeth. She bit lightly. Stephanie shuddered and gasped, the orgasm still in her body, the bite provoking an aftershock. Jasmina, seeing what Venetia was doing, cupped Stephanie's other breast and embedded her teeth in its corrugated nipple too. It was a sensation Stephanie had never had before – both breasts held, both nipples bitten and sucked and teased.

'You could have a competition,' she said.

They did. They vied for her feelings, each hoping for the prize of a gasp of pleasure, a shudder of delight. And they got it. Stephanie moaned, rolling her head from side to side as she abandoned herself to her feelings, as she felt her body begin to want again.

It was her cunt that wanted. It felt neglected. Stephanie lay with her legs open, her knees bent, her labia swollen and wet and sulking. Stephanie could feel her clitoris throbbing, crying for attention.

Venetia's hand was the first to run down over her taut navel to the thick forest of black public hair, but Jasmina's was not far behind. While Venetia delved into her labia, Jasmina's hand caressed her thigh. Not for a moment did their mouths lose contact with her nipples.

Venetia found Stephanie's clitoris. It felt hard, engorged already by her first orgasm. Jasmina's hand went under her thigh to find the entrance to her sex.

Only minutes before Venetia's fingers had been deep in her cunt. Now it was Jasmina who pushed into her wetness. But this felt so different. This was two hands, two women. Stephanie felt her excitement racked up another notch, like the cogged gears of a jack, oiled and engaged, turning with slow, jerky movements, each notch sending her higher, harder.

She was sweating now, like both women. Sweat ran down between her breasts, down to pool in her navel. Now she was really hot, and she revelled in that too.

Their pace was increasing. However much they wanted to work as one, the two hands were different, responded differently, caressed, pounded, pummelled, penetrated differently. Jasmina's hand gave way to Venetia's who slipped her fingers up into Stephanie's body, while Jasmina worked her clitoris. Then they reversed again. Or did they? Stephanie couldn't tell, couldn't keep track of anything other than the sensations they were squeezing out of her. She levered herself against their bodies on either side of her. She pushed her thighs between their legs, wanting to feel their cunts pressing into her flesh. With so little pubic hair she soon got what she wanted, feeling their labia, thick and wet, on the tops of her thighs. Immediately, they moved their bodies on her, using her thigh muscles, riding them, using them as wanking posts.

The sweat made their bodies slippery, frictionless and greasy. Three women laced together in a single passion.

If there was any plan, any co-ordinated design, any collusion between the women, it had disappeared, each suddenly aware only of her own need, an urgent, vital need. The three bodies rolled together, a *mélange* of cunt and tit and thigh, of arse and hips and mouths. It became impossible to tell who was doing what to whom. It didn't matter. It was all one.

Stephanie felt her orgasm break, felt herself racked up the final notch, and then falling, falling into a tunnel of slippery, female flesh. She knew the other women were coming too, that's what made it better. She could feel them. Their orgasm was part of hers. She felt them come, felt their bodies tremble, their gasps of pleasure, felt them as if they were her own, tripling what she experienced.

And it seemed to go on forever. Her orgasm was like a fire, orange and purple flames, everything she felt stoking the flames, everywhere she looked more fuel for the roaring fire inside her. She felt Jasmina's sex melting on her thigh, Venetia's teeth embedded in her nipple, fingers – whose, she did not know – deep in her cunt. She saw their beautiful bodies, their long legs twined with her own, their breasts crushed against her, a writhing tableau of naked sex.

Very slowly her body regained control. All of them were panting for air, as though there wasn't enough oxygen in the room for three women engaged in such endeavours. Stephanie extracted herself from their bodies gradually, limb by limb.

She stood up. The two women on the bed cuddled together, closing the gap she had left.

Stephanie felt renewed. She felt strong again. She felt in control again. She felt powerful. The experience with Gianni was behind her. It was like the feeling she had experienced the first time she had come to the castle, a feeling Devlin had promoted in her, or created in her, she was not sure which. It was a feeling she had come to love, a feeling that filled her with a satisfaction that was more than sexual pleasure. She was in control.

She walked into the bathroom to shower off the sweat from her body. She set the shower on hot before she stepped in, but then, once the water was playing over her body, she turned the mixer to cold. She wanted to test her resolve. The ice-cold water jetted over her, chilling her instantly. But the chill had no psychological impact. There was no emotional shock, no wish to dash back into the warm. The experience with Gianni *was* behind her.

She turned the water off and towelled herself dry. She felt strong enough to think about Gianni again. He was not going to get away with what he'd done to her. She would have her revenge. Carefully planned, carefully executed, perfect, sweet revenge. This time there would be no mistakes, no way out for him. No way he would ever be able to retaliate.

Back in the bedroom, Venetia and Jasmina lay on the bed. They had cuddled together almost unconsciously when Stephanie got up, moving together the better to enjoy the aftermath of orgasm, the need for contact at its greatest.

It was Jasmina who had taken it further, Jasmina who had started kissing Venetia's ear lobe, then her shoulder; who had cupped Venetia's heavy breast in her hand to feel its weight, who had murmured, 'You are so beautiful, my cherie,' before she trailed her kisses down over the large, soft curves of Venetia's breasts, licking and nibbling at the flesh, down over her navel to the hard mound of Venetia's pubis, sparsely covered with short, fair hair, almost like it had been shaved and the hair re-grown, except the hair was fine and soft, not stubbly, down into her labia, wet and sticky from her orgasm.

Stephanie came out of the bathroom in time to see Jasmina dipping her head down between Venetia's legs, as Venetia rolled on to her back, to lick, eagerly, at her thick clitoris. From where she stood Stephanie watched, for once uninvolved, as Jasmina used her tongue – as pink in contrast to her black flesh as her cunt lips were – with her new found expertise on the supine Venetia. Venetia's excitement was only too apparent. Her eyes had rolled back and she was breathing in short, irregular gasps; her fingers were taut and stretched out as she tried to claw at the sheets of the bed, as if trying to get some purchase, trying to save herself from falling. Her mouth was loose too, whimpering little meaningless sounds.

Stephanie watched. She did not touch. She felt a curious detachment from the spectacle, appreciating the beauty of the two women, but no longer being sexually involved with it.

Even Venetia's keening call as Jasmina's mouth, and her sharp tongue, drove her to another orgasm, did not rouse Stephanie. She watched Venetia's body arch up off the bed, as her orgasm pulled her sinews and tendons involuntarily taut, before releasing them again and letting Venetia flop back on the bed, like a puppet whose strings had been cut.

Jasmina looked up, looked into Stephanie's eyes, her face shining with pleasure, the pleasure of victory, of conquest, of finding a new skill at which she was adept.

But Stephanie was not tempted to join in again. Another need had asserted its priority in her body and, at the moment, it was not one she could ignore. She was starving hungry again. She had got over the feeling of cold, now she had to eat herself out of the feeling of hunger that three days on bread and gruel had left churning in her stomach.

THIRTEEN

It was only when they were out on the terrace downstairs waiting for lunch that Stephanie realised that Devlin had not come back. It was well after one o'clock now.

'Where's Devlin got to?'

'He should have been back by now,' Venetia said.

'He'll have to be punished,' Stephanie laughed.

'Perhaps that's what he had in mind.'

Jasmina was puzzled by this brief exchange, as puzzled as she was by the relationship between Venetia and Stephanie, but she said nothing. There were things that went on in the castle she did not understand. But Stephanie had promised her a guided tour, promised her she would see all the secrets. And there was no hurry. She had already learnt a great deal about herself at the hands of this extraordinary woman. She didn't mind waiting for the next revelations.

Venetia and Jasmina lunched on salad while Stephanie devoured a rack of local Umbrian lamb, even chewing the threads of meat from the bone, as well as eating all the potatoes, fritto misto legume and, when she was still hungry, a local goat's cheese with a hunk of focaccia. Melon ice cream and cappuccino followed that.

It was as her second cup of foaming coffee came to the

table that she saw the power boat heading across the water towards the castle, leaving a long wake stretching back into the distance. As the boat got closer, Stephanie could see Devlin's distinctive figure sitting on the transom. The boat disappeared from view under a canopy of vegetation as it came in to dock. A few minutes later Devlin bounded up the terrace steps from the courtyard in front of the main doors.

'Stephanie,' he said, bending to kiss her cheek. 'You look so much better.'

'I feel it. Where on earth have you been?'

'I thought I should gather a little more information. I went to see a friend of mine, an Italian.'

'Information?'

'On Gianni.'

Stephanie felt herself tense at the mention of his name. She could feel her eyes narrowing.

'What sort of information?'

'This chap knows the family.' Devlin sat at the table and ordered the waiter to bring him an expresso. 'He's retired now, but apparently he used to do business with the wife's family. According to him, Gianni was nothing before he married. All his money, all his deals, it's all controlled by his wife. Everything is in his wife's name, too. Gianni likes to pretend he's made a fortune, that he's come from nowhere and made a mint, but all he did was marry into money. His wife is from one of the richest families in Italy.'

'Interesting.'

'Oh yes. Apparently the family were so against the marriage they tried to buy him off. They did everything they could to stop it. Her father hated him. Still does. But they got married despite that. She was besotted with him.'

'I can't imagine why.'

'Oh, I'm sure he could be very persuasive. Anyway, then it all started to go wrong. Gianni was given some of the wife's money to play with and lost a lot of it straight away. When his wife found out, she was so furious she took control. He'd set up this business. Well, she took it over. She made it a success. Gianni just sits around in a big office doing very little while she runs everything. She's made the money grow.'

'Well good for her.'

'Now she only tolerates him because she wants to prove her family wrong. They told her he was a good-for-nothing and she wouldn't believe them. She doesn't want them to be able to say "I-told-you-so". Well didn't, at least.'

'Didn't?'

'Apparently, she's now so fed up with him she doesn't even care about that anymore. She's looking for a way out. Any excuse, and he's out.'

Devlin sipped at his coffee, then popped one of the chocolate truffle petit fours, that had been served with the coffee, into his mouth. Devlin had an unrepentant sweet tooth.

Stephanie smiled. 'Oh, I'm sure we can find her an excuse, can't we?'

'In spades,' Devlin said.

Jasmina started to laugh at the reference to spades. 'Oh yes, you can count me in. Bien sûre.'

'I didn't mean . . .' Devlin looked embarrassed.

'I know,' Jasmina said, touching his arm. 'But I have an idea. In Madrid, when I was there, I learnt something that might be of use. It is a very special talent. I have all the equipment. I kept it. I thought I might use it again one day. I think it would be the perfect, revenge.'

'What is it?' Stephanie asked.

Jasmina was grinning from ear to ear. 'I don't know the English.' She explained with a mime. It did not take long for them to understand what she meant. And she was right. It would be perfect. The perfect revenge.

They talked for a while longer, but Stephanie's energy had begun to wane, the excitements of this morning, and now the food, taking their toll. She wanted to sleep.

'I'm going to bed. Wake me at seven, will you?' she said.

'Shouldn't you just sleep on?' Devlin said.

'No. I wouldn't sleep tonight, then. And anyway I'll want another meal tonight. So wake me.'

'D'accord,' Jasmina said. 'I'll wake you.'

'And bring Devlin with you.' She looked Devlin in the eye, and immediately had an image of his huge cock. 'Right, Devlin?'

'If you're feeling better,' he said.

'Oh, don't worry about that.' She patted his hand, the massive banana fingers making his coffee cup look like doll's house crockery. 'I'll be feeling much better by then.' Despite her tiredness, Stephanie felt a frisson of passion at the thought of what she would have Devlin do to her.

Leaving them at the table, she walked through the castle to her room. Without taking off the white track suit she had worn for lunch, she curled up on the bed, pulling a sheet over her. If she hadn't felt so tired she would have had Devlin come up with her. She was looking forward to reasserting her authority as well as feeling that massive cock inside her again. Not, of course, that she would let him know that. That was not the nature of their relationship any more. That was not what Devlin wanted from her and not what she wanted to give him either.

She remembered the excitement she had felt at the idea of introducing him to Jasmina, how excited she'd felt on the phone telling him about her, and how Jasmina had reacted, in turn, when Devlin was first mentioned. All before Gianni had intervened. Well, now the time had come, or almost. Tonight, when she woke up, she would share Devlin with the beautiful, athletic women and show her another aspect of the sexual nexus she had created.

Stephanie slept, a deep, dreamless sleep.

Jasmina opened the door of Stephanie's room at exactly seven, with Devlin at her side. She tiptoed over to the bed and, like Prince Charming, managed to wake Stephanie with a kiss.

'Mm . . .' Stephanie said, opening her eyes. 'Nice . . .' She stretched out on the bed, throwing the sheet off. 'I feel good.'

Jasmina was wearing a yellow bikini. She had swum in the lake that afternoon, then lain in the sun.

'Where's Devlin?' Stephanie asked.

Jasmina looked round, surprised not to find him standing beside her. 'He was with me.'

'He'll be in the hall.'

'What goes on between you two? It is very strange.'

'You'll see. You said you wanted to learn.'

'Mais oui.'

'Well this is going to be your second lesson.'

Stephanie got up from the bed and stripped off the track suit. She felt wonderful, rested, warm and full of delicious sexual anticipation. No doubt, while she slept her unconscious had been busy with thoughts of Devlin.

'I'm going to shower.'

'Moi aussi?' It was a question.

'Yes. There's lots of room. Let's give Devlin a treat. Devlin, come in here.'

Devlin came in, closed the bedroom door behind him and stood, his eyes looking firmly at his feet. For him, the game had already begun. It was a game he wanted to play very badly.

'We're going to have a shower. You can watch. Aren't I good to you?'

'Yes,' he hesitated, glancing up at Jasmina as he said, 'mistress.'

Stephanie unhooked the bra of Jasmina's bikini, then pulled the briefs off from the back. 'She's beautiful. Look at her, Devlin.'

'Yes, very.' Devlin's eyes roamed over Jasmina's tight body. His erection was already prodding from his trousers.

'Follow us,' Stephanie ordered.

The two naked women walked into the bathroom. Stephanie set the shower and they climbed under the powerful jet together, soaping each other vigorously, then washing the suds off their bodies. Devlin watched. He stood by the bathroom door and watched. By the side of Jasmina's dark pelt, Stephanie seemed so white, like fine china.

They stepped out of the shower and towelled each other dry with big, fluffy, white towels from the heated towel rail. Devlin watched the towels rubbing between their legs, drying their pubic hair, massaging their breasts and their nipples. They both rubbed aggressively, ignoring the sexual implications for the moment, wanting only to be dry.

'He likes to watch?' Jasmina asked tentatively, unable to ignore Devlin's presence.

'Sometimes he's not allowed to do anything but watch. You see how hard he is?'

Jasmina looked at the massive bulge in Devlin's loose-fitting slacks.

'He is big.'

'Very. Open a bottle of champagne Devlin,' she ordered, as she got Jasmina to dry her hair.

Back in the bedroom, Devlin had opened a bottle from the supply kept in the bedroom fridge, discreetly hidden in the silk panelling of the wall. He'd poured two glasses. Stephanie handed one to Jasmina.

'Cheers,' she said, clinking her long, crystal champagne flute against the side of Jasmina's.

'Salute,' Jasmina replied. The cold wine made their nipples pucker.

'All right, Devlin,' Stephanie said, turning to him. 'We'd better show Jasmina how much you've missed all your special treats, hadn't we? Or shall we just keep you waiting?' Stephanie went over to the chest of drawers where she kept her lingerie. As she rifled through the drawers, thinking of what she might wear, she suddenly remembered the clothes she had ordered from Jasmina's shop.

'Have the things arrived from your shop?'

'Mais oui. There.' She pointed to the wardrobe. 'I did not unwrap them.'

'Take your clothes off, Devlin. I think it's time we showed our guest what you have to offer.'

As Devlin began to unbutton his shirt, Stephanie opened the wardrobe. Neatly stacked on the floor were a series of distinctive red and green boxes, bearing the logo of the lingerie shop where she had met Jasmina. The third box she opened had what she was looking for. From the tissue paper inside she pulled a shiny, wet-look leotard cut high on the hip. But unlike a conventional leotard this garment was cut at the front to fit under the bosom, leaving the breasts exposed. It also

201

had another unusual feature. The material that ran down the curve of the pubis to the deep cleft of the buttocks was fitted with a zip, a zip which, opened, would expose the whole slit of her sex. She pulled the garment up over her naked body. It was beautifully made, shaping itself perfectly to her rich contours, the elastic material stretched tight over her waist and hips and the flatness of her navel.

She found a pair of high-heeled shoes with the same black, wet-look shine. They were very high, the tapering heels thinning to a wicked spike.

Stephanie looked at herself in the mirror, her breasts standing out firmly above the halter, her long legs shaped by the high heels. The tongue of the zip was fitted with a soft leather tab to make it easy to grasp. The tab hung down between her legs, from a distance like a tiny, black cock.

'Well now I'm ready for you, Devlin.'

Jasmina clapped. 'Such a good fit.'

'Well Devlin, what do you think?'

Devlin had discarded his shoes, socks and shirt. He looked up at Stephanie.

'Well?' she said with mock irritation.

'Fantastic.'

'You'd better get the rest of your clothes off, then. Jasmina's waiting to see what you've got.'

With difficulty, his erection still sticking out from the front of his trousers, Devlin unzipped his fly. He let his trousers fall to the floor before stepping out of them. He pulled his boxer shorts off. Once upon a time, when Stephanie had first met Devlin, his ability to have a spontaneous erection had been virtually nil. Stephanie had been responsible for changing all that. She had reached into Devlin's psyche and, like a Delphic oracle, had exposed its inner-workings, the entrails laid out before her.

'Mon dieu,' Jasmina said, as Devlin's monstrous cock was exposed.

Stephanie came over to him, took it in her hand and, as though exhibiting a prize bull, displayed it to Jasmina, turning it from side to side, pushing it up and down, weighing his balls too. It was hers, after all, hers to do with as she pleased.

'I have never seen such an enormous . . . It is so big.'

'You want him?'

'Oh yes. I think I cannot take him, but I try. Oh yes, I try.' Stephanie could see the excitement burning in Jasmina's eyes. She put her hand out to touch the gnarled flesh as if she were touching some alien thing from another world.

'Bend over the bed.'

Jasmina obeyed, resting her hands on the counterpane and sticking her bum in the air.

'Such a lovely arse, don't you think, Devlin?' Stephanie ran her hand down the black rump. 'Beautiful, isn't she?'

Stephanie let her fingers caress the sharp curves of Jasmina's arse before running then down between her legs to her labia. Jasmina moaned at her touch. Stephanie delved up higher to find her clitoris. She wanted to make sure Jasmina was wet. She needn't have worried. Jasmina was already a well of liquid passion.

'Come on then, Devlin.' Stephanie sat on the bed next to Jasmina's thigh. She transferred her hand from the back to the front, caressing Jasmina's navel before dropping her finger down on to her clitoris again. 'Aren't you the lucky one.'

'Yes, mistress.'

He positioned himself behind the black rump. Stephanie took his cock in her other hand and centred it on Jasmina's pouting cunt.

'Slowly,' she ordered, and he pushed.

Jasmina felt him nose between her labia.

'Deeper,' Stephanie ordered again, stroking at Jasmina's clitoris, feeling it stretched by Devlin's cock.

'Oh oui, oui . . .' Jasmina said, as it went deeper.

'You are not to come, Devlin. You know that.'

'Yes, mistress.'

Stephanie saw his cock pulse as he said the word 'mistress'.

'More, more . . .' Jasmina wriggled her arse back on to the massive cock, pushing it deeper. Stephanie caressed her straightened arms, pinched her knob-like nipples, squeezed what there was of her breasts, then ran her hand down to her clitoris again.

'Fuck her, Devlin.'

With Stephanie in this mood, Devlin knew better than to start moving his cock without permission. Now he started to move, pushing as deep as he could go, then pulling out again, feeling the pink lips of this magnificent woman folded around his cock.

Stephanie concentrated on Jasmina's clitoris. She could feel her excitement as Devlin moved inside her. She knew what she was experiencing. She would never forget the first time Devlin had taken her, the first time that cock had pressed into her cunt. She'd never forget that feeling – how it had filled her, swamped her, brought her off. Jasmina was whimpering now, like an animal, as Devlin moved faster, probed deeper. Even at its deepest, there was still a length of inches left outside.

'Tu me fais venir,' Jasmina cried. She could hardly think of the English. 'Come . . .' was all she could say.

'Come then,' Stephanie urged.

She didn't need any further bidding. She felt herself opened like she had never been opened before, every nerve stretched like her cunt was stretched, defenceless against the onslaught of sensation, like the centre of a flower, its petals peeled back to reveal the delicate stamen shrouded in pollen.

It was Stephanie who took her over the edge though, pulling her head up and kissing her full on the mouth, filling her mouth with her hot, wet tongue. Her orgasm exploded. She wanted to scream, but was gagged by Stephanie's mouth. She pushed back on Devlin, seeing if she could get him deeper still, seeing if she could make her body respond more, climax more, wring another ounce of feeling from her nerves. She quivered, finding it hard to stay on her feet as every muscle locked in her spasm of delight.

The kiss promoted Stephanie's need. She felt Jasmina's orgasm in her mouth, felt her mouth go hot and slack. As Jasmina collapsed on to the bed, unable to stay on her feet any longer, as Devlin's cock popped out of her cunt, glistening with Jasmina's juices, Stephanie's need was urgent.

'Get on to the bed,' she ordered. 'On your back.'

Devlin scrambled up on to the bed and lay next to Jasmina, his cock almost vertical.

Stephanie knelt by his head, her knees apart.

'Unzip me.'

He put out his hand and caught the leather tab of the zip. He pulled it down slowly, its jaws parting to reveal the thickness of her pubic hair. He pulled it down and then up, up into the curves of her arse, until her whole sex was revealed.

'Now lick me,' she said, swinging one knee over his face until her crotch was poised above him. He had to lever his head off the bed to get at her, his neck muscles straining. It was difficult to get his tongue between the jaws of the zip, but he tried.

'Harder, Devlin.' She lowered her sex on to his face.

He worked with his tongue, trying to get past the folds of material, past the harsh jaws of the zip, past her thick pubic hair to the soft flesh of her cunt. It wasn't easy.

'Over there.' Stephanie touched Jasmina's arm and pointed. Jasmina followed the direction of her finger. By the bedside table was a riding crop. 'Yes, the crop.'

Jasmina pulled herself off the bed and took the crop in her hand. Her eyes were full of curiosity, but there was no hiding her excitement.

'We have to punish him for doing so badly. I tell him to lick me out and this is the best he can do.'

Stephanie swung off Devlin's face and lay on her back.

'Fuck me, Devlin.'

She didn't think she'd ever seen his cock harder. The veins on its surface were so pronounced they looked as though they wanted to burst. Each vein was a different colour: reds, blues, purples.

'Jasmina's going to beat you while you fuck me.'

'No, please,' he said, meaning that's what he wanted more than anything in the world.

'I beat him,' Jasmina said, looking hesitant.

'Yes. On his arse. Hard, Jasmina.'

Devlin was on top of her, his cock trying to press between the zip. The zip scratched at his cock. He pushed harder, the tender skin of his circumcised glans trying to find a passage.

'Come on, Devlin,' Stephanie taunted.

Suddenly, he was through. Suddenly she felt his heat invading her cunt. She was wet. He pushed on, into her, up her. He was inside her now. The jaws of the zip still hurt him, pinching at him, making every movement painful, but it was worth it now. He worked himself deeper. He felt Stephanie's hands on his back, holding him to her.

'Do it, Jasmina,' Stephanie said.

The black woman knelt on the bed, raised the crop and cut it down across Devlin's buttocks. It hit much harder than she'd intended. Devlin moaned.

'Fuck me, Devlin,' Stephanie said. 'Again . . .'

Jasmina swiped the whip across Devlin's arse again. It was exciting. It was another experience. She felt herself getting hot, she felt her cunt demanding attention. With her free hand, she groped for her own clitoris.

Stephanie felt Devlin's cock ramming home inside her. It filled her, possessed her, sated her. Oh, how good it felt to have him inside her again. His cock swelled with every cut of the whip. She knew he was going to come.

'I want your spunk, Devlin.'

She wriggled herself down on him, trying to take more, trying to get every last millimetre of his flesh into her, knowing she was coming now, as she looked over at Jasmina and saw her wanking herself as she raised the whip. Her wetness lubricated the zip of the leotard. It still bit into his flesh, but he could move now, fuck her, bring himself off. He had her permission. His mind was full of images, the silky folds of Jasmina's cunt, her sharp arse split by his cock. His body was full of sensations: the whip on his buttocks, the harshness of the zip at his cock. Stephanie could take him deeper, hold him tighter, than any woman that he'd known but it was not her body that had given him most pleasure, but her mind. She knew what he wanted, she knew what he was. She knew his secrets and used her knowledge.

'Spunk,' she said. The authority in her voice, her dominance, made him come. He was being used, used for her pleasure.

He bucked faster, and deeper, then stopped,

207

knowing he was ready, feeling his spunk spasming out of his cock, past the tight confines of the zip that held him like a vice, up and out into her liquid cunt. Stephanie felt it too, his cock swelling even more as he came, stretching her cunt the short distance between being in control of her body and being totally out of control, as her orgasm plunged her down, into a blackness where the only sensation was waves of pure pleasure. She heard herself scream.

She opened her eyes as she felt Devlin's cock slip from the lips of her cunt. Jasmina was still on her knees, her hand hugging at her labia, holding on to the remnants of her orgasm, the riding crop discarded on the bed.

'Mon dieu,' she said. 'C'est un zob extraordinaire.'

Devlin lay on the bed. 'You never cease to amaze me,' he said. The game was over.

Jasmina pulled the shoulder strap of the leotard down over Stephanie's arm. 'I take this off.' She pulled the other strap down too and continued to pull, the garment reversing itself as it came off Stephanie's body. Stephanie arched her buttocks off the bed as Jasmina pulled the wet-look material over her arse and down her thighs.

'Better?' she said.

'Yes.'

'Good. I want to feel your body.'

'Jasmina . . .'

'Yes.'

Jasmina stroked Stephanie's long hair. She stroked both her cheeks with the back of her hand. She kissed her on the mouth. She lay, her body alongside Stephanie's black on white. She kissed her neck and her breast, expecting perhaps for Stephanie to object, to say she'd had enough. But she didn't.

She kissed her between her breasts, and then up over the hillock of each breast to lick at her nipples. Despite herself, Stephanie felt aroused. Jasmina's mouth dipped on to her navel, her tongue exploring the dimple of Stephanie's belly button, then the fringes of her lush pubic hair.

Devlin was watching. Jasmina parted Stephanie's thighs. She kissed along her thigh, down to her knee, down to her foot, trailing her tiny breasts against Stephanie's waist. Down the length of one leg, up the length of the other until she was at the triangle of her pubis again.

'I want his spunk,' she said, in perfect English.

Stephanie opened her leg wider, raising one leg, its knee bent. The trail of Jasmina's tongue curved down between her thighs, down to where her hair was plastered to her flesh with wetness. She teased out Stephanie's clitoris and heard her gasp. It was hotter than it had ever been. Then she tongued lower, running her hands under Stephanie's arse and lifting it up off the bed so she could get her tongue right into her cunt, right into the dark walls, to lap at the gobs of spunk she knew she would find there.

She lapped with her tongue, not caring what Stephanie felt, what she made Stephanie feel, wanting only to taste spunk. She found it there and lapped it up. All she could find, all she could taste. She felt her body beginning to come again. The taste was making her come – though somewhere deep inside her she knew perfectly well it was everything else: the situation, the whipping, Devlin's cock, Stephanie's fingers, everything was making her come. As she rubbed her thighs together, grinding on her clitoris, she felt Stephanie's cunt contracting. She was coming too.

Her orgasm sang through her body, building into a

crescendo. As every instrument joined in, every nerve singing, as the music got so loud she screamed for her release, it came. Suddenly her legs were pushed apart and Devlin's huge banana finger was pushing up inside her. She had never felt a sensation like it, a finger the size of a cock. It released her. She came over it, flooded over it, melted over it as her tongue tasted spunk and her mind gave up on trying to make sense of all the things that were happening to her.

When she opened her eyes, nothing had moved. Stephanie's cunt was in front of her as she lay between her white thighs. And Devlin's finger was still buried deep in the folds of her molten and exhausted sex.

FOURTEEN

Naturally enough, Stephanie was starving again.

Venetia joined them for dinner. Sitting round the glass-topped table the three women were all dressed to the nines. Venetia wore a deep green satin dress, strapless but with a full length, tight skirt, though a kick pleat meant she could walk with slightly less diminutive steps than the tightness would suggest. The dress, worn over a strapless basque, presented a cleavage which any man would have found difficult to avoid with his eyes.

Jasmina wore a cat-suit in a clinging, leopard-skin print. The material followed every curve, every muscle of her hard, fit body, the print disguising the smallness of her breasts and the pout of her nipples.

Stephanie wore black leather: a short pencil skirt, and a little bolero jacket in the softest glove leather, over a plain white blouse that was almost transparent. She wore no bra tonight. Devlin's eyes could feast themselves – from Venetia's cleavage to her near-naked breasts.

Stephanie ate heartily again but by the end of the meal felt, for the first time since her return, that her appetite was slaked. The last vestige of her experience was, she hoped, behind her.

But not behind Gianni. Over coffee they hatched

their plot. Devlin was sure that Gianni's wife would leave him if she got even the faintest whiff of scandal.

'She's at the end of her tether,' he said. 'The man I went to see has known her since she was a child.'

'And this time, he's not going to squirm out of it.'

'I'll make him a permanent reminder,' Jasmina said, smiling. She had never imagined the skill she had learnt in Madrid would be put to such a use. But then, there were so many things she had never imagined before she had met Stephanie . . .

'But we have to act quickly. His wife gets back to Rome tonight and goes away again the day after tomorrow.'

'It has to be tomorrow then,' Stephanie said.

'Unless we wait until she gets back.'

'I don't want to wait,' Stephanie said emphatically.

They talked it all through. They made their plan. They considered every detail, tried to think of everything that could go wrong. This time, there were going to be no mistakes.

It was ten o'clock by the time Stephanie was ready, her lines rehearsed. She picked up the phone and dialled Gianni's number while the others listened. She heard the phone ringing and saw the huge mansion in her mind's eye.

Someone answered. It was Angelina's voice.

'Signor Gianni per piacere,' Stephanie said, in her best Italian.

'Momento.' Stephanie heard a click. There was a pause. Another click.

'Sì?'

'Gianni. It's Stephanie.'

'What do you want, bitch?' he said. He did not sound happy to hear her voice.

'I've been thinking about what you said.'

'What do you want with me?'

'Listen and I'll tell you.'

'I don't think I want to listen, bitch.'

'I've been thinking about what you said,' Stephanie persisted. 'About setting up an alternative to the castle.'

'This is some trick, no?'

'Somewhere that would be useful to you – '

'You back with Devlin now?'

'Devlin bores me,' Stephanie said, looking straight into Devlin's eyes across the table. 'I need more excitement. You excite me, Gianni.'

'This is a trick. What you try?'

'If that's what you want to think.'

'It is.'

'You excite me. Simple as that.' She let his egoism do its work. 'What you did to me. What you made me do.'

'I heard this before. You gave me this bullshit before. You think I'm stupid.'

'You excite me. Wasn't I wet when you fucked me, soaking wet? Wasn't I running with excitement when you fucked me? You think my body can lie?' When he'd fucked her last he hadn't even got inside her. She gambled he wouldn't remember much.

'Yes.'

'I didn't realise, Gianni. It was hard for me to understand. You treat me badly. I must like it. I didn't know I did till I met you. But you're a real man. You know how to give a woman what she wants.'

'So?' he said. It sounded as though Stephanie had hooked her fish. Now she had to reel the line in gently.

'So, I told you I'm bored here, with Devlin. This is his operation. He set it up. I want my own place, to use my own ideas. You said yourself it would be worthwhile. We could find a house somewhere near Rome. I'd run it for you.'

'And what do you get for this?'

'Oh, I'd be handsomely paid, Gianni. And . . .'

'And?'

'And I get you, don't I? Whenever I want you.'

'Is a trick,' he said decisively, the fish pulling against the line and swimming away. But the hook was still in its mouth.

'OK, if that's what you think . . .' She let him think she was about to hang up.

'No. Wait.' The reel took up the slack again.

'I'm coming to Rome tomorrow. Come to my hotel. I can hardly chain you to the wall there, can I? And you can't pull any stunts either. Neutral ground.'

'No . . .' Gianni was clearly trying to think if there was anything nasty she could do. He decided there wasn't. 'I come.'

'We can talk, and maybe . . .'

'Maybe what?'

'I'm sure you could think of something, Gianni. You know what turns me on.'

'Do I?'

'Don't you remember? I'm offended.'

'I remember,' he said.

'Good. Tomorrow night at eight.'

'No, not tomorrow.'

'Gianni, it has to be tomorrow. Otherwise forget it.'

'Why does it have to be?' She thought she heard suspicion in his voice again.

'I have to come to Rome for Devlin tomorrow. I can't just go to Rome on a whim. He'd suspect something. He knows I'm bored.' She held her breath, waiting for his response.

'Eight o'clock tomorrow, then.'

'The Excelsior,' she said.

'But of course.'

'Can't wait,' she said. That, at least, was true.

She dropped the receiver back on to its cradle. 'Got him!' she said with delight. 'Got him.'

'Now we go over everything again. Everything. He's a nasty character. We don't want anything to go wrong again,' Devlin said.

And they did. This time there would be no mistakes. They would be flown to Rome in the morning and check into the hotel. Jasmina would go to her flat and pick up the equipment she needed, and they would have the rest of the day to prepare for Gianni's arrival. This time the plan was going to work, Stephanie knew it. This time Gianni's marriage would be ended, his fortune lost and, with it, his power. This time it would be a lesson he would never able to forget.

They moved from the table to the fireside. Instead of brandy, Devlin suggested they open a bottle of champagne, so they sat drinking a vintage Taittinger. Jasmina sat at Stephanie's feet on the thick cream rug, Devlin and Venetia on a small sofa opposite. Stephanie had planned to take Jasmina down to the cellars tonight, to show her the rest of the castle and its secrets now she had been introduced to the eccentricities of its creator. But with the exertions that lay ahead tomorrow she thought better of it. Tonight they should relax. Which didn't mean they had to be celibate.

She looked over at the beauty of Venetia, stark, model-like beauty, her full cleavage revealing the marvellous curves of her breasts, the rest of the body, bar her slim, pinched ankles, hidden in deep green satin. She looked at the lithe beauty of Jasmina, her body like an athlete, radiating strength and health. And then there was Devlin, a thorn between three roses if there

215

ever was one, but a man who had given her more sexual pleasure than she would have believed possible, a man that in so many ways had made her come alive. Three beautiful women and a man. A world of possibilities.

Stephanie lowered the lights so the flames from the fire flickered in the room, lighting everything in flaring orange. She pulled off the little leather jacket and the white blouse, her firm, up-tilted breasts lit by firelight. Then she bent in front of Venetia, bent to kiss her red lips. She slipped on to her lap, not breaking the kiss, and pulled the front of the green satin down, pulled the bra of the basque down too so Venetia's breasts were pressed, naked, against her own.

She arched herself back so she lay across Devlin's lap, her back on his thighs now, and pulled his mouth down on to hers. She felt Venetia's hands unzipping her skirt, pulling it down. She lay across their laps, naked, breaking the kiss, wanting their hands to explore her. Jasmina pulled the zip of the cat-suit down. In one fluid movement, like some simple ballet, she pulled it off so that she was naked too.

Six hands explored her, caressed her, massaged her as she lay naked. The firelight flickered on her body. She felt Devlin's erection nudging into her back.

Six hands lifted her to the floor. She watched as Venetia's dress fell away, as she unhooked the basque, as Devlin stepped out of his shirt and slacks. Then they were all naked. But she was the centre, she was the hub of the wheel. It was she who made the wheel go round.

They spread her, spread her legs, spread her labia, fingered her and split her and covered her in mouths and hands and fingers until she thought she would go mad with so much feeling. They held her when she came, and she came over and over again. They turned

216

her on to her stomach, then round again on to her back. She moaned and screamed and gasped and whimpered. Mouths on her cunt, fingers in her mouths, every opening of her body probed and penetrated, every curve moulded and held, her nipples pinched and licked and sucked. Each orgasm was harder, stronger, lasted longer. They held her trembling body tight, thinking only of her pleasure, not of their own.

But for all her coming she still had a need. She opened her eyes to find Devlin. She moved her head so it was between his knees, his massive erection above her. Hands were still everywhere, fingers in her cunt, two fingers, three fingers, she was so wet she could not tell. Fingers in her arse too and at her breasts. But she knew what she wanted for her completion. She reached up with her mouth, sucked Devlin's balls into it. At first she could only ensnare one, but when he saw what she was doing he knelt lower and her lips closed on the other. She held them in her mouth, sucking them gently. A hand felt her body and came to circle Devlin's cock. It was replaced by a mouth, then the hand again, wanking him more easily with the wetness from the mouth.

Stephanie wanted him to come. She wanted to feel his hot spunk on her breasts, wanted that to be her final orgasm. She knew it would make her come. It was Jasmina's black hand that wanked him, pulling him harder, as Venetia worked on Stephanie's cunt. Devlin tensed; his whole body locked. He fought to keep his eyes open, to look at the beautiful body lying underneath him to see Venetia and Jasmina in the flickering fire, their flawless bodies next to his. But he felt his spunk rising, felt his eyeballs roll back in his head, and he cried out as he jetted spunk over Stephanies breasts.

It seemed it would never stop. So much. A tiny spot

went as far as the black curls of her pubic hair. As she felt its heat, she came, his balls slipping from her mouth as she trembled helplessly, her body taking no commands except from the centre of its pleasure. They held her tight and waited for the orgasm to die away. It was a long time before she was completely still.

Stephanie awoke feeling refreshed and strong. She showered and packed a small case with everything she needed. Bruno had delivered a list of things from the cellars last night. She checked them all carefully before packing them in the case.

Downstairs, Venetia and Jasmina were already sitting with Devlin, having breakfast. The terrace was a little too cold in the morning now; the sun was much lower in the sky and was still wet with dew. Stephanie had coffee and orange juice and was delighted to find she did not want to eat more than half a croissant.

It had been decided that Devlin should stay at the castle just in case Gianni should phone, and to avoid the slim, admittedly very slim, chance that he'd be seen by Gianni in Rome. He was vehemently opposed to the idea of them going alone, until they had pointed out that with three of them in a place as public as a hotel there was really very little that Gianni could do. Though not entirely convinced, he agreed. Certainly, if Gianni rang the castle and discovered Devlin was not there he might get suspicious, and that was the last thing they wanted.

Two hours later they were in the plane to Rome. The Rolls Royce met them at the airport and took them to the Excelsior, taking Jasmina on to her flat to pick up the equipment she needed. By five o'clock she was back, and everything was prepared. The trap was set.

Stephanie dressed carefully for the rendezvous. She

wore white: an under-wired, white bra, in silk and lace, that pushed her breasts up into a firm cleavage, a suspender belt that was a thick panel of lace, with thin satin suspenders clipped into white stockings, and a pair of lacy French knickers. Her dark pubic bush was clearly visible under the thin knickers. She wore a white dress too, its skirt short enough to show a flash of stockings if she crossed her legs, the material just thin enough to give a faint suggestion of what she was wearing underneath.

At seven, the phone rang. Stephanie's heart almost stopped when she heard Gianni's voice.

'Stephanie?' it said.

'Yes, Gianni?'

'You are there?'

'Of course.'

'Just checking.'

'Gianni, don't you trust me?' she said, in a mocking tone.

'No. You have to teach me to trust you.'

'Gianni, I'm so hot. I've been in this suite, thinking about what you're going to do to me when you get here. You are coming, aren't you, Gianni? I'm so hot for you.' She hoped she wasn't being too obvious. She tried her best to make it sound convincing.

'I'll be there.' Apparently it was not obvious to him.

'I can't wait,' she said, managing to sound breathless, her voice fogged with passion.

The three women were together in the sitting room of the suite.

'What was all that about?' Venetia asked, having heard only one end of the conversation.

'He's still suspicious.'

'As long as he is still coming,' Jasmina said.

'He's coming.'

219

Sooner than they thought. Exactly four minutes later, there was a knock on the outer door of the suite. Stephanie knew immediately who it was. Gianni had called her from the lobby. He had come early as a precaution. If she was planning something at eight, when they'd arranged to meet, he might catch her out by arriving at seven. He didn't.

'Gianni!' Stephanie said with mock surprise. Behind her, Jasmina and Venetia retreated into the bedroom. 'You're early.'

'You said you couldn't wait.'

'So come in.'

He looked nervous. As he entered the sitting room, his eyes searched every corner.

'Drink?' Stephanie offered.

'Scotch.'

The hotel mini-bar yielded a miniature of Johnnie Walker. She poured it into a tumbler for him. She opened a bottle of champagne for herself with no intention of drinking it, not yet at least.

'I'm disappointed,' she said.

'Why?'

'No whip. Where's your whip, Gianni? Aren't you going to punish me?'

'Business first.'

'OK.'

'You meant what you say on the phone?'

Stephanie sat down and crossed her legs. The white welt of the stocking came into view under the skirt. Above the stocking, the white made her flesh seem very tanned.

'Yes,' she said, in a businesslike tone. 'We have to find the right place. It has to be remote. We don't want the neighbours complaining about the screams, do we?'

'I think I know a place.'

220

'Good. I'll need to recruit some girls to start with, and some men. Once we get started we do what Devlin does. How many people do you have working in your companies?'

'Two or three hundred.'

'So anyone caught up to no good is given a choice. The police, or our little hideaway.'

'Yes, very good.' Gianni was thinking aloud.

'And,' Stephanie continued, 'I've persuaded Venetia to join us. You remember Venetia? She can look after the women guests like your friend . . .'

'Gina.'

'Was that her name.'

'Venetia. She was very beautiful, yes?'

'Yes. And I have another beauty. Our first recruit. You want to see?'

'Yes,' Gianni said hesitantly. He had not relaxed. He was still on his guard.

Stephanie got up, the skirt falling back over the tantalising glimpse of stocking that she had seen Gianni's eyes light on during the conversation. She went to the bedroom door and opened it, then came back and sat down, this time next to Gianni.

'I thought you should have a little foretaste of what I'm capable of,' she whispered in his ear. 'Of course, you're early. They may not be quite ready.' She bit his ear, then put her tongue into the hollow curl of flesh. She felt him shudder. At the same time, she slipped her hand into his lap and groped for his cock. Gianni ran his hand up under her skirt, feeling the sheen of the nylon, looking down at her finely-sculpted thighs. She felt him getting hard. He stared at the bedroom door.

At that moment, Venetia appeared in the door of the bedroom. She was wearing a pair of thigh-length black leather boots with four inch heels, a pair of soft leather

221

bikini knickers cut high on the hip with nothing more than a tiny triangle at the top of the cleft of her arse, so her buttocks were completely nude – and nothing else. Her breasts, plump crescents of flesh, were exposed, their nipples rouged and hard. Wound around her right hand was a thin, chrome chain, like a dog leash and, like a leash, it was attached to a studded, black leather collar strapped around Jasmina's neck.

As Venetia strode into the room like an Amazon, the heels adding extra inches to her height, she pulled on the leash, and Jasmina came forward. She was on all fours, completely naked but for a black lace G-string that barely covered the slit of her sex. Her body glistened. They had oiled every inch of it: her neck, her tiny breasts, her powerful thighs, the curve of her arse. Every inch of her flesh.

'This is your first slave. Do you approve?'

Gianni's apprehension disappeared like a puff of smoke. He did not know where to look first – at Venetia's magnificent breasts, trembling slightly as she walked, leading Jasmina round the room like a dog, at Jasmina's rump glistening with oil, at the thin strap of black satin that rose from between her legs to divide her buttocks, or at Venetia's legs clad to the thigh in black leather. Let alone at Stephanie, and her white nylon thighs.

'Would you like a little action now, Gianni, or do you still want to talk business?'

He said nothing as Stephanie kneaded his now fully-erect cock. He greedily watched the way Jasmina's buttocks moved against each other as she was led around, her black skin shimmering, the oiled body suggesting a wetness in other areas.

Stephanie unzipped his fly and pulled his cock out.

'Does this answer my question?' she said.

'Yes.' His voice was throaty, his mouth dry.

'After all, you should sample the goods before you buy, shouldn't you?'

'Yes . . .'

Stephanie got to her feet and pulled him up too, his cock poking horizontally out of his trousers. She led him into the bedroom, where the curtains and shutters were already drawn, and a thick scarf had been draped over the bedside light. Venetia and Jasmina followed them in and then closed the bedroom door. The room was lit now only by the dimmed light on the bedside table.

'Take your clothes off. The slave is going to oil you, Gianni, so you can slip and slide against her.'

Gianni took his clothes off in a flash, throwing caution aside as quickly as he threw his clothes off, his eyes never leaving the Amazon and the African as they waited for him. His cock throbbed. It was hard, bone hard.

'Lie on the bed, Gianni,' Stephanie said. She went over to Venetia, who unzipped her dress, then went back to stand by the bed as she let it fall from her shoulders to reveal her lingerie. 'Virginal white, you see.'

Gianni saw. His eyes took in this latest spectacle: Stephanie's body shaped by the expensive underwear, her breasts pressed together to make a dark tunnel of cleavage, the dark pubic hair veiled by a thin gauze of white, her thighs bisected by the welts of the stockings, the suspenders pulled taut over her tanned, creamy, soft skin.

Stephanie unclipped the chain leash from the collar on Jasmina's neck and handed her the body oil. Immediately, she knelt up on the bed. Her hands started at his chest, rubbing the oil deep, circling and kneading. Venetia came to stand at the head of the bed, on one side, and Stephanie stood at the other. Gianni looked from side to side: two visions of sexual perfection. Stephanie had certainly shown him what she was capable of. If this was what she could do – if her imagination was so active – he wanted her, whatever the price. After all, he had the money, albeit his wife's money, and he could do with it whatever he pleased . . .

'Good, isn't it?' Stephanie said, as if reading his mind. 'So sexy . . .'

Jasmina moved her oiled body on to his, rubbing against him as she worked more oil in, oil on oil, slippery, hot, frictionless, like a cock in a cunt.

'Now your back, master,' Jasmina whispered, trying to sound servile.

He turned over and immediately felt oil poured on to his spine and her strong hands rubbing it in. This time he felt her kneeling above him, her oiled thighs at his oiled sides as she knelt in the small of his back. He could feel the heat of her sex through the tiny black panties.

She stretched her hands along his back up to his arms, working oil over his shoulders. She pushed his arms up over his head then massaged the oil around his upper arms. She stretched out more, lying on him – he could feel her nipples pressing into his shoulder blades, her whole chest satiny with oil – as she worked the oil higher up his arms, stretching them further out towards the headboard of the bed.

Gianni closed his eyes. The sensation of this oiled, near naked woman slipping and sliding over his back was wondrous. Her weight and strength pushed his buttocks rhythmically into the bed so his hard cock was, in turn, pushed into the sheets. He abandoned himself to sensation, though in the back of his mind he was still thinking about Stephanie. What a sexual imagination. It was going to be fantastic to have her on tap, to do his bidding for his friends, for his business associates. It would make him successful, especially if he managed to take a few photographs of the men and women he did business with indulging in the more perverse sexual activities. That would do him no harm at all. Perhaps he could even trap his father-in-law, who hated him. Now that would be something . . .

She was working on his wrists now, stretched right out over his body, working oil into the joint of his wrists, circling them with her thumb and forefinger, massaging the oil deep while her body wriggled against his. He didn't feel the steel hoops curl around his wrists. They had padded them so they wouldn't feel cold. He felt only Jasmina's hard body worming down on him. It was only the clicks, almost simultaneous, that made him open his eyes in alarm, and by then it was too late. The cuffs were locked in place on his spread-eagled wrists, and secured to each corner of the bed. The trap was sprung.

He struggled wildly, kicking and pulling at the cuffs.

'I wouldn't do that, Gianni, you'll hurt yourself.'

'You bitch. You bitch. I knew. I knew . . .' he screamed.

They dealt with his legs quickly. Venetia and Stephanie simply sat on a leg and grabbed his ankle while Jasmina attached the cuffs they had prepared. They had planned each manoeuvre. Gianni did not have the strength to kick a woman off his leg. In seconds, he was bound and helpless, his ankles, like his wrists, cuffed to each side of the bed.

'You bitch. Lupa!' he screamed, over and over again.

They had planned how to gag him. Venetia held his head while Jasmina held his nose. Stephanie held the leather gag, borrowed from the cellars, against his lips.

He firmly refused to open his mouth, but, already out of breath from his exertions in trying to struggle free, his air supply cut off from the nose, it was only a matter of seconds before he was forced to open his mouth to breathe. The gag was rammed home and Gianni was theirs.

'Well,' Stephanie said, 'I think we deserve a drink.' There was no hurry now. Venetia got the bottle of champagne and the glasses from the sitting room, while Stephanie double-checked all Gianni's bonds. She wanted no mistakes this time. Satisfied, she took the glass that Venetia handed her.

'To a job well done.'

'I hope we didn't disturb the other guests,' Venetia said as they drank the wine.

'They probably thought it was a TV on too loud,' Stephanie said, running her hand down Gianni's rump. All three women were sitting on the edge of the bed looking casually at their prisoner. 'He looks so sexy with all that oil. When we get back, I want to try it. The three of us all oiled up together – '

'And Devlin?' Jasmina said.

'Oh, I don't know if we can allow that. Not after last night.'

'When we return, I want a lot of everything.' Jasmina stood up. 'I think it is the tattooing, it makes me very sexy.'

'When we get back to the castle, my little hussy, you will have no cause to say that you want anything,' Stephanie said.

'Is that a promise?' Jasmina said playfully. 'I must take off this oil before I start. I do not want my hand to slip.'

As soon as Jasmina had returned from the bathroom, Venetia picked up the phone on the bedside table and dialled the number they had memorised. It was answered on the second ring.

'Signora Gianni, per piacere.'

At the mention of his wife's name, Gianni, who had remained quiet, seeing no point in struggling, began to thrash about on the bed, pulling at his bonds. They did not give. What were they calling his wife for? They must be completely mad.

'Signora Gianni. Hold the line one moment,' Venetia said, in her best Italian. She handed the phone to Jasmina, who had pulled on a pair of jeans and a white T-shirt.

In her fluent Italian, Jasmina explained to the Signora that she had been asked to call by the manager of the Excelsior Hotel. There had been some kind of incident, a rather unpleasant scene, in fact, and the manager would be grateful if she could come and pick her husband up. No, she had no idea what Signor Gianni was doing at the hotel, Jasmina said, in answer to her question, but he had booked a suite for the evening. The manager had asked her to make it clear, however, that Signor Gianni would not be welcome at the hotel again, after this incident. They were trying to run a decent and respectable establishment and the use of the hotel for the activities that Signor Gianni had undertaken was not to be condoned. What is more, several guests had complained at the noise. If Signora Gianni was not prepared to come and pick her husband up, the hotel management would have no alternative but to call the police, though they were reluctant to do so because of the scandal it would cause. Nevertheless, there would be no alternative.

Signora Gianni was keen to know precisely the nature of her husband's activities, and why he could not come home by himself. Jasmina replied that she would prefer not to discuss such matters over the phone, but that Signora Gianni should come straight up to Suite 214–215 as soon as she got to the hotel.

The latter remark, as Jasmina hung up, provoked another frantic bout of struggles from Gianni and a string of muffled curses. Had he not been gagged, they would have heard a panoply of verbal abuse mixed with desperate pleading: threats of violence alternating with pleas for mercy and extravagant bribes. But nothing more than a mumbled moan could actually be heard.

Jasmina translated the conversation. Signora Gianni had said she would be at the hotel within the hour.

'No time to waste then,' Stephanie said.

Jasmina laid out her equipment: a large bottle of surgical spirits, bottles of coloured inks, cotton wool pads and a bulbous instrument that looked like a large fountain pen attached to an electrical flex. While Jasmina loaded the pen with blue ink, Stephanie plugged it in.

'Ca va,' Jasmina said, satisfied she was ready. She turned the pen on. A high-pitched buzzing filled the room. Gianni twisted in his bonds to try to see what was going on. He felt the cold sting of surgical spirits as she smeared it with a cotton pad on to his left buttock. He caught only a fleeting glimpse of the instrument in Jasmina's hand, but knew at once what it was. They were going to tattoo him. He immediately fought against his bonds, struggling with all his strength. It was no use.

'You must not struggle,' Jasmina said. 'If you are not very still, it will hurt more.'

He remained still. She wiped his buttock with spirit again and applied the nib of the pen to his flesh. The vibrating nib broke the skin, injecting ink just under the surface. Gianni was about to receive his first tattoo.

228

Gianni's face was purple with rage, horror and despair. He could not stop himself from struggling, wriggling his arse away, but the nib of the pen only slipped and bit deeper into his flesh.

'I warned you, you must stay still,' Jasmina scolded.

She worked slowly and meticulously while Stephanie and Venetia packed up and changed into street clothes. It had been some time since she had used her equipment, but after a few minutes it became mechanical again: a wipe of surgical spirit, a stroke of the pen – often accompanied by a muffled cry of pain from her victim – and another letter took shape. Normally, with a large design like this, she would have made a transfer on to the skin first, as a guide; but today they weren't that interested in precision. As long as the ten letters on the left buttock and the seven on the right were clear. She worked in three colours – red, blue and green – reloading the pen, watching the ink seep under the epidermis, where it would remain more or less forever. Operations to remove tattoos were always painful and only moderately successful, especially on such large areas of soft, absorbent flesh.

The final two letters of the ten on the left cheek needed Stephanie to hold the buttock so Jasmina could tattoo right into the cleft. The seven letters of the right were much easier.

It was forty-five minutes after the phone call that Jasmina finally stood back and called for the girls to admire her work. She had done a good job. Tattooed across Gianni's ample arse, in coloured, ornate calligraphy two inches high, was a simple inscription: 'STEPHANIE'S REVENGE'.

'Wonderful, you're wonderful,' Stephanie said, kissing Jasmina on the cheek. Gianni was trying to look down over his shoulder, contorting himself to see. Of course, he could see nothing. He would never see what was written on his arse except with the letters reversed in a mirror.

'She'll be here any minute,' Venetia warned.

They gathered their bags together. Jasmina quickly packed away her equipment.

Stephanie knelt at the head of the bed so she could look straight into Gianni's eyes. 'We have to go now, Gianni. But don't worry. Your wife is coming to pick you up. She'll be here in a minute. This time I don't think your secretary will save you.'

The look in Gianni's eye changed from pleading, to hatred, to despair, and back again to pleading. He would do anything, he tried to tell her with his eyes, anything in the world if she would just let him go . . .'

Standing up, Stephanie patted his tattoo. It stung.

'The medium is the message,' she said, laughing.

They had planned everything. They were going to take no chances this time about anything. Not the slightest chance. While Venetia and Jasmina went down to the waiting Rolls Royce with all the bags, Stephanie waited by the lifts.

It was not a long wait. After five minutes, Signora Gianni strode out from between their opening doors, a look of thunder on her face, and followed the signs to 214–215. She was wearing the same short, black, mink jacket. She strode out purposefully, her Bally court shoes clacking on the wooden floor of the corridor. Stephanie followed her, pretending to look for a room number.

They had left the key in the outer door of the suite. Signora Gianni checked the number on the door, turned the key and went inside.

Stephanie could hear her calling out Gianni's name. She called three times, and then there was silence. If

Signora Gianni said anything, Stephanie could not hear what it was. In fact, she said nothing.

It was a matter of no more than a minute before she re-emerged from the suite, walking just as purposefully. She saw Stephanie and gave her a strange look, but said nothing. She did not bother to close the suite door behind her, nor take the key from the lock. She walked quickly to the lift and pressed the call button. Stephanie came to stand beside her. She pressed the call button too. While they waited side by side for the lift to arrive, Signora Gianni took out a silver cigarette case from her snake-skin Gucci bag and lit a Sobraine cocktail cigarette with a gold Cartier lighter. As she brought the cigarette to her lips, Stephanie could see that her hand was trembling slightly. She took a long drag on the cigarette, and blew the smoke out in a long stream. Then her thin lips formed into the merest suggestions of a smile.

They did not normally have the newspapers at the castle; it was too isolated. But the following day, in the afternoon, Devlin took the power-boat to the mainland and came back with all the Italian tabloid press. It did not take an impressive command of the Italian language to understand the headlines accompanying the pictures of Gianni alongside separate pictures of his wife. Signora Gianni had acted swiftly. Gianni had been served with a writ preventing him having anything more to do with the business: from setting foot in its offices, from drawing a cheque on its bank account, from even so much as taking a paper clip. Another matrimonial writ barred him from the house, his car, his private bank account. All these things were, Signora Gianni claimed, her property and the property of her family. She was suing for divorce on the grounds of adultery.

She had even called a press conference. With her father at her side, she told the assembled reporters than she had discovered that her husband was a sexual deviant, that he was and always had been a lover of miniscule proportions and that, as far as she was concerned, he could rot in hell. Her father had added that his son-in-law had simply ceased to exist, and he would use his considerable power and influence to see that the hurt done to his daughter by her monstrous husband would make him unemployable.

They read the stories over and over with glee, Jasmina and Devlin translating every word. By the time they had finished, darkness had fallen, and the time had arrived for another adventure, an adventure Gianni had been responsible for delaying.

It was time to take Jasmina down to the cellars. Stephanie had promised her, and she was eager to learn. And Stephanie would teach her, teach her to be dominant as she had been with Devlin. And teach her to submit.

Upstairs, they stripped her naked. Venetia brought a white cloak of heavy satin. It fastened only at the neck, feeling cold against Jasmina's body, making her nipples pucker.

'Is it time?' Jasmina said quietly.

'Is it what you want?'

'Mais oui.'

'Then I have to bind you. That is the first lesson.'

Taking a silk rope, Stephanie bound Jasmina's hand behind her back. Venetia helped her into white shoes. Stephanie kissed her on the mouth, remembering the first time she had been kissed with her hands bound.

They walked down the wide staircase on either side of her. As she walked the cloak flowed open, revealing her black and naked body, her hard, stone-like nipples, the cultured muscles of her thighs. With her hands bound behind her back she was unable to prevent it.

Stephanie held aside the tapestry that revealed the door to the cellars. Jasmina felt her pulse racing, her breathing short and shallow.

The door swung open. She saw the well-worn stone steps. She felt a rush of cold air.

'Are you ready?' Stephanie said.

'Yes,' she said, then added, wanting to tell them she understood what was going to happen to her, 'yes, mistress.'

Stephanie led her forward, her shoes echoing on the stone. She would give Jasmina undreamt-of pleasure, fill her imagination with lusts and longings, swamp her body with sensations, just as she remembered being swamped the first time she had come to the castle.

In a sense, it was her reward, her prize for helping Stephanie, for giving her the means to complete Stephanie's Revenge.

Letter from Esme

23¢

Dear Readers

Another month, another letter. I'm writing this in
November, in the midst of shortening days, falling
leaves, and urchins begging for fireworks money.
And thanks to the miracles of modern book
production, you're reading this next Spring, or
sometime thereafter, and dreary Winter is already
a memory. It's rather like time travel, isn't it?

Now I must tell you about the Nexus books that
are being published in March 1993, and in the
back of one of which you've found this little
message.

Stephanie's Revenge and *Castle Amor* are the brand new novels; *A Man with a Maid 3* is the classic reprint. Which one have you got your fingers into?

Stephanie has come a long way since we first met her as an ordinary but increasingly sex-obsessed working girl in the book called *Stephanie*. In *Stephanie's Castle* she discovered the mingled pleasures and pains of the high life in an Italian castle with a very interesting set of cellars. Now, in *Stephanie's Revenge*, she plays tit for tat with an Italian gangster. I won't spoil your fun by telling you who wins in the end, but I can assure you there's plenty more of that delicious mingling along the way.

Castle Amor is a much more light-hearted affair. It's excellent bed-time reading, and one way or another it'll send you off to sleep with a smile on your face. Completely silly, but wittily written, fast-paced, and chock full of well-bred young ladies throwing off their crinolines and having fun with stable boys. I won't give away the plot, but if I were to say nineteenth century, middle of Europe, small principality overburdened with randy aristos, and *The Prisoner of Zenda*, I'm sure you'd get the idea.

A Man with a Maid 3 is, of course, the third volume of a trilogy. Yes, I know I'm stating the obvious, but anyway: if you like it, go and look for the previous two books – new editions have only just been published. I'm not sure just how much of the trilogy is authentically Victorian and how much is more recent, but it remains one of my favourite Olde English reads. The third book sends me quite weak at the knees with indecision: should I identify with the gorgeous and severe Helen Hotspur, or with one of the thoroughly chastised young women who endure and enjoy punishment at Helen's hands in the sound-proofed privacy of the Snuggery?

Coming along next month we have: *Ms Deedes on Paradise Island*, in which the lovely Ella investigates a particularly nasty trade in aphrodisiacs; *Obsession*, the third book by Maria del Rey, author of *The Institute* and *Paradise Bay* – another very different story, but once again very powerful; and the classic reprint is *Violette*, real French naughtiness from the nineteenth century.

Sometimes I am asked, 'Esme, how did a gentle, sweet, innocent, beautiful flower such as you become involved in the seedy world of smutty books?' Actually that's not true: I made it up because I want to talk about where Nexus authors come from.

It's not a seedy world, actually. The people at Nexus are young, very friendly, very open about erotic writing, and work in light and airy modern offices on Ladbroke Grove. It must come as a surprise to anyone who expects to find a team of scruffy old men in dirty raincoats leering over page 3 girls in a dark East End warehouse.

And the people who write Nexus books are surprising, too: they're so downright ordinary. I've bumped into some of them at the Nexus office, and honestly, you wouldn't be able to tell them from a bunch of teachers, accountants, and housewives. Because that's exactly what they are! Not all of them, of course: some make all of their living from writing, and one or two of these are quite well-known, and write under pseudonyms.

And although many of them look ordinary, they're not, of course. Because unlike so many people, who gleefully read every tiny detail of the tabloids' reports about awful rape cases and books by Madonna but moan about declining moral standards and inadequate obscenity laws, Nexus authors aren't hypocritical about sex. We all do it, we all like it, and we all enjoy reading about it. More power to their elbows, say I.

And how do you become one of this select band of literary convention-busters? You do what I did: send a letter and a large, stamped, self-addressed envelope to the Nexus office, and they will send you a copy of their guidelines for prospective authors. This document is more than a tip sheet: it contains everything you need to know — how to present your work, what kinds of stories are acceptable, how much material to send in for consideration. If you have any questions, the Nexus editors are happy to answer specific enquiries by phone.

I've been looking at the latest version of the guidelines. Here are a few tips that might save you some time and trouble if you're thinking about having a go at writing for Nexus.

A few subjects, not surprisingly, are completely unacceptable: sex involving children or animals, for instance. The editors say that they are increasingly wary of stories that even hint at underage sex; they advise authors that all the characters in a Nexus book should be adults, and that if any character appears childish, or in a situation where you might expect to find a child, the author should make it unmistakably clear that the character is over sixteen years old *at least*. For the same reason, stories which include incest are unlikely to find favour.

There's not much point sending in a short story: Nexus books are full-length novels, and a short story will give the editors only the vaguest of ideas about your ability to write a novel.

And the standard of presentation is important: a story produced with a rickety old typewriter with uneven keys and a fading ribbon on dog-eared paper will not impress as much as a story laser-printed on to fresh white pages. It's not just that the latter is easier to read: it also suggests that the author is a professional writer who takes his writing seriously.

Finally, when you've written your piece, jiffy-bagged it and consigned it to the post, don't expect a quick answer. Sometimes (the editors claim) unsolicited typescripts (see, I'm learning technical terms!) are read and returned within a few days. But sometimes a backlog develops, and it takes months. Patiently waiting for publishers is one of the necessary disciplines of being an author, it seems. And one of the less pleasant ones!

That's about it for this month. I'd like to know what you'd like to know about Nexus, so please write in and tell me what I can do for you!

But remember – I'm writing these letters six months in advance, so you won't notice any changes for some time. My response is going to be unusually slow!

And don't, whatever you do, send me anonymous letters full of your wild sexual fantasies. Any such letters will (after I've read them, of course) be turned over the the Nexus editors and made into a book. Well, maybe. So there!

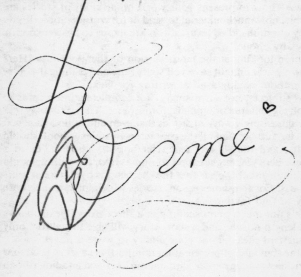

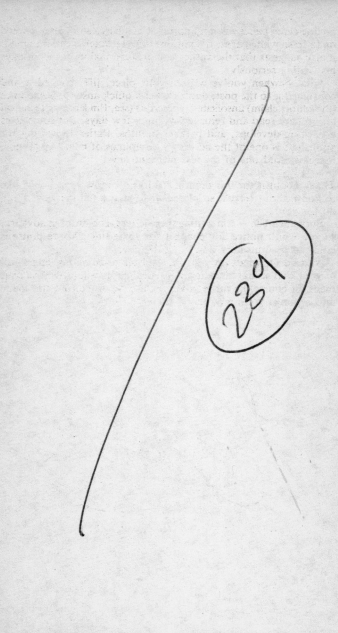

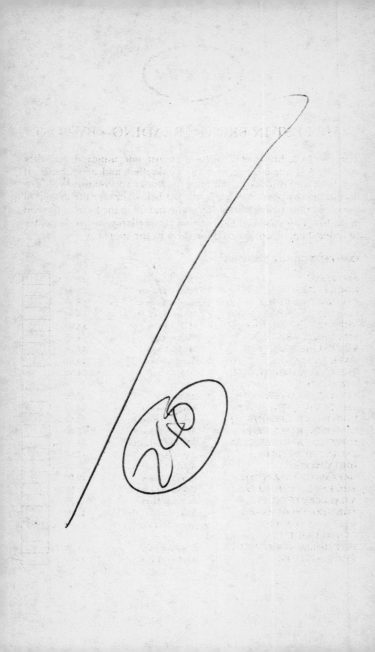

THE BEST IN EROTIC READING – BY POST

The Nexus Library of Erotica – almost one hundred and fifty volumes – is available from many booksellers and newsagents. If you have any difficulty obtaining the books you require, you can order them by post. Photocopy the list below, or tear the list out of the book; then tick the titles you want and fill in the form at the end of the list. Titles marked 1993 are not yet available; please do not try to order them – just look out for them in the shops!

CONTEMPORARY EROTICA

AMAZONS	Erin Caine	£3.99	
COCKTAILS	Stanley Carten	£3.99	
CITY OF ONE-NIGHT STANDS	Stanley Carten	£4.50	
CONTOURS OF DARKNESS	Marco Vassi	£4.99	
THE GENTLE DEGENERATES	Marco Vassi	£4.99	
MIND BLOWER	Marco Vassi	£4.99	
THE SALINE SOLUTION	Marco Vassi	£4.99	
DARK FANTASIES	Nigel Anthony	£4.99	
THE DAYS AND NIGHTS OF MIGUMI	P.M.	£4.50	
THE LATIN LOVER	P.M.	£3.99	
THE DEVIL'S ADVOCATE	Anonymous	£4.50	
DIPLOMATIC SECRETS	Antoine Lelouche	£3.50	
DIPLOMATIC PLEASURES	Antoine Lelouche	£3.50	
DIPLOMATIC DIVERSIONS	Antoine Lelouche	£4.50	
ENGINE OF DESIRE	Alexis Arven	£3.99	
DIRTY WORK	Alexis Arven	£3.99	
DREAMS OF FAIR WOMEN	Celeste Arden	£2.99	
THE FANTASY HUNTERS	Celeste Arden	£3.99	
A GALLERY OF NUDES	Anthony Grey	£3.99	
THE GIRL FROM PAGE 3	Mike Angelo	£3.99	
HELEN – A MODERN ODALISQUE	James Stern	£4.99	1993
HOT HOLLYWOOD NIGHTS	Nigel Anthony	£4.50	
THE INSTITUTE	Maria del Ray	£4.99	

LAURE-ANNE	Laure-Anne	£4.50	
LAURE-ANNE ENCORE	Laure-Anne	£4.99	
LAURE-ANNE TOUJOURS	Laure-Anne	£4.99	
A MISSION FOR Ms DEEDS	Carole Andrews	£4.99	1993
Ms DEEDES AT HOME	Carole Andrews	£4.50	
Ms DEEDES ON PARADISE ISLAND	Carole Andrews	£4.99	1993
MY SEX MY SOUL	Amelia Greene	£2.99	
OBSESSION	Maria del Rey	£4.99	1993
ONE WEEK IN THE PRIVATE HOUSE	Esme Ombreux	£4.50	
PALACE OF FANTASIES	Delver Maddingley	£4.99	
PALACE OF SWEETHEARTS	Delver Maddingley	£4.99	1993
PARADISE BAY	Maria del Rey	£4.50	
QUEENIE AND CO	Francesca Jones	£4.99	1993
QUEENIE AND CO IN JAPAN	Francesca Jones	£4.99	1993
QUEENIE AND CO IN ARGENTINA	Francesca Jones	£4.99	1993
THE SECRET WEB	Jane-Anne Roberts	£3.99	
SECRETS LIE ON PILLOWS	James Arbroath	£4.50	
SECRETS IN SUMATRA	James Arbroath	£4.99	1993
STEPHANIE	Susanna Hughes	£4.50	
STEPHANIE'S CASTLE	Susanna Hughes	£4.50	
STEPHENIE'S DOMAIN	Susanna Hughes	£4.99	1993
STEPHANIE'S REVENGE	Susanna Hughes	£4.99	1993
THE DOMINO TATTOO	Cyrian Amberlake	£4.50	
THE DOMINO ENIGMA	Cyrian Amberlake	£3.99	
THE DOMINO QUEEN	Cyrian Amberlake	£4.99	

EROTIC SCIENCE FICTION

ADVENTURES IN THE PLEASURE ZONE	Delaney Silver	£4.99	
EROGINA	Christopher Denham	£4.50	
HARD DRIVE	Stanley Carten	£4.99	
PLEASUREHOUSE 13	Agnetha Anders	£3.99	
LAST DAYS OF THE PLEASUREHOUSE	Agnetha Anders	£4.50	
TO PARADISE AND BACK	D.H.Master	£4.50	
WICKED	Andrea Arven	£3.99	
WILD	Andrea Arven	£4.50	

ANCIENT & FANTASY SETTINGS

CHAMPIONS OF LOVE	Anonymous	£3.99	
CHAMPIONS OF DESIRE	Anonymous	£3.99	

CHAMPIONS OF PLEASURE	Anonymous	£3.50	
THE SLAVE OF LIDIR	Aran Ashe	£4.50	
THE FOREST OF BONDAGE	Aran Ashe	£4.50	
KNIGHTS OF PLEASURE	Erin Caine	£4.50	
PLEASURE ISLAND	Aran Ashe	£4.99	
ROMAN ORGY	Marcus van Heller	£4.50	

EDWARDIAN, VICTORIAN & OLDER EROTICA

ADVENTURES OF A SCHOOLBOY	Anonymous	£3.99	
THE AUTOBIOGRAPHY OF A FLEA	Anonymous	£2.99	
BEATRICE	Anonymous	£3.99	
THE BOUDOIR	Anonymous	£3.99	
CASTLE AMOR	Erin Caine	£4.99	1993
CHOOSING LOVERS FOR JUSTINE	Aran Ashe	£4.99	1993
THE DIARY OF A CHAMBERMAID	Mirabeau	£2.99	
THE LIFTED CURTAIN	Mirabeau	£4.99	
EVELINE	Anonymous	£2.99	
MORE EVELINE	Anonymous	£3.99	
FESTIVAL OF VENUS	Anonymous	£4.50	
'FRANK' & I	Anonymous	£2.99	
GARDENS OF DESIRE	Roger Rougiere	£4.50	
OH, WICKED COUNTRY	Anonymous	£2.99	
LASCIVIOUS SCENES	Anonymous	£4.50	
THE LASCIVIOUS MONK	Anonymous	£4.50	
LAURA MIDDLETON	Anonymous	£3.99	
A MAN WITH A MAID 1	Anonymous	£4.99	
A MAN WITH A MAID 2	Anonymous	£4.99	
A MAN WITH A MAID 3	Anonymous	£4.99	
MAUDIE	Anonymous	£2.99	
THE MEMOIRS OF DOLLY MORTON	Anonymous	£4.50	
A NIGHT IN A MOORISH HAREM	Anonymous	£3.99	
PARISIAN FROLICS	Anonymous	£2.99	
PLEASURE BOUND	Anonymous	£3.99	
THE PLEASURES OF LOLOTTE	Andrea de Nerciat	£3.99	
THE PRIMA DONNA	Anonymous	£3.99	
RANDIANA	Anonymous	£4.50	
REGINE	E.K.	£2.99	

THE ROMANCE OF LUST 1	Anonymous	£3.99	
THE ROMANCE OF LUST 2	Anonymous	£2.99	
ROSA FIELDING	Anonymous	£2.99	
SUBURBAN SOULS 1	Anonymous	£2.99	
SUBURBAN SOULS 2	Anonymous	£3.99	
THREE TIMES A WOMAN	Anonymous	£2.99	
THE TWO SISTERS	Anonymous	£3.99	
VIOLETTE	Anonymous	£4.99	

"THE JAZZ AGE"

ALTAR OF VENUS	Anonymous	£3.99	
THE SECRET GARDEN ROOM	Georgette de la Tour	£3.50	
BEHIND THE BEADED CURTAIN	Georgette de la Tour	£3.50	
BLANCHE	Anonymous	£3.99	
BLUE ANGEL NIGHTS	Margaret von Falkensee	£4.99	
BLUE ANGEL DAYS	Margaret von Falkensee	£4.99	
BLUE ANGEL SECRETS	Margaret von Falkensee	£4.99	
CAROUSEL	Anonymous	£4.50	
CONFESSIONS OF AN ENGLISH MAID	Anonymous	£3.99	
FLOSSIE	Anonymous	£2.50	
SABINE	Anonymous	£3.99	
PLAISIR D'AMOUR	Anne-Marie Villefranche	£4.50	
FOLIES D'AMOUR	Anne-Marie Villefranche	£2.99	
JOIE D'AMOUR	Anne-Marie Villefranche	£3.99	
MYSTERE D'AMOUR	Anne-Marie Villefranche	£3.99	
SECRETS D'AMOUR	Anne-Marie Villefranche	£3.50	
SOUVENIR D'AMOUR	Anne-Marie Villefranche	£3.99	

WORLD WAR 2

SPIES IN SILK	Piers Falconer	£4.50	
WAR IN HIGH HEELS	Piers Falconer	£4.99	1993

CONTEMPORARY FRENCH EROTICA (translated into English)

EXPLOITS OF A YOUNG DON JUAN	Anonymous	£2.99	
INDISCREET MEMOIRS	Alain Dorval	£2.99	
INSTRUMENT OF PLEASURE	Celeste Piano	£4.50	
JOY	Joy Laurey	£2.99	
JOY AND JOAN	Joy Laurey	£2.99	

JOY IN LOVE	Joy Laurey	£2.75	
LILIANE	Paul Verguin	£3.50	
MANDOLINE	Anonymous	£3.99	
LUST IN PARIS	Antoine S.	£4.99	
NYMPH IN PARIS	Galia S.	£2.99	
SCARLET NIGHTS	Juan Muntaner	£3.99	
SENSUAL LIAISONS	Anonymous	£3.50	
SENSUAL SECRETS	Anonymous	£3.99	
THE NEW STORY OF O	Anonymous	£4.50	
THE IMAGE	Jean de Berg	£3.99	
VIRGINIE	Nathalie Perreau	£4.50	
THE PAPER WOMAN	Francois Rey	£4.50	

SAMPLERS & COLLECTIONS

EROTICON 1	ed. J-P Spencer	£4.50	
EROTICON 2	ed. J-P Spencer	£4.50	
EROTICON 3	ed. J-P Spencer	£4.50	
EROTICON 4	ed. J-P Spencer	£4.99	
NEW EROTICA 1	ed. Esme Ombreux	£4.99	
THE FIESTA LETTERS	ed. Chris Lloyd	£4.50	
THE PLEASURES OF LOVING	ed. Maren Sell	£3.99	

NON-FICTION

HOW TO DRIVE YOUR MAN WILD IN BED	Graham Masterton	£4.50	
HOW TO DRIVE YOUR WOMAN WILD IN BED	Graham Masterton	£3.99	
HOW TO BE THE PERFECT LOVER	Graham Masterton	£2.99	
FEMALE SEXUAL AWARENESS	Barry & Emily McCarthy	£5.99	
LINZI DREW'S PLEASURE GUIDE	Linzi Drew	£4.99	
LETTERS TO LINZI	Linzi Drew	£4.99	1993
WHAT MEN WANT	Susan Crain Bakos	£3.99	
YOUR SEXUAL SECRETS	Marty Klein	£3.99	

Please send me the books I have ticked above.

Name   ....

Address   ....

            ....

            ....Post code ....

Send to: **Nexus Books Cash Sales, PO Box 11, Falmouth, Cornwall, TR10 9EN**

Please enclose a cheque or postal order, made payable to **Nexus Books**, to the value of the books you have ordered plus postage and packing costs as follows:

   UK and BFPO – £1.00 for the first book, 50p for the second book, and 30p for each subsequent book to a maximum of £3.00;

   Overseas (including Republic of Ireland) – £2.00 for the first book, £1.00 for the second book, and 50p for each subsequent book.

If you would prefer to pay by VISA or ACCESS/MASTERCARD, please write your card number here:

— — — —   — — — —   — — — —   — — — —

Signature: _____